THE LYNCH MOB WAS ON ITS WAY!

The crowd's angry bellow made the hairs on Smoke Jensen's neck rise and vibrate.

They were coming for him.

How many were there? Would they be able to get in? Smoke had been scared many times before in his life . . . but nothing compared to what he experienced now.

He was absolutely paralyzed . . . he was so helpless, so vulnerable. Death rode the mob like a single steed, a hound out of hell, and it made Smoke think about his own fragile mortality. How easily they could take him!

NO! He had to find a way out of this! Somehow he had to escape . . . and if he couldn't escape, he had to take as many of the mob with him as he could . . .

TODAY WAS A GOOD DAY TO DIE!

WILLIAM W. JOHNSTONE

CUNNING OF THE MOUNTAIN MAN

ZEBRA BOOKS
KENSINGTON PUBLISHING CORP.

ZEBRA BOOKS are published by

Kensington Publishing Corp.
850 Third Avenue
New York, NY 10022

First Printing: October, 1994

Printed in the United States of America

One

Sound came to him first. It might be the buzz of an insect, only faint and teasingly erratic. Feeling slowly returned in the form of a throbbing stab of pain in his head. Light registered in a dimly perceived slash of pale gray rectangle, intersected by dark lines. Last to return was memory. Fragile and incomplete, it at least gave him a name, an identity. Jensen. Smoke Jensen.

For many, that name conjured images of a larger-than-life hero, as featured in over a hundred penny dreadfuls and dime novels. Legend had indeed drawn Smoke Jensen larger than his six-foot-two, although broad shoulders, a thick, muscular neck, big hands, and tree-trunk legs left him lacking in nothing when it came to physical prowess. He could truly be considered of heroic proportions.

In the opinion of others, Smoke Jensen was a killer and an outlaw. Some claimed he had killed three hundred men, not counting Indians and Mexicans. The truth was closer to a third of that. And, there was no back-down in Smoke Jensen. He had shot it out with the fastest, fought the toughest, outrode the swiftest. Now he found himself helpless as a kitten.

With an effort that nearly failed to overcome the pulses

of misery-laden blackness, Smoke Jensen forced himself up on his elbows. The back of his head felt like he had been kicked by a mule. Where was he? With the fuzziness of a swimmer emerging from murky water, his vision managed to focus on the gray smudge above his head.

A window . . . a barred window. How had he gotten here?

Slowly, scraps of memory began to solidify. "Yes," said Smoke Jensen in a whisper to himself. "I am—or was—in Socorro, New Mexico."

He had been on his way back to the Sugarloaf from selling a string of horses to the Arizona Rangers. They had been fine animals, big-chested and full of stamina. The Rangers wanted some sturdy, mountain-bred mounts for the detachment patrolling the areas around Flagstaff, Globe, and Show Low. Smoke's animals, raised in a high valley deep in the Rockies, answered their needs perfectly. The sale had been arranged through an old friend, Jeff York, now a Ranger captain. His recollection gave Smoke a sensation of warmth and contentment. Even though he was in jail, the money he had received would be safe. It had been forwarded to Big Rock, Colorado, by telegraph bank draft.

None of this told him why he had awakened with a gut-wrenching headache in a jail cell.

A new scrap of memory made itself known. He had three hands along. Where were they? Sitting up proved even more agonizing than rising to his elbows. For a moment the brick walls and bars swam in giddy disorder. Gradually the surge of nausea receded, and his eyes cleared. Full lips in a grim slash, Smoke Jensen examined his surroundings.

He soon discovered that outside of himself—and two drunks sleeping it off in adjacent cells—the jail was empty. The snores of one of the inebriates had provided the insect noises he had first heard. Again he asked himself what had gotten him in jail. Another wave of discomfort sent a big hand to the back of his head.

Gingerly, Smoke Jensen inspected the lump he found there. It was the size of a goose egg and crusted with dried blood. At least it indicated that he didn't have a hangover. Smoke then tried to focus his thoughts on the past few hours. All his effort produced another blank. Suddenly, a door of flat iron straps banged open down the corridor from Smoke's cell. Two men entered, both with empty holsters. Obviously the jailers, Smoke reasoned. At least now he would have some answers.

In the lead came a slob whose belly slopped over a wide, thick leather belt to the point of obscuring his groin. He waddled on hamlike thighs and oddly skinny, undersized calves. His face was a bloated moon, with large, jiggly jowls; the lard of his cheeks all but buried his small, pig eyes. He carried a ring of keys and a ladle.

Behind him came a smaller man lugging a heavy kettle, filled with steaming liquid. Shorter by a head than the fat one, by comparison he managed to look frail and undernourished. His protuberant buck teeth and thin, pencil-line mustache, over an almost lipless mouth, gave him a rodent appearance. In a giddy moment, Smoke Jensen thought the man would be more suited to be jailer in Raton, New Mexico. Their presence roused one of the drunks.

"Hey, Ferdie, what you got for breakfast?"

Ferdinand "Ferdie" Biggs worked his small, wet, red mouth and spoke in a surprisingly high, waspish tone. "Ain't gonna be any breakfast for you, Eckers. I ain't gonna have you go an' puke it up . . . an' me have to clean up the cell! Got some coffee, though, if you can call this crap coffee."

"How 'bout me, Ferdie Biggs?" whined the other boozer. "You know I don't spew up what I eat after a good drunk."

"It's a waste of the county's money feedin' you, Smithers. If you want som'thin' to fill your belly, suck yer thumb."

Smithers's face flushed, and he gripped the bars of his cell door as though he might rip them out. "Damn you, Biggs. If you didn't have these bars to protect you, I'd beat the livin' hell out of you."

"Says you," Biggs responded. By then he and his companion had reached the neighboring cells. Biggs turned and dipped the ladle into the light brown liquid and poured a tin cup half-full. "Since you gave me so much lip, you get only half a cup, Smithers."

"I'm ravin' hungry," Smithers protested.

Biggs gave him a cold, hard stare. "You want to be wearin' this?" Smithers subsided, and Biggs shoved the cup through the access slot cut in the bars above the lock case. He served Eckers next. Three steps brought him to the cell occupied by Smoke Jensen. He paused there, his small mouth working in a habitual chewing motion.

When he took in Smoke's shaky condition, Biggs produced a wide grin that revealed crooked, yellowed teeth.

"You're gonna hang, Jensen. You killed Mr. Tucker in cold blood, and they're gonna string you up for it."

Smoke nodded dumbly. Murder called for a hanging, he silently agreed.

Who is Mr. Tucker?

Martha Tucker sat on the old horsehide sofa in the parlor. Head bowed, hands covering her face, she sobbed out her wretchedness. Larry gone, dead, murdered they had told her. She vaguely recalled hearing the name Smoke Jensen, who the sheriff had informed her had killed Lawrence Tucker. Only her abysmal grief kept her from now recalling who or what Smoke Jensen was. What was she going to do?

What about the children? What about the ranch? Could she legally claim it? Most states, like her native Ohio, considered women mere chattel—property like a man's house, horse, or furniture. At least New Mexico was still a territory and under federal law. That might offer some hope. Martha's shoulders shook with greater violence as each pointed question came to her. For that matter, would the hands stay on with Larry gone? She knew with bitter certainty that no one who considered himself a "real" man would willingly work for a woman. Martha broke off her lamentations at the sound of soft, hesitant footsteps on the large, hooked rug in the center of the parlor floor.

She dabbed at her eyes with a damp kerchief and looked up to see her eldest child, Jimmy. At thirteen, albeit small for his age, he had that gangly, stretched-out appearance of the onset of puberty. His cottony hair had a shaggy look to it; Larry was going to take him into town Saturday for a visit to the barber. Oh, God, who would do it now?

"Mother . . . Mommy? Please—please, don't cry so. Rose and Tommy are real scared." The freckles scattered across his nose and high cheekbones stood out against the pallor of his usually lightly tanned face.

For his part, Jimmy had never seen his mother like this. Her ash-blond hair was always meticulously in place, except for a stray strand that would escape to hang down in a curl on her forehead when she baked. She was so young, and the most beautiful woman Jimmy had ever seen. His heart ached for her, so much so that it pushed aside the deep grief he felt for his father's death.

"Jimmy . . ." Anguish crumpled Martha's face. "Oh, my dearest child, what are we . . . what *can* we do?"

At only thirteen, Jimmy Tucker lacked any wise adult suggestions to offer. All he could do was at last give vent to the sorrow that ate at him, and let large, silent tears course down his boyish cheeks.

Quint Stalker sat his horse in the saddle notch of a low ridge. A big man, with thick, broad shoulders, short neck, and a large head, Stalker held a pair of field glasses to his eyes; bushy, black brows seemed to sprout from above the hooded lenses. Down below, to Quint Stalker's rear, in a cactus-bristling gulch, waited the seven men who would be going with him. His attention centered on a small, flat-roofed structure with a tall, tin stove pipe towering above its pole roof at the bottom of the slope.

Old Zeke Dillon had run the trading post beyond the crest for most of his life, Quint reflected. You'd think a feller in his late sixties would be glad to get away from all that hard work and take some good money along, too. But not Zeke.

Bullheaded, was Zeke. A stubborn, old coot who insisted on hanging onto his quarter-section homestead until he dropped dead behind the plank counter of his mercantile, where he traded goods for turquoise and blankets with the Hopi and Zuni. Well, today he'd get an offer he could not turn down.

It just happened that Zeke Dillon's trading post occupied ground far more valuable than he knew. But Quint Stalker's bosses knew. That's why they had sent Quint to obtain title to the 160 acres of sand and prickly pear, roadrunners and cactus wrens. Quint lowered the field glasses, satisfied that Zeke, and no one else, occupied the pole-roofed building half a mile from his present position. He raised a gloved hand and signaled his men.

Twenty minutes later, Quint and his henchmen rode up to the front of the trading post. Dust hazed the air around them for a while, before an oven-breath of breeze hustled it away. Quint Stalker and three of his men had dismounted by the time Zeke Dillon came to the door. He stood there, squinted a moment in hopes of recognizing the visitors, and rubbed wet hands on a stained white apron.

"Howdy, boys. Step down and bide a spell. There's

cool water an' lemonade inside, whiskey, too, if you ain't Injun."

"Whiskey and lemonade sound good, old-timer," Quint Stalker responded.

Zeke brightened. "Like in one o' them fancy cocktails I been hearin' about out San Francisco way, eh?"

With a nod, Quint shoved past the old man. "Sort of, old-timer." Inside, he let his eyes adjust to the dimness, his sun-burnished skin grateful for the coolness. Then he turned on Zeke Dillon. "Business first, then we'll get to the pleasure."

"How's that?"

"Before we leave here this afternoon, you're gonna sell us your trading post."

"Nope. Never on yer life. I've done turned down better offers than the likes of you can make."

Suddenly a .44 Merwin and Hulbert appeared in Quint Stalker's hand. "What if I were to say you'd sign a bill of sale and take what we offer, or I'll blow your damned brains out?"

Zeke Dillon swallowed hard, blinked, gulped again, and kept his eyes fixed on the gray lead blobs that showed in the open chambers of the cylinder. Tears of regret and humiliation filled his eyes. Not ten years ago, he'd have beaten this two-bit gunney to the draw, and seen him laid out cold on the floor with a bullet in his heart. But not now. Not ever again. With a soft, choked-off sob, Zeke said goodbye to his beloved way of life of the past fifty years.

Quint Stalker produced a filled-out bill of sale and a proper transfer of title form, and handed a steel-nibbed pen to the thoroughly intimidated old man. With a sink-ing heart, Zeke Dillon dipped the pen in an inkwell on the counter and affixed his signature to both. Then, sighing, he turned to Stalker.

"All right, you lowlife bastard. When do I get my money?"

"Right now," Quint Stalker replied evenly, as he shot Zeke Dillon through the heart.

Sheriff Jake Reno, of Socorro County, New Mexico, who looked every bit an older—but less sloppily fat—version of his chief jailer, stepped into the hall from an office above the Cattlemen's Union Bank in Socorro. He gleefully counted the large sheaf of bills, using a splayed, wet thumb. Nice doing business with fellers like that, he concluded.

All he had to do is see that one Mr. Smoke Jensen gets hanged all right and proper, and he'd get another payment of the same amount. Not bad for a couple of day's work. Given the sheriff's nature, he didn't even bother to wonder why it was that these "business men," as they called themselves, were so set on disposing of Smoke Jensen.

God, the man was a legend in his own time, a dozen times over. Sheriff Reno knew *who* Smoke Jensen was, and a thousand dollars went a long way to insuring he didn't give a damn why those fancy-talking men—clearly the one with a dash in his name sounded like an Englishman—wanted Smoke Jensen sent off to his eternal reward; it was none of the sheriff's business. Time, Sheriff Reno decided, to celebrate his good fortune.

Down on the street, he walked the short block and a

half to the Hang Dog Saloon. The building front featured a large, scalloped marquee, heavy with red and gold paint, lettered in bold black. It had a big, ornately bordered oval painting in the middle, which showed a dog, hanging upside down, one foot caught by a strand of barbed wire. It served as a point of amusement for some of the town wags. For others, more involved with the war against the "wicked wire," it represented a political statement. For still others, the sign pointed out man's indifference to cruelty to animals.

Sheriff Reno entered through tall, glass-filled wooden doors. The bevel-edged panels sported a cheery, six-wide border of mixed red, green, and black checks. He waved to several cronies and headed directly to the bar, where he greeted the proprietor and bartender, Morton Plummer.

"Howdy, Mort. A shot and a beer."

"Sort of early for you, ain't it, Sheriff?"

Reno gave Plummer a frown. "I'm in a mood to celebrate."

"Celebrate what, Jake?" Morton Plummer asked as he poured a shot of rye.

"I got me a notorious killer locked up in my jail. And enough evidence to hang him for the murder of one of our more prominent citizens."

"I heard something about that," Mort offered, a bit more coolly than usual. "D'you really believe a gunfighter as famous as Smoke Jensen would do something so dumb as let himself get knocked out right beside a man he'd just killed?"

Jake Reno's face pinched and his eyes narrowed. "Who told you that, Mort?"

"Hal Eckers was in for his usual morning bracer a while ago. Said he was locked up acrost from Smoke Jensen most of the night. Ferdie Biggs was shootin' his mouth off about the killin'."

An angry scowl replaced the closed expression on the face of Sheriff Reno. "Damn that Ferdie. Don't he know that even a drunk like Eckers remembers what he hears. Especial, about someone as famous as Smoke Jensen. Might be some smart-ass lawyer"—he pronounced it *liar*—"got ahold of that and could twist it to get Jensen off."

Reno downed his shot and sucked the top third off his schooner of beer. What he had just said set him to thinking. To aid the process, he signaled for another shot of rye. With that one safely cozied down with the other to warm his belly, he saw the problem with clarity. It might be he could use some insurance to see that he collected that other five hundred dollars. Slurping up the last of his beer, Jake Reno signaled Mort Plummer for refills and sauntered down the mahogany to where Payne Finney stood doing serious damage to a bottle of Waterfill-Frazier.

"Is Quint Stalker in town?"

Payne Finney gave the sheriff a cold, gimlet stare. "I wouldn't know."

"I find that odd, considerin' you're his—ah—foreman, so's to speak."

"I've got me a terrible mem'ry, when it comes to talkin' with lawdogs."

Sheriff Reno gave a friendly pat to Finney's shoulder. "Come now, Finney, we're workin' on the same side, as of . . . uh . . ." He consulted the big, white face with the black Roman numerals in the hexagonal, wooden case of the Regulator pendulum clock over the bar. "Ten minutes ago."

Finney's cool gaze turned to fishy disbelief. "That so, huh? Name me some names."

Jake Reno bent close to Payne Finney's ear and lowered his voice. The names came out in the softest of whispers. Finney heard them well enough and nodded.

"I guess you wouldn't know them, if you weren't mixed up in it. What is it you want?"

Sheriff Reno spoke in a hearty fashion after gulping his whiskey. "Thing is, of late, I've come to not trust the justice system to always function in the desired way."

"That a fact, Sheriff?" Finney shot back, toying with the lawman. "And you such a fine, upstanding pillar of the law. Now, what is it you don't trust about the way justice is done in the Territory?"

"Well, there's more of these smooth-talking lawyers comin' out here from back East. They got silver tongues that all too often win freedom for men who should damn-well hang."

"You may have a point," Finney allowed cautiously.

"Of course, I do. An' it's time something was done about it."

"Such as what?"

"Well, you take that jasper I've got locked up right now. Think how it would distress that poor Widow Tucker if some oily haired, silver-tongued devil twisted the facts an' got him off scot-free? It'd vex her mightily, you can be sure."

"What are you suggesting?" Finney pressed, certain he would enjoy the answer.

"Depends on whether you think you're the man to be up to it. For my part, I'd sleep a lot better knowin' some alternative means had been thought up to see that Smoke Jensen gets the rope he deserves."

TWO

Ranch hands, local idlers, and a scattering of strangers crowded into the two saloons closest to the Socorro jail by midafternoon. Talk centered on only one topic—the killer the sheriff had locked up in the hoosegow.

"That back-shooter's needin' some frontier justice, you ask me," a florid-faced, paunchy man in a brocaded red vest and striped pants declared hotly from the front of the bar in the Hang Dog Saloon.

"Damn right, Hub," the man on his left agreed.

Several angry, whiskey-tinged voices rose in furtherance of this outcome. Payne Finney kept the fires stoked as he flitted from group to group in the barroom. "This Smoke Jensen is a crazy man. He's killed more'n three hunnard men, shot most in the back, like poor Lawrence Tucker."

Finney added to his lies as he joined a trio of wranglers at the back end of the bar. "Remember when it was in the papers how he killed Rebel Tyree?" He put an elbow to the ribs of one cowhand and winked. "In the back. Not like the paper said, but in the back."

"Hell, I didn't even know you could read, Payne."

"Shut up, Tom. You never got past the fourth grade,

nohow. I tell you, this Jensen is as bloodthirsty as Billy Bonney."

"Bite yer tongue, Finney," Tom snapped. "Billy Bonney is much favored in these parts. He done right by avengin' Mr. Tunstill."

Payne Finney gave Tom Granger a fish eye. "And who's gonna avenge Mr. Lawrence Tucker?"

"Why, the law'll see to that."

"An' pigs fly, Tom. You can take my word for it, somethin' ought to be done."

"You talkin' lynch law, Payne?" The question came from a big, quiet man standing at a table in the middle of the room.

Turning to him, Payne Finney blinked. Maybe, he considered, he'd pushed it a bit too far. Gotta give them the idea they thunked it up on their own. That's what Quint Stalker had taught him. Payne silently wished that Stalker was there with him now. He had no desire to get on the wrong side of Clay Unger, this big, soft-spoken man who had a reputation with a gun that even Quint Stalker respected. He raised both hands, open, palms up, in a deprecating gesture.

"Now, Clay, I was just sayin' what if . . . ? You know a lot more about how the law works than I do—no offense," Payne hastened to add. "But from what little I do know, it seems any man with a bit of money can get off scot-free."

"And you were only speculating out loud as to, what if it happened to Smoke Jensen?"

"Yeah . . . that's about it."

Clay Unger raised a huge hand and pointed his trigger finger at Payne Finney. It aimed right between his eyes.

"Don't you think the time to worry about that is *after* it's happened?"

"Ummm. Ah—I suppose you're right, there, Clay."

Finney made his way hastily to the doors and raised puffs of dust from his bootheels as he ankled down the street to Donahue's. There he set to embellishing his tales of Smoke Jensen's bloody career. His words fell on curious ears and fertile minds. He bought a round of drinks and, when he left an hour later, he felt confident the seeds of his plan would germinate.

After Clay Unger and his friends had left the Hang Dog, two hard-faced, squint-eyed wranglers at the bar took up Payne Finney's theme. They quickly found ready agreement among the other occupants.

"What would it take to get that feller out of the jail and swing him from a rope, Ralph?"

Through a snicker, Ralph answered, "If you mean co—oper—ation, not a whole lot. Ol' Ferdie over there surely enjoys a good hangin'. Especially one where the boy's neck don't break like it oughtta. Ferdie likes to see 'em twitch and gag. Might be, he'd even hand that Jensen over to us."

" 'Us,' Ralph?" a more sober imbiber asked pointedly.

Ralph's mouth worked, trying to come up with words his limited intellect denied him. "I was just talkin'—ah—sorta hy-hypo—awh, talkin' like let's pretend."

"You mean hypothetically?" Ralph's detractor prodded.

"Yeah . . . that's it. Heard the word onest, about a thang like this."

Right then the batwings, inset from the tall, glass-paneled front doors swung inward, and Payne Finney strode in. "What's that yer talkin' about, Ralph?"

Puppy-dog eagerness lighted Ralph's face. "Good to see you, Payne. I was jist sayin' that it should be easy to get that Jensen outta the jail and string him up."

Finney crossed to the bar and gave Ralph a firm clap on one shoulder. "Words to my likin', Ralph. Tell me more."

Seated in a far corner, at a round table, three men did not share the bloodthirsty excitement. They cast worried gazes around the saloon, marked the men who seemed most enthused by the prospect of a lynching. Ripley Banning ran short, thick fingers, creased and cracked by hard work and callus, through his carroty hair. His light complexion flushed pink as he leaned forward and spoke quietly to his companions.

"I don't like the sound of this one bit." He cut sea-green eyes to Tyrell Hardy on his right.

Ty Hardy flashed a nervous grin, and stretched his lean, lanky body in the confines of the captain's chair. "Nor me, Rip. Ain't a hell of a lot three of us can do about it, though."

From his right, Walt Reardon added a soft question. "How's that, Ty? Seems a determined show of force could defuse this right fast."

Tyrell Hardy cut his pale blue eyes to Walt Reardon. He knew the older man to be a reformed gunfighter. Walt's fulsome mane of curly black hair, and heavy, bushy brows, gave his face a mean look to those who did not know him. And, truth to tell, Ty admitted, the potential for violence remained not too far under the surface. He flashed a fleeting smile and shook his head, which set his longish, nearly white hair to swaying.

"You've got a good point, Walt. But, given the odds, I'd allow as how one of us might get killed, if we mixed in."

"There's someone sure's hell gonna get killed, if this gets ugly," Rip Banning riposted. "What'er you sayin', Walt?"

Walt's dark brown eyes glowed with inner fire, and his tanned, leather face worked in a way that set his brush of mustache to waggling. "Might be that we should keep ourselves aware of what's going on. If this gets out of hand, a sudden surprise could go a long way to puttin' an end to it."

Martha Tucker went about her daily tasks mechanically. All of the spirit, the verve of life, had fled from her. She cooked for her children and herself, but hardly touched the food, didn't taste what she did consume. She had sat in stricken immobility for more than two hours, after word had been brought of Lawrence's death. Now, anger began to boil up to replace the grief.

It allowed her to set herself to doing something her late husband had often done to burn off anger he dare not let explode. Her hair awry, her face shiny in the afternoon light, an axe in both hands, Martha set about splitting firewood for the kitchen stove. With each solid smack, a small grunt escaped her lips, carrying with it a fleck of her outrage.

She cared not that at least a full week's supply already had been stacked under the lean-to that abutted the house,

beside the kitchen door. Neither did Martha have the
words or knowledge to call her strenuous activity ther-
apy; neither she, nor anyone in her world, knew the word
catharsis. She merely accepted that with each yielding
of a billet of piñon, she felt a scrap of the burden lift,
if only for a moment.

"Mother," Jimmy Tucker called from the corner of the
house.

He had to call twice more, before his voice cut into
Martha's consciousness.

"What is it, son?"

Jimmy's bare feet set up puffs of dust as he scampered
to his mother's side. "There's a man coming, Maw."

Cold fear stabbed at Martha's breast. "Who . . . is it?"

"I dunno. He don't . . . look mean."

"Go in the house, Jimmy, and get me the rifle. Then
round up your sister and brother and go to the root cellar."

"Think it's Apaches?"

"Not around here, son. I don't know what to think."

Jimmy's eyes narrowed. "I had better stay with you,
Maw."

"No, Jimmy. It's best you are safe . . . just in case."

"If it's that Smoke Jensen, I'll shoot his eyes out,"
Jimmy said tightly.

A new fear washed over Martha. "You hush that kind
of talk, you hear? If I had time, I'd wash your mouth
with soap."

Almost a whine, Jimmy's voice came out painfully. "I
didn't cuss, Maw."

In spite of the potential danger of the moment, Martha
could not suppress a flicker of smile. Since the first time,

at age four, that Jimmy had used the *S*-word, a bar of lye soap had been the answer, rather than his father's razor strap. Oh, how Jimmy hated it.

"Go along, son, do as I say," Martha relented with a pat on the top of Jimmy's head, something else he had come to find uncomfortable of late.

In less than a minute, Jimmy returned with the big old Spencer rifle that had belonged to his father. One pocket of his corduroy trousers, cut off and frayed below the knees, bulged with bright brass cartridges. Martha took the weapon from her son and loaded a round. She held it, muzzle pointed to the ground, when the stranger rode around into the barnyard two minutes later.

"Howdy there," he sang out. "I'm friendly. Come to give you the news from town."

"And what might that be?" Martha challenged.

"Well, ma'am, it looks like it's makin' up for a hangin' for that Smoke Jensen feller. Folks is mighty riled about what happened to your husband."

Unaccountably, the words burst out before she had time to consider them. "Is it certain that he is the guilty party?"

The young rangler did a double take. "Pardon, ma'am? I figgered you'd consider that good news."

Committed already, her second question boiled out over the first. "They've held a trial so soon?"

A sheepish expression remolded the cowboy's face. "In a way. Sort of, I mean, ma'am. In the—in the saloons. The boys ain't happy, an' they're fixin' to string that feller up."

"Good lord, that's—*barbaric.*"

Self-confidence recovered, the ranch hand responded

laconically. "There's some who might consider what he done to your husband to be that, too, ma'am."

"You're not a part of this?"

"No, ma'am. I just rode out to bring you the word."

"Then—then ride fast, find the sheriff, and have him bring an end to it. I don't want another monstrous crime to happen on top of the first."

"You don't mind my sayin' it, that's a mighty odd attitude, ma'am."

"No, it's not. Now you get back to town fast and get the sheriff."

"I say now's the time, boys!" Payne Finney shouted over the buzz of angry conversation in the Hang Dog. "Somebody go out and get a rope. Do it quick, while we still got the chance."

"Damn right!"

"I'll go over to Rutherford's, they got some good half-inch manila."

"No, a lariat will do," Forrest Gore sniggered. "Cut into his neck some that way."

"We'd best be making time, then," another man suggested. "Who all is with us?"

Twenty-five voices shouted allegiance.

"I'll go wind up the fellers at Donahue's," Finney informed them. "Take about half an hour, I'd say. Then we do it."

Covered by the shouts of approval, Ty Hardy leaned toward his companions. "Oh-oh, it looks like the boil's comin' to a head."

"Best we think fast about some way to lance it," Walt Reardon prompted.

"Yeah, an' quick," Rip Banning urged.

Long, gold shafts of late afternoon sunlight slanted into the office above the Cattlemen's Union Bank. Dust motes rose as a strong breeze battered the desert-shrunken window sashes and found the way inside. Crystal decanters sat squat on a mahogany sideboard; glasses had been positioned precisely in front of the three very different men who sat around the rectangular table.

Seated at one end, head cocked to the side, listening to the growing uproar from the saloons down the street, Geoffrey Benton-Howell pursed his thin lips in appreciation. Tufts of gray hair sprouted at each temple, creating a halo effect in the sunbeams, the rest of the tight helmet remained a lustrous medium brown. Long, pale, aristocratic fingers curled around the crystal glass, and he raised it to his lips.

Smacking them in appreciation, he spoke into what had become a long silence. "It appears that our designs prosper." Geoffrey's accent, although modulated by years in the American West, retained a flavor of the Midlands of England. "Miguel, you were wise indeed to suggest we take the sheriff into our confidence. It sounds to me that he is an inventive fellow."

Miguel Selleres glowed in the warm light of this praise. *"Gracias, Don* Geoffrey. *Mi amigos,* I would safely suggest that we have killed two birds, so to speak, with a single stone."

Although not quite as much the dandy as Benton-How-

ell, Selleres dressed expensively and had the air of a
Mexican grandee. Short of stature, at five feet and six
inches, he had the grace and build of a matador. Age
had not told on him, though already in his mid-forties;
he seemed every bit at home in this rough frontier town
as in the salon of a stately hacienda. One side of his
short-waisted, deep russet coat bulged with the .45 Mendoza copy of the Colt Peacemaker, which he wore concealed.

"Señor Selleres," the third man at the table said, pro-
nouncing the name in the Spanish manner; *Say-yer-res*.
"What, exactly, are you getting at?"

"May I answer that, Miguel?" Benton-Howell interrupted when he saw his partner's danger signal, a writhing of his pencil-line mustache.

"Go right ahead, *Señor* Geoffrey," Selleres grunted,
containing his anger.

"What he's getting at, Dalton, is that Tucker is out of
our way, with the perfect man to pin it on."

"Umm. You do make things so much clearer, Geoff,"
Dalton Wade said with a lip curl, to make clear his attitude toward Miguel Selleres.

Miguel Selleres cut his jet-black eyes from one partner to the other. He saw affability in the expensive
clothing and impeccable manners of Geoffrey Benton-
Howell, whom he had referred to as *Sir* Geoffrey. His
obvious affluence radiated security to their ambitious
goals.

Across the table from him sat a man Miguel thought
ill-suited to their company. Although he masked it with
sugared words and no overt insult, Dalton Wade's intense
dislike of anyone or anything Mexican radiated from his

pig face in waves of almost physical force. His swelling paunch matched his heavy jowls, and emphasized his porcine appearance. Wade dressed in the tacky manner of a local banker—which he was—in a rumpled suit of dark blue with too wide pinstripes. Miguel Selleres felt a genuine wave of revulsion rise within himself. Like a seller of secondhand buggies, Miguel thought with a conscious effort to throttle his rising gorge. It further angered him to acknowledge that he was the youngest of this unholy trio.

"In light of our obvious success, I'd suggest that you contact Quint Stalker and ensure that he moves with dispatch on the properties we desire," Selleres aimed at Wade.

"It has already been done," Wade snapped, barely in the boundaries of civility.

Benton-Howell stepped in to keep the peace. "Let me expand on that. As we speak, Stalker and some of his men should be acquiring the trading post at Twin Mesas. When that is accomplished, they will move on to the next, and the next. So there is little left we must address today. However, I have come upon a third benefit we can count as ours in this affair."

"Oh, really? What's that?" Dalton Wade remained cool, even to the man to whom he was beholden for being included in the grand design.

"Why, the most obvious of all, gentlemen. I propose a toast to us—the men who are about to put an end to Smoke Jensen."

Three

Sheriff Jake Reno eased his belly through the doorway to his office in the Socorro jail. His small, dusty boots made a soft pattering on the floorboards, as he crossed to a tiny cubicle set in the wall that divided the office from the cellblock. He poked his head in the open doorway and grunted at a snoozing Ferdie Biggs.

"Open up, Ferdie. I want to talk with that backshooter."

A line of drool glistened on Ferdie's ratlike face. It flashed as he wobbled the sleep out of his head and came to his boots. "Sure 'nuff, Boss. You gonna give him what for?"

"Do you mean beat hell out of him? No. No entertainment for you this afternoon, Ferdie. I only want to talk to him."

Disappointment drooped Ferdie Biggs's face. He reached for a ring of keys and unlocked the laced strap iron door that opened the cellblock for the sheriff. Reno stalked along the corridor, until he reached the cell that held Smoke Jensen.

Smoke reclined on his bunk, head propped up by both forearms. He didn't even open an eye at the sound of the lawman's approach. Heedless of possible damage to the weapon, Reno banged a couple of bars with the barrel of his Merwin and Hulbert. When the bell tone faded, Smoke opened one eye.

"What?" he asked with flat, hard menace.

"I come to get a confession out of you, Jensen."

"Fat chance. I didn't do anything."

"Sure of that, are you?" Reno probed.

"Yes. I'm sure I didn't back-shoot that man."

"You don't sound all that positive to me."

"Sheriff, I'm not sure about what exactly happened to me, how I got here, or when, but I *do* know that I have never deliberately back-shot a man in my life."

"Smoke Jensen, gunfighter and outlaw and he's never shot a man in the back before? I find that hard to believe. You're pretending, Jensen. I know it and so do you."

"Humor me, Sheriff. Tell me about it."

Taken aback, Sheriff Jake Reno gulped a deep breath. "All right. If it will help you see the light and give me a confession. It happened last night, about ten-thirty. Some shots were heard by customers in the Hang Dog Saloon. They rushed out to find out what was going on. In the alley at the edge of town, they came upon a body lying on the ground, and you.

"You were cold as a blowed-out lamp. The body was dead," Reno explained further.

"Mr. Tucker?"

Reno brightened. "Then you do admit knowing him?"

"No. Your jailer gave me the name early this morning."

"That idiot. Handed you a way out on a platter, didn't he? I'll fix his wagon later. Yes, it was Mr. Lawrence Tucker, a highly popular and respected local rancher.

He'd been shot. You were laying not far from him, with a .45 in your hand."

"I don't carry a .45," Smoke began to protest.

"You had it in your hand, damnit," Reno snapped. Then he drew a deep breath to regain his composure. "It had been fired twice. There were two bullet holes in Mr. Tucker's back. End of case."

"That's ridiculous, Sheriff."

"Oh, yeah?"

"Yes. I normally carry a .44. Two of them, in fact."

"Don't matter, Jensen. No .44s were found anywhere around you, or on Mr. Tucker, and no double rig. Your cartridge belt had a pocket for only one iron, and that .45 fit in it like in a glove."

"Did you or anyone recognize the gun and belt, Sheriff? Ever see it before?"

But Reno had already turned away. Over a shoulder he softly purred his last words for Smoke Jensen. "I'd like to stay and chat, Jensen, but I have important business outside town. You all just sit tight, an' we'll get you hanged all legal and proper."

Hank Yates turned from the batwings of the Hang Dog Saloon. "He's ridin' out of town now."

A wide grin turned the cruel, thin line of Payne Finney's mouth into something close to happy. Leave it to Jake Reno to cover himself. "Good. Now, boys, we can really get to work. Some of you go out the back way and wait in the alley between here an' the saddler's. The rest come with me. Spread out across the street and hold yer place, while I go get the fellers from Donahue's."

"You really think we can just walk down there and take Jensen out?" Yates asked, doubtful.

Finney started for the door as he spoke. "Matter of fact, I know we can."

With a surge of action, the men in the saloon obeyed Finney's commands. For a moment, their alcoholic confusion marred any smooth departure, as men bumped into one another aimed in opposite directions. They ironed it out quickly enough and left the barroom almost empty. All except for three men at the corner table they had occupied since the establishment opened.

"I think we'd best stay here awhile," Walt Reardon suggested.

"We've gotta do something to help," Rip Banning urged, his face nearly the color of his flaming hair.

"We will. In due time."

"Dangit, Walt, every second means more danger."

"Relax, Rip. Those boys have got to get all fired up with more whiskey and brave words, before they do anything drastic. Believe me, I know. I've been on the receiving end of more'n one lynch mob."

Neither Ty nor Rip wanted to dispute Walt over that. Rip eased back in his chair and stared balefully at the front doors. Ty examined his empty beer schooner. Walt eyed the Regulator clock on the wall above the bar. Sound exploded inside the barroom, as boot heels drummed on the planks of the porch outside.

Two rough-looking characters burst in, demanding bottles of whiskey. They took no note of the trio in the corner. After they left, Walt and the other two waited out ten long, tense minutes. Then Walt eased his six-gun from leather and put the hammer on half-cock. He rotated the cylinder to the empty chamber and inserted another cartridge. Then he closed the loading gate and returned his weapon to the holster.

"Rip, you go fetch our gear, an' go saddle up the horses."

Rip nodded and departed. Then Walt turned to Tyrell Hardy. "Ty, why don't you slip out the back door and go to the hotel. Bring our long guns back with you."

"Sure, Walt, right away." Ty Hardy was gone faster than his words.

Smoke Jensen heard the ruckus coming from the saloons and correctly interpreted its meaning. He needed to find some way out of this, before they drank enough liquid courage to come and do what they wanted to do. He had to think. He had to find out what had happened after the middle of the previous afternoon, when he and his hands arrived in Socorro.

"We checked into a hotel," Smoke muttered softly to himself. "Got our gear settled in the rooms, then stopped off at a saloon for a drink before supper." It felt like invisible hands were ringing his mind like a washcloth. "What did we eat? Where?"

The silence of the jail and in his mind mocked him. Smoke came up on his boots and paced the small space allowed in his tiny cell. "Something Mexican," he spoke to the wall. "Stringy beef, cooked in tomatoes, onions, and chili peppers. *Bisték ranchero*, that's it."

A loud shout interrupted his train of thought. One voice rose above the others, clear though distant; the cadence that of someone making a speech. It floated on the hot Socorro air through the small window high in his cell.

"I knew Lawrence Tucker for fifteen years. From when he first moved to these parts. He was a good man. Tough as nails when he had to be, but a good father and husband. Know his wife, too. An' those kids, why they're the most polite, hard-working, reverent younguns you'd ever want to know."

"Yeah, that's right," another voice joined the first. "Larry smoked cigars, like y'all know. Right fancy ones, from a place called Havana. Now, I'll tell you what. I'll buy a box of those special cigars for the first man who fits a rope around the neck of Smoke Jensen!"

Loud cheering rose like a tidal wave. Smoke Jensen stared unbelievingly at the stone wall and gritted his teeth. The testimonials went on, and Smoke could visualize the bottles being passed from hand to hand. In his mind he could see the faces, flushed with whiskey and blood-lust, growing shiny with sweat, as the crowd became a mob.

"In the fifteen years Lawrence Tucker has been here," the first orator went on, "he never done a mean or vicious thing. Oh, he shot him a few Apaches, and potted a couple of lobo wolves who wandered down from the San Cristobals, but he never traded shots with another man, white or Mezkin. Didn't hardly ever even raise his voice. Yet, he was respected, and his hands obeyed him. If it wasn't for havin' to tend the stock and protect the ranch, they'd be here now, you can count on that. And they'd be shoutin' loudest of any to hang that back-shooting sumbitch higher than Haymen."

More cheers. The whiskey, and the rhetoric, were doing their job.

Smoke Jensen climbed on the edge of the bunk and stretched to see beyond the walls of his prison. It did him little good. He found that his cell fronted on the brick wall of a two-story bakery. It had been the source of the tormenting aromas since his awakening. So far he had received not one scrap of food—only that swill laughingly called coffee, shortly after first light.

Never one to worship food, Smoke's belly cramped constantly now at the yeasty scent of baking bread and sugary accompaniment of pies and cakes. No doubt, the sadistic Biggs had placed him in this cell deliberately, and denied him anything to eat. For a moment it had taken his mind off his very real danger.

More shouts from the distant street soon reminded him. "What're we waitin' for?"

"The fellers at Donahue's are fixin' to join us," Payne Finney bellowed. "Y'all stay here, I'll hurry them on."

Smoke Jensen knew he had to do something before they got the sand to carry out their threats. To do that, he needed help. The question of getting it still nagged him. What *had* happened to the hands he had with him?

Three men sat on their lathered horses under a gnarled, aged paloverde tree that topped a large, red-orange mound overlooking the Tucker ranch. The one in the middle pulled a dust-blurred, black Montana Peak Stetson from his balding head, and mopped his brow with a blue gingham bandanna. He puckered thick lips and spat a stream of tobacco juice that struck an industrious dung beetle, which agitatedly rolled his latest prize back toward the hole it called home.

"That woman down there," he said to his companions. "She's got lots of grit. Say that for her. Wonder what the Big Boss will have to come up with to get her off that place?"

A soft grunt came from the thick-necked man on his right. "I say we jist ride down there, give her what her old man got, an' take over the spread."

Contempt curled the bald man's lips. "Idiot! You'd kill a woman? That's why you take orders from me, and I take 'em from Quint Stalker. It's gotta be all proper and legal, idjit."

"Didn't used to be that way," the bellicose one complained.

"Right you are. But ever since ol' Lew Wallace was territorial governor, we've had an extra large helpin' of law and order."

"You tell me? I done three years, breakin' rocks, because of him."

"Then don't open that grub hole of yours and spout such stupid ideas, or you'll do more than that."

"Sure, Rufe, sure. But I still say it would be the easiest way."

"All we're here to do is drop in and scare her a little."

"Then why don't we get on with it?"

They came down in a thunder of hooves. Dust boiled from under their horses, which rutched and groaned at the effort, adding to the eerie howls made by the men who rode them. Quint Stalker had sent only three men because it was such an easy assignment. In less than two minutes, the overconfident hard cases learned how badly their boss had read the situation.

A skinny, undersized boy with snowy hair popped up out of a haystack and slid down its side, yelling as he went. "Mom! Mom! Hey, they're comin' again!" The callused soles of his bare feet pounded clouds from the dry soil.

He cut left and right, zigzagging toward the house. A woman's figure appeared in one window. Rufe and his henchmen had no time to take note of that. With a whoop, the bald one bore down on the lad and bowled him over with the churning shoulder of his mount. A wild squawk burst from Jimmy Tucker, as he went tail over top and rolled like a ball. He bit down hard, teeth grinding, and cast a prayerful glance toward his mother.

In a flash, that became the last bit of scaring they did.

A puff of smoke preceded the crack of a .56 caliber slug that cut the hat from bald Rufe's head. He let out a squall of his own and grabbed uselessly at the flying Montana Peak, then set to cursing. Another bullet forced his companions to veer to the side and put some distance between them.

"Git back here! It's only a damn woman," Rufe bellowed.

Martha Tucker refined her aim some, her left elbow braced on the windowsill, tapered fingers holding the forestock. Calmly she squeezed off another shot from the Spencer. Her third round smacked meatily into Rufe's right shoulder, and exploded terrible pain through his chest. It also convinced him that this was no simple damn woman.

He'd had enough. He, too, reined to his left and put

spurs to the flanks of his horse. Another shot sounded behind him and sped all three on their way.

It started with a sound like an avalanche. A low, primal growl that swelled as it advanced, metamorphosing into the roar of a tidal bore, bent on smashing up an estuary and inundating everything along the river. Although coming from a distance, the angry bellow echoed from the brick wall of the bakery. It made the hairs on the nape of Smoke Jensen's neck rise and vibrate.

They were coming.

How many? Would they get in? Smoke Jensen had been scared in his life many times before. Yet nothing compared to what he experienced now—not the grizzly that had nearly taken off his face before he killed it with a Greenriver knife . . . not the dozen Blackfeet warriors who had surrounded him, alone in camp, with Preacher out running traps . . . not when he faced down a dozen hardened killers in the street of Banning. None of them compared. This absolutely paralyzed him for the moment. He was so helpless, vulnerable. Death rode the mob like a single steed, a hound out of Hell, and it made Smoke reexamine his own fragile mortality. How easily they could take him.

NO! He could find a way to get out of this. Somehow, he could hold off the mob. Think, damnit!

The rattle, squeak, and clang of the cellblock door interrupted Smoke Jensen's fevered speculation as it slammed open. He left the window at once, pressed his cheek to the corridor bars, and looked along the narrow walkway. Waddling toward him, Smoke saw the fat figure of Ferdie Biggs. The keys jangled musically in one pudgy paw.

"Turn around and back up against the bars, Jensen."

"You're taking me out of here?"

"Yep. Jist do as I say."

Smoke turned around and put his hands through the space between two bars. Biggs reached him a moment later, puffing and gasping. Cold bands of steel closed around the wrists of Smoke Jensen. A key turned in the small locks.

"Now step back. All the way to the wall."

"Am I being taken to some safer place?" Smoke asked, his expectations rising.

"Get back, I said." Biggs snarled the words as he reached behind his back and drew a .44 Smith and Wesson from his waistband. He stepped to the door and turned a large key in the lockcase. The bar gave noisily, and the jailer swung the barrier wide. He motioned to Smoke with the muzzle of the Smith, and a nasty smirk spread on his moon face. "Naw. I'm gonna give you over to those good ol' boys out there."

Four

Ferdie Biggs prodded Smoke Jensen ahead of him along the cellblock corridor. At the lattice-work door he passed on through without closing it. He had done the same with the cell, the keys hanging in the lock. The sudden rush of adrenaline had cleared the fuzziness from Smoke's head. He realized that for all of Biggs's slovenly appearance and illiterate speech, he was at least clever enough to lay the groundwork for it to appear the mob had overwhelmed him and broke into the jail.

"You're not smart enough to fake a forced entry, Ferdie," Smoke taunted him. "You're going to get caught."

Biggs gave him a rough shove that propelled Smoke across the room to the sheriff's desk. The narrow edge of the top dug into his thighs. Bright pinpoints of pain further cleared Smoke's thinking. He was ready, then, when Biggs barked his next command.

"Turn around, I wanna have some fun, bust you up some, before I let the boys in."

Smoke turned and kept swinging his right leg. The toe of his boot connected with the hand that held the six-gun and knocked it flying. It discharged a round that cut a hot trail past Smoke's rib cage, and smashed a blue granite coffeepot on a small, Acme two-burner wood stove in the corner. Biggs bellowed in pain and surprise, a moment before Smoke reversed the leg and planted his boot heel in the jailer's doughy middle.

Ferdie Biggs bent double, the air *whoosh*ing out from his lungs. Meanwhile Smoke Jensen recovered his balance and used his other foot to plant a solid kick to the side of Ferdie Biggs's head. From where it made contact came a ripe melon *plop!,* and Ferdie went to his knees.

"The keys, Ferdie," Smoke rasped out. "Give me the keys to these handcuffs."

"Ain't . . . gonna . . . do it."

Smoke kicked him again, a sharp boot toe in the chest. Ferdie gulped and sputtered, one hand clawed at his throat in an effort to suck in air. He turned deep-set, piggish eyes on Smoke Jensen in pleading. Smoke belted him again, from the side. A thin wail came from far down Ferdie's throat—he'd been able to gulp some breath.

"I keep kicking until I get the keys."

Smoke's hard, flat, unemotional voice reached Ferdie in a way nothing else might. One trembling hand delved into a side pocket of his vest. Shakily, he withdrew a single key on a small ring. He dropped it twice, while he knee-walked to where Smoke Jensen stood beside the desk.

"Now, reach around behind me and unlock these manacles." Smoke shoved the tip of one boot up in Ferdie's crotch. "Try anything, and you'll sing soprano for the rest of your life."

Sobbing for breath, and in desperation, Ferdie complied. It took three fumbling attempts to undo the first lock. Then Smoke took the key from Ferdie's trembling fingers and shoved the bleeding, glazed-eyed jailer back against the wall that contained a gun rack. Smoke freed his other wrist, then snapped the cuffs on Ferdie.

"Is there a back way out of here?"

Before Ferdie could answer, a loud pounding began on the closed and barred front door. "C'mon, Ferdie, open up!" a man bellowed.

"Bring him out! Bring him out! Bring him out!" the mob chanted in the background.

"Don't be a fool, Ferdie. He ain't worth gettin' hurt over."

"Your 'good ol' boys' don't seem to like you much, Ferdie," Smoke taunted. "Answer me. Is there a back way out?"

"N-no. Usedta be, but the sheriff had it bricked up."

"How brilliant of him. Nothing for it but to face them down."

Ferdie Biggs blinked incredulously. "How you gonna do that, all alone?"

"I won't be alone," Smoke advised him as he reached to the gun rack. "I'll have Mr. L. C. Smith with me."

He selected a short-barrel, 10-gauge L. C. Smith Wells Fargo gun and opened the breech. From a drawer at the bottom of the rack, he took six brass buckshot casings. Two he inserted into the shotgun. A loud crash sounded from the direction of the front door. Ferdie Biggs cringed.

"They shouldn' do that. It was all set—" He snapped

rubbery lips tightly closed, and lost his porcine appearance as he realized he had said too much.

"Set up or not, it isn't going the way they expected, is it?"

A rhythmic banging sounded as four men rammed a heavy wooden bench against the outer face of the door. Ferdie worked his thick lips.

"Oh, hell. Sheriff's gonna have my butt, if that door gets broke."

"The thing you should be worried about is that I've got your butt right *now.*"

Ferdie Biggs looked at Smoke Jensen with sudden, shocked realization. "You ain't gonna shoot me, are you?"

"Not unless I have to." The door vibrated with renewed intensity, and Smoke cut his eyes to it. He saw signs of strain on the oak bar.

"Get something heavier," came advice from the mob.

"Hell, get some dynamite."

That sent Ferdie Biggs on a staggered course to the shuttered window. He shouted through the thick wooden covers and closed the lower sash. "Oh, Jeeezus, don't do that. I'm still in here."

"Who cares?" a laughing voice told Ferdie.

"Great friends you've got." Smoke Jensen added a cold, death-rattle laugh to increase the effect of his words.

From a drawer in the sheriff's desk, Smoke took a very familiar pair of cartridge belts. One had the pocket slung low, for a right-hand draw. The other rode high on the left, with the butt of a .44 pointing forward, canted at a sharp angle.

Smoke cut his eyes to a thoroughly shaken Ferdie. "And here the sheriff told me they found no sign of my own guns. Now they show up in his desk. Wonder how that happened?"

"Don't ask me. All I saw was that old .45."

Smoke hastily strapped himself into the dual rigs. His hand had barely left the last buckle, when the door gave a hollow *boom* and the cross-bar splintered apart and fell to the floor. Another *slam* and the thick oak portal swung inward. Three men spilled into the room. The one in the lead held a rope, already tied into a hangman's knot.

To his left stood another, who looked to Smoke Jensen to be a saddle tramp. His wooden expression showed not the slightest glimmer of intelligence. The rifle he held at hip level commanded all the respect he needed. To the other side, Smoke saw a pigeon-breasted fellow, who could have been the grocery clerk at the general mercantile. Indeed, the fan of a feather duster projected from a hip pocket.

Triumph shone on their faces for only a second, until they took in the scattergun competently held in the hands of Smoke Jensen. Payne Finney reacted first. He let go of the noose and dived for the six-gun in its right-hand pocket.

"For godsake, shoot him, Gore," he yelled.

"You shoot him, Payne," came a wailed reply.

Smoke Jensen had only one chance. He swung the barrels of the L. C. Smith into position between the two gunmen, so that the shot column split its deadly load into two bodies. The deafening roar filled the room. A scream of pain came from the suddenly animated man named Gore. A cloud of gray-white powder smoke obscured the view for a moment. Smoke Jensen had already moved and gazed beyond the huge puffball.

His finger had already found the second trigger; Smoke guided the shotgun unerringly to the next largest threat. When that man made no move to carry on the fight, he sought out the two he had shot. Both lay on the floor.

Payne Finney had taken the most of the 00 pellets, and bled profusely from five wounds. Gore had at least three pellets in his side and right forearm. He lay silent and still now. Shock had knocked him unconscious. A third man, who had been unlucky enough to be in the open space between Finney and Gore, was also down, his kneecap shot away. He writhed and whined in agony. Smoke's keen sight also took in something else.

Sputtering trails of sparks arched over the heads of the mob, who stood stunned on the stoop and in the street. Instinctively, Smoke dived away from the open door, expecting a shattering blast of dynamite. Instead, the red cylinders fell among the members of the lynch mob and went off with thunderous, though relatively harmless roars. Starbursts of red, white, and green fountained up to sting and burn the blood-hungry crowd. Immediately, three six-guns opened up from behind the startled men of Socorro. Yells of consternation rose among the would-be hangmen.

More shots put wings to the feet of the least hearty of them. Movement away from the jail became epidemic when Smoke Jensen stepped into the doorway, shotgun ready. Laughing, yelling, and shooting, Smoke Jensen's three missing ranch hands, Banning, Hardy, and Reardon, dusted some boot heels with lead to speed the lynchers on their way.

"Hey, Walt," Ty Hardy shouted over the tumult. "I told you those Mezkin fireworks I bought in Ary-zona would come in handy."

Walt Reardon looked upon Smoke Jensen with a near-worshipful expression. "Kid foolishness I called them. Reckon I was wrong. Smoke, good to see you."

"Alive, you mean," Smoke returned dryly.

Reardon brushed that aside. "What the hell happened? You disappeared, and the next thing we know, folks are sayin' you killed a man; back-shot him—which means it sure as the devil weren't you."

"What took you so long?" Smoke smiled to take the sting out of his words.

"We had to have a plan. You should have seen them. Half a hunnerd at least." Reardon tipped back the brim of his hat and wiped a sweaty brow. "What now?"

"I suggest we leave the lovely town of Socorro for better parts," Smoke advised.

"Suits," Reardon agreed. "We—ah—took the precaution to get your horse saddled and ready. It's down the block."

All four started that way. Behind them, Ferdie Biggs tottered out onto the stoop. "What about me? What's gonna happen to me?"

Smoke Jensen swiveled his head and gave Ferdie Biggs a deathly grin. "You'll have quite a story to tell the sheriff now, won't you, Ferdie?"

* * *

Through no fault of their own, Geoffrey Benton-Howell, Miguel Selleres, and Dalton Wade erroneously toasted the demise of Smoke Jensen when they heard the commotion coming from the jail. Beaming heartily, Benton-Howell refilled their glasses and raised his again.

"And here's to our prospects of becoming very wealthy men."

"Here, here!" Dalton Wade responded.

"I think it is fortuitous that our man found Quint Stalker so quickly," Miguel Selleres remarked. "Now that he is rounding up his men, we can put our next phase in operation."

"I'd like to see Smoke Jensen swinging from a tree." Bitterness rang in Wade's words.

Benton-Howell gave him a hard look. "It would be more politic for us to remain here, out of the sight of others. If you would be so kind, why is it you have such a hatred for Smoke Jensen?"

Dalton Wade considered a moment before answering. "Three close friends are in their graves because of that damned Smoke Jensen."

Geoffrey Benton-Howell said, "They were all good friends?"

"Yes, they were. Two of them were doing quite well, running a small town up in Montana with iron fists. Some of their henchmen stepped on the toes of someone related to Smoke Jensen. Jensen took exception to it. When Jensen finished, fifteen men were dead, another twenty-seven wounded. Among them, my friends."

"What about the third?" Benton-Howell asked.

"Jeremy and I were very close friends. He fancied

himself a good hand with a gun. Fast, exceptionally fast in fact. But . . . not fast enough. He braced Smoke Jensen one day. Jensen was actually a bit slower on the draw, but oh, so much more accurate. Jeremy didn't have a chance."

"I see. So all along this has been personal with you, not just a means to an end. For my part, and Don Miguel's, when our involvement in this is known, we'll be considered clever heroes to many people. It will make what comes after . . . ah . . . more palatable to them." His smile turned nasty. "From now on, events are going to turn rather rough. It's necessary that they are blamed on a mythical Smoke Jensen gang, seeking retribution for his death."

Benton-Howell poured more brandy, and his laughter filled the room.

Sheriff Jake Reno rode into a town oddly quiet for the scene of a lynching. Socorro slumbered under the hot New Mexico sun. A deep uneasiness grew when he saw no signs of a dead Smoke Jensen hanging from any tree on the northern edge of town. He found the jail door open, as expected, though no sign of Ferdie Biggs. He dismounted and entered.

Ferdie Biggs lay slumped on the daybed used by the night duty jailer. He had a fist-sized lump on the side of his head—bandaged in yards of gauze—a fat, swollen lip, and more tape and bandage around his ribs.

"What the hell happened to you?" Reno blurted.

"Smoke Jensen's what happened. He kicked the crap out of me and escaped. Had three fellers with him, outside the jail when the mob came. Set off some kind of explosives, shot up the place, and they all got away."

Rage burned in the sheriff's chest as he saw his five-hundred-dollar bonus flying away. He crossed to where Biggs lay and grabbed a double handful of shirt, yanking the slovenly jailer upright. "Goddamnit, can't you do anything right?"

"Ow! Oh, damn, I hurt! I meant what I said, Jensen *kicked* me."

"I suppose because he was in handcuffs?" Reno said scornfully.

Ferdie gulped. "Yep. I had him cuffed, right enough."

"But you got too close. Pushed your luck, right?"

"Uh-huh. I wanted to punch him up a little, have some fun before they hung him. Next thing I knew, he was usin' them of his boots on me."

"Idiot. Get that lard butt of yours out there and round up some men to form a posse. We're going after Jensen." Sheriff Reno's decision came automatically, without a thought of consulting the men who had bought his co-operation.

There'd be hell to pay when they found out his means of disposing of Smoke Jensen had failed, he reckoned. Best to put that off for a while. Chances were he'd run Jensen to ground easily, and come back to collect his five hundred. Sure, Reno's growing self-confidence told him, Smoke Jensen or no, the man was on the run in strange territory. It would be easy.

It would take all of the cunning of the last mountain man to evade the posse Smoke knew would be sent to pursue him and his hands. Ten miles out of town, Smoke had called a halt and sincerely thanked his men for the rescue. He saw clearly now, that they had laid low in order not to become ensnared in whatever skullduggery had put him in line for a lynching. He also explained the options open to them.

". . . so that's about it. You can all take off for the Sugarloaf, or take your chances with me."

"What do you reckon to do?" Walt Reardon asked.

"I'm going to find out who killed Tucker, and why. That should clear my name in these parts."

Reardon, used to being a wanted man, nodded soberly. "Might be a big undertakin'. I allow as how you could use some help."

"Same for me," Ty Hardy chimed in.

"I'll stick it out with you, Smoke," Rip Banning added.

"It can get rough. There's a chance some of us will draw a bullet."

"Way I see it, Smoke, that's an everyday experience. Long as it's not a stacked deck, count me in for the game."

Smoke Jensen looked hard at Walt Reardon, appreciating his staunch support and his knowledge. Smile lines crinkled around Smoke's slate-gray eyes, and he nodded curtly. "Best I could come up with is to head for the nearest mountains. Wear the posse down, confuse them. Sooner or later they'll give up and go home."

Walt grinned. "Now, that shines. I 'member the time me an' old Frisco Johnny Blue did just that up in Dakota Territory. Worked fine as frog hair. Is there . . . ah . . .

somethin' else we could be doin', while givin' that posse the slip?"

"Maybe. I'll think on it. Now, let's put some distance between us and them. Next stop's the Cibola Range."

Five

Sheriff Jake Reno trotted his blotched gray along the main trail leading north out of Socorro. The posse had covered eight miles at a fast trot, then slowed the pace to look for tracks. They found them easily. Reno held them to a leisurely pace from then on.

"My guess is they'll be cuttin' west soon," he advised the man on his left.

"Why's that?" the uncomfortable store clerk asked.

"Smoke Jensen's got him a rep'tation of bein' a mountain man. The last mountain man. I reckon he'd feel more at home in the hills. Too open to keep on north toward the Rockies. Those three saddle bums is wanted for jail break, along with Jensen, an' you can add murder on Jensen's head. No, they won't want to run into a lot of folks."

Snorting doubt through a nose made red by whiskey, the clerk issued his own opinion. "If he wanted mountains, there's plenty around Socorro."

"But too close to town for his likin'. Smoke Jensen's nothin' if he ain't clever. If he was to sneak around outside town, we could keep resupplied forever and wear him down. Now, you be for keepin' a close eye out for where they turn off."

They almost missed it, as it was. A bare, wide slab of rock led into the bed of an intermittent stream, presently made liquid by heavy rains in the mountains. A fresh scrape, made by the iron shoe of a heavy horse, told the story to the sheriff's favorite scout. He waved the posse down as they approached.

"They went into the water."

"Not too smart under the best of conditions," Jake Reno opined.

"It will run dry in an hour or two," the scout suggested.

"Or it'll come a flash flood gushin' down on us. We'll ride the banks, let them take the risk. Jensen and his trash friends'll come out sooner than later, I figger."

Five miles to the west, the posse came upon the spot where four horses began to walk on wet sand. Sheriff Reno halted the men and tipped back the wide brim of his hat. A blue gingham bandanna mopped at the sweat that streaked down his temples and brow.

"Yep. They're headin' into the Cibolas. Eb, you an' Sam head back for town. Get us some pack animals and lots of grub. This is gonna be a long hunt."

"Like I said, boys. This ain't like the High Lonesome, but at least it's mountains." Smoke Jensen dismounted and continued to speak his observations aloud. "I'd say the sheriff is a good ten miles behind. Time to fix up something for him to remember us by."

"How's that?"

"Walt, you were with the Sugarloaf back when those

Eastern dudes tried to attack the place. Perhaps you could enlighten young Rip here."

"Sure, Smoke." Walt proceeded to tell Ripley Banning about the deadfalls, pits, and the great star-shaped log obstacles that had so befuddled the army of Eastern thugs, who had been sicked on the Sugarloaf hands only a year past. Rip started to grin early on, and his eyes danced with mischief by the time the tale had been told.

"Considerin' your fondness for ornery tricks, Walt, it couldn't be that maybe you thought up some of those nasty traps?"

Walt Reardon pulled a face. "Rip, you wound me. Though I confess, it was my idea to gather up them yeller jacket nests in the night whilst they was restin', and flang gunnysacks full in among the sleepin' outlaws." He clapped his hands in approval. "They folks danced around right smartly."

Under the direction of Smoke and Walt, several large snares and a deadfall were rigged on the trail they left. "We'll cut south a ways now," Smoke suggested. "If I was making a way through these hills, I reckon I'd pick me a way through that pair of peaks yonder. Looks like a natural pass to me."

"You've got a hell of an eye, Smoke," said Walt admiringly.

Sheriff Jake Reno heard a faint *twang,* a second before a leafy sapling made a swishing rush through the air and cleaned two possemen off their mounts. One's boot heel caught in the stirrup, and the frightened horse he had been riding set off at a brisk run along the trail. The man's screams echoed off the high sandstone walls that surrounded them.

Not for long, though, as his head plocked against a boulder at the side of the narrow passageway, and he lost consciousness. Wide-eyed and pale, the sneering clerk lost some of his cockiness. He cut his eyes to the sheriff and worked a mouth that made no sound for a moment.

"What was that?"

"A trap, you dummy. Nobody move an inch, hear?"

The sheriff's advice proved wise indeed. The riders cut their eyes around the terrain and located two more of Smoke Jensen's surprises; a deadfall and another swing trap. Reno ordered the men to dismount and search on foot. That worked well enough, until a second *swoosh* of leaves and a startled scream froze them in place.

Jake Reno found himself looking up at a man suspended some ten feet off the ground, his ankles securely held in a rope snare. "Just like a damn rabbit," the lawman grumbled. "Some of you get him down. We'll stick to the center of the trail. Walk your mounts. And . . . keep a sharp eye, or you'll be swingin' up there next . . . or worse."

Smoke Jensen stood looking south at the summit of a natural pass through the Cibola Range, and studied the land beyond. "I figure that bought us a good three hours. It appears to me there's a small box canyon about a half hour's ride along this trail. We'll camp there for the night."

From that point on, Smoke and his wranglers took care to hide their tracks. Walt Reardon took the rear slot with a large clump of sagebrush, which he used to wipe out their prints on soft ground. They reached the overgrown entrance to the side canyon in twenty minutes. Smoke went ahead and made sure they could navigate the narrow passage without leaving obvious signs of their presence. At the back of the small gorge, they found a rock basin of water, cool and clear. Called a tank in these parts, from the original Spanish designation of *tanque,* these natural water reservoirs had saved many a life on the barren deserts of the Southwest.

Some, like this one, were even big enough to swim in. Of course, Smoke advised his ranch hands, that would have to wait until they and the horses had drunk their fill, and used all they needed for cooking.

"Though I don't mind leavin' behind some dirt for the good Sheriff Reno to swallow," he concluded with a chuckle.

Ty Hardy and Walt Reardon set about locating pine cones and dry wood to make a nearly smokeless fire. Smoke figured they had a good three hours in which to prepare food for that night and the next morning. Once well-accustomed to the outlaw life, Walt Reardon had prepared well, stuffing their saddlebags with coffee beans, flour, sugar, salt, side pork, and dry beans. Smoke got right down to mixing dough for skillet bread. Resembling a giant biscuit, baked over coals in a cast-iron skillet, and sealed with the lid of a Dutch oven, it was served in pie wedges. Not as tasty as the flaky biscuits Smoke's lovely wife, Sally, made, but it would serve, and could be eaten hot or cold. Rip Banning watched intently, until Smoke sent him for water for the Dutch oven to soak beans. Rip returned with a broad, boyish grin.

"Found me a bee tree. It's jam packed with honey. Reckon it'll go good on that skillet bread."

Smoke cocked an eye on him. "How you reckon on getting that honey without having an argument with the bees?"

"Why, I'll just smoke . . . uh . . . dumb of me, huh? Can't drowse 'em out with a big ol' puff of pearly white that'd let the sheriff know where we'd gone."

"You're learnin'. We'll just have to forego the honey tonight. And," Smoke continued, "I'm appointin' you to make sure all fires are well out before sundown."

"Make the lesson stick, huh?"

"You got the right of it, Rip."

Walt returned from his last trip for wood with four plump squirrels. Excitement filled Rip Banning. "We're gonna feast. How'd you git 'em without firing a shot, Walt?"

Walt made light of it, but could not avoid a tiny brag. "I come up on them, frolickin' on the ground. So I just locked eyes and mesemer . . . mesariz . . ."

"Mesmerized," Smoke provided.

"Yeah, that's right. I done stared them down."

Rip nodded with youthful enthusiasm, then produced a frown over his green eyes. "Squirrels are hard to dress out."

Walt gestured with his russet-furred contribution to dinner. "That's why you're cleaning all of 'em."

"Awh, Walt—"

"You fixin' to sink a tooth into one of 'em, you can do the honors."

They tasted delicious, roasted over the fire, helped along with skillet bread, thick beans, wild onions, and watercress from the tank. Half an hour before sundown, Rip poured water on the fire, raked the ashes, and distributed the stones that had formed the fire ring. With muttered good nights, Smoke and the two older hands rolled up in their blankets and fell into deep sleep. Rip, being youngest, had the first watch. He would wake Walt for second shift, who in turn would roll out Ty Hardy. Smoke took the last trick, usually the most likely for a surprise attack.

Setting down the empty tin cup, Sheriff Jake Reno wiped a drop of coffee off one thick lip and rested the hand on the swell of his belly. He was beginning to suspect that they had taken the wrong trail. This one led nowhere, if he recollected correctly. It would take them half a day to cross south over the ridges between them and the pass that led to the great inner valley of the Cibola Range. There they could get reinforcements and resupply at Datil, or further on at Horse Springs.

Provided, of course, that Smoke Jensen didn't get there first and tie up with some local guns. That could get nasty. The heavy breakfast the sheriff had eaten rumbled in his gut. Oh, lord, all he needed was to work up a burnin' stomach. Those damned traps set out by Jensen had cost them half a day. Just thinking about them put him in a stew.

"Herkermer, I want you to round up a dozen of the

boys and take the shortest route to Cristoforo Pass. I got me a feelin' we're in the wrong part of the Cibolas."

"The trail led us northwest," Herkermer protested. "Besides, the shortest way is the longest. All them ridges to climb."

"You'll pick up speed goin' down the other sides," Reno snapped back.

"What'll you be doing in the meantime?"

"Look, Herkermer, I'm runnin' this posse, not you. We'll be havin' a look-see at this trail; the canyons yonder link up, make for hard goin', but a body can get through. We have to be certain which way Jensen went. Then we'll join you in Datil. I've a hunch Jensen is makin' for the main part of the range."

"He'd sure have to know a hell of a lot about the country for him to figger that out," Payne Finney said obstinately, the pain in his side making him more irritable than usual.

"What's to say he don't have a map, you ninny? Those buckshot holes is makin' you dizzy-headed. Truth to tell, you ain't in fit condition to ride with us. I think I'm goin' to send you back to Socorro with a message for some certain gentlemen."

"Our mutual employers, you mean," Payne prompted nastily. "Suits me. I ain't feelin' all that whippy, no how."

"You tell 'em where we are and what we're doin'," came the sheriff's command.

You're splittin' the posse, an' makin' a fool of yerself, Payne Finney thought silently. He knew only too well how damned dangerous Smoke Jensen could be. *Goddamn you, Smoke Jensen,* Payne Finney vowed to himself, *I'm gonna fix your clock sure as shootin'.*

* * *

Geoffrey Benton-Howell and his partners already knew of the fiasco in the jail. Miguel Selleres and Dalton Wade fumed, while Geoffrey Benton-Howell tried to calm his partners and get some positive thoughts out of them about a bit of news just delivered. The bearer of the good tidings, Axel Gundersen, watched the two would-be tycoons vent their spleens with mild amusement. At last, he spoke into the silence after their tirade.

"Ja, sure, Sir Geoffrey, it's exactly like I say. The gold is there, true enough, *hufda.* Make no mistake about that. Some of it is exposed on the surface. The problem is getting it out."

Miguel Selleres rounded on him. *"Hijo de la chingada!* Make sense, *Señor!* Didn't you just say that gold was to be found on the surface? What's to make it difficult getting it out?"

Gundersen drew a straight face and called on his ample knowledge of English idiom. "About eight hundred angry White Mountain Apache warriors, *ja* sure."

"Ah . . . ummm, yes, Miguel. There is a small difficulty to get around the Apaches."

"What's the problem in that?" Dalton Wade snapped.

"The gold is on their land," Geoffrey Benton-Howell reminded his listeners.

"Land they've got no goddamned right to," Wade thundered. "What do those stupid savages know about gold?"

Benton-Howell tried a soft approach. "That we white men desperately want the yellow rocks, as they call the gold. That we go absolutely mad over possessing it."

Wade's lip curled downward in a parody of a pout. "There you go. To those stinking Apaches, they are just rocks. If people can't appreciate what they have on their land, it should be taken from them."

"Which we are in the process of doing. Here, take some brandy and relax. Well, Gunderson, you've done a fine job. Your compensation will be in keeping with your achievements."

"*Ja,* sure, I expected no less. Now all you need to do is follow through with the politicians."

During the lonely hours of his watch, Smoke Jensen had thought through the situation in which he found himself. The previous day had been given over to surviving long enough to examine conditions and options. He announced the result of his deliberations over breakfast the next morning.

"We're going to split up."

"We done anything that don't suit you?" Walt Reardon asked cautiously.

"No, nothing like that. We can stick together and run that posse ragged, but in a way, that's spinnin' a wagon wheel over a gorge. Someone needs to get word to the Sugarloaf. Ty, I'm going to leave that up to you."

"I'd rather ride beside you, Smoke."

"I know you would. But Sally has to hear about this from someone on our side. Besides, it might be we'll need help from the other hands, before this is over. Or from Monte Carson. He knows you, so does Sally. Walt, I want you and Rip to head back to Arizona. Contact Jeff York, the Ranger captain we sold those horses to.

Tell him what's going on, and ask if he knows what's behind it."

"Want us to bring him here?"

"Out of his jurisdiction, Walt. But if he offers, carry him along."

"I've got the feeling there's gonna be hell to pay 'fore long."

Smoke came to his boots, put a hand on Walt's shoulder. "You're right. And I aim to see the ones payin' it are Sheriff Reno and his posse. I'm headin' on. Lead your horses up the trail a ways in the direction you're going, then wipe out every sign of this camp."

Walt nodded curtly. "Keep a wall to your back, Smoke."

"I will, whenever I can, Walt."

"Hell, this ain't gettin' us anywhere, Sheriff," a disgruntled posseman complained.

Jake Reno considered that a moment. "You're right, Jim. We ain't seen a sign of them in hours. Might be we're following the wrong trail. What we need to do is fan out, follow ev'ry game and people path heading south. I know it in my bones that Smoke Jensen is headed toward Horse Springs. There's a telegraph there, and he can get help if he wants it."

"What would any wanted man go into a town for?" Jim asked.

"It's not like he really kilt—" Reno realized what he was about to say and bit off the words.

Two of the citizens of Socorro exchanged nervous glances. Doubt wrinkled the brows of several others.

"Now, I want you to keep this in mind. This whole affair has gone too damn far. Check out everything that moves, and if you see Jensen, shoot to kill."

Six

Smoke Jensen ghosted through the trees in a low ground mist that had drifted in around three in the morning. Only his wranglers had left the northern slopes of the Cibola Range. Smoke had kept his place, expecting to catch Sheriff Jake Reno off guard. And he had.

A crackle of brush made Smoke Jensen cut his eyes to the left. Only a second passed before he heard soft, murmured words from that direction. His keen vision marked the shapes of two heads, close together. The sheriff had been smart enough to put out pickets, but he hadn't been too smart about who he had assigned the duty, Smoke reckoned. The mountain man had exchanged boots for moccasins earlier, and now moved with utter silence.

Half a dozen carefully placed strides brought him up behind the unwary pair. One of the possemen had just fished the makin's out of a vest pocket. When he started to roll a quirley, Smoke Jensen reached out with two big, hard hands to the off sides of the duo's heads, and slammed them together. He made quick work of binding their hands and feet with short lengths cut from a rope he had taken off another unattentive sentry earlier.

Smoke stuffed the neckerchiefs of the unconscious

men into their mouths. Satisfied with his work, he moved on. A surprisingly short distance inward of the camp, he came upon a line of picketed horses. A reassuring pat on the muzzles of the critters gained their silence, while Smoke undid their reins from the tightly stretched lariat that served as an anchor. A sudden, cold thought speared at him. This was entirely too easy.

"I figgered you'd come lookin' for us. So, I left you a few tidbits to whet your appetite," said Sheriff Reno, as he clicked back the hammer of his Smith and Wesson .44 American.

Smoke Jensen turned his way and made a draw in one smooth motion. Jake Reno had never seen anything like it. One second he was looking at Smoke Jensen's back, a split-second later, Jensen faced him, the black hole of a .44 muzzle settling in on the lawman's belly. Without conscious direction, Reno's body took over, flexed at the knees, and he flew backward into the sharp thorns of a clump of blackberry bushes. Smoke's .44 roared and spat fire, before Reno could even think to trigger his.

Hot lead cut a shallow trail across the upper curve of the sheriff's buttocks. With wild squalls, the horses took off at a run, and so did Smoke Jensen.

"Goddamnit, he's shot me! Smoke Jensen's shot me," Jake Reno roared, more angry than hurt.

Bent double, the famous gunfighter streaked along, parallel to the camp and at a right angle to the direction taken by the frightened critters. From behind, Smoke heard new, painful yelps from the sheriff, who was learning why any man with good sense sent his woman and kids out to pick berries.

Sleepy cries of alarm rose from the disturbed camp.

Men began to curse hotly, when they realized what the sound of pounding hooves meant. Smoke Jensen ignored them and forced his way through the underbrush to where he had left his mount. He'd give them some time to settle down, he reasoned, then hit again about midnight.

Five of Quint Stalker's gang, who had ridden with the posse, paused at the dark entrance to a side canyon. Not even the full moonlight could penetrate the gorge. Under the frosty starlight, they cut uncertain glances at one another.

"Don't know why the hell the sheriff wants us checkin' this out in the middle of the night," one complained.

"Says he's got a hunch. You ask me, it's a little in-digestion proddin' his belly."

"Or his sore butt stingin'," another opined.

At the rear of the loose formation, the last man saw a brief flicker of movement right before his eyes. Then he let out a short, startled yelp, as the loop tightened and pinned his arms to his sides above the elbows. The others turned in time to see him disappear from the saddle.

"What the hell!" the nominal leader exploded. "Hub! Where the hell are you?"

But Hub wasn't saying anything. He was too busy sucking on the barrel of a .44 in the hand of Smoke Jensen. Smoke gave an unseen nod of satisfaction and bent low to whisper in Hub's ear.

"You want to stay alive, you keep real quiet." Smoke removed the steel tube from Hub's mouth at the man's energetic nod of agreement. "I'm going to tie your legs together and string you up in that tree."

"You said I could live," Hub blurted in confusion and fear.

"Upside down, idiot. And you will live, if you give me five minutes to get clear of this place. Then you can yell your fool head off."

Hub Peters had no problem believing everything Smoke Jensen told him. He felt the rope circle his ankles and the tension increase. The tight band around his chest eased off, and he swung free of the ground. His fear somewhat abated, he could again hear his companions.

"D'you see that? Where in hell did he go?"

"I don't know, but it's some more bad news from Smoke Jensen, count on it."

"We goin' in after Hub?"

"You crazy?" the leader challenged. "Want to wind up disappearin' before yer friends' eyes?"

"What about Hub?"

"Nice friends you have, Hub. If I was you, I'd light me a shuck for some place far, far away from them." Smoke's soft chuckle faded off into the distance.

Silently, Hub Peters agreed with Smoke Jensen.

Had they been looking in the right direction, the men of the posse would have seen a telltale spurt of gray-white powder smoke, some three seconds before the blue granite coffeepot gave off a metallic clang and leaped from the fire. Boiling liquid flew everywhere, then the sound of the shot came. Three hard cases—brought by the sheriff to keep the townies in line—squawked in alarm as the hot brew scalded their flesh.

They tore at their shirts and trousers in an effort to

escape their torment, unmindful of the danger. Most of the others had already bellied down in the dirt.

"Over there!" came a frightened cry as another blossom of gray rose from the hillside.

This time, one of Quint Stalker's gunnies went down with a bullet through his right thigh. He flopped and cursed and moaned in the dust, while his companions skittered off to find better cover. One outlaw hanger-on with better foresight had brought a long-range Express rifle. He unlimbered it from its scabbard, adjusted the sight, and took aim. After levering three rounds through the Winchester, he had to acknowledge that only a fool would have stuck around after the second shot. He'd wasted the ammunition.

When the sniper fire did not resume after five minutes, the possemen picked up the remains of their breakfast and fell into their routine. A crack-whisper of sound above their heads turned faces upward, to receive a shower of shredded leaves. Right on the tail of the high round, another snapped into camp and split the cross-tree of a pack saddle.

Once more, everyone dove for cover. One pudgy townsman didn't take as much care as his comrades, and paid for it with the heel of one boot. The howl he put up might have convinced someone his foot had been shot off.

"Goddamn you, Smoke Jensen!" Sheriff Jake Reno roared, shaking a fist above the boulder behind which he sheltered. A .45-70-500 Express bullet whipped past his knuckles, close enough to feel its heat. He gave a little yelp and hunkered down.

This time no one moved for fifteen minutes. Two of

Stalker's hard cases came out in the open first. "We'd best go look for a trail," one opined.

"What for? It'd only lead to an ambush," the other outlaw complained.

"Damn you, men, you're my deputies now, and you'll do as I say," Reno raved. "Get on your horses and go out there and hunt down Smoke Jensen."

"Temp-orary deputies, Sheriff," the reluctant one reminded Reno. "And, right about now, I'm figgerin' that short time has runned out."

"You're not leaving," an unbelieving Sheriff Reno gasped.

"Reckon to. I sure ain't gonna stand around and git shot at by a man who don't miss lest he wants to."

"You're cowards, that's what you are."

Eyes narrowed with sudden anger, the hard case faced off with the sheriff. "Now, I don't 'zactly take kindly to that, Sheriff. Y'all want to back up them bad-mouthin' words with gunplay?"

Ooops! Sheriff Reno suddenly realized he had gone too far. "Ah—ummm, no, not at all. I spoke out of hand, gentlemen. Go if you want. Besides, I need someone to take a message to our mutual friend."

"You mean Quint?"

Sheriff Reno winced. "Uh . . . tell him what's going on, and have him send some more men."

"Don't reckon he'll be able to do that. We've got other irons in the fire."

"Damnit, man, nothin's more important than stopping Smoke Jensen. Just carry the message, and I'll be satisfied."

"Sure 'nuff, Sheriff," the grinning hard case responded as he headed for his horse.

He made it three-quarters of the way there, before a bullet from Smoke Jensen took him in the meaty point of his left shoulder. Little pig squeals came from skinned-back lips, along with bloody froth from a punctured lung as he went to the ground.

"Oh. Sweet . . . Jesus!" Sheriff Reno shouted to the sky. And to those around him it sounded like a prayer.

Smile lines crinkled around Smoke Jensen's gray eyes, and the corners of his mouth twitched. After this, those townies would be afraid to drink anywhere in the mountains. Of course, it would be hard on anyone who happened on the stream before it washed clear.

He'd left the carcasses out to bloat and ripen in the sun for two days. They had become so potent, that Smoke needed to cover his face with a wet kerchief to cut down the stench. Even then, it near to gagged him when he rigged the rope that held them in the water. He made sure it was easy to see.

A final look around the clearing by the stream, and he got ready to leave. Carefully, Smoke wiped out any sign of his presence as he departed. Within a minute, only the muted echo of a soft guffaw remained of the last mountain man.

"What's that awful smell?" a townsman asked of Sheriff Reno.

"Smells like skunk. Mighty ripe skunk," the lawman replied.

"It's coming from the crick," one of Quint Stalker's outlaws advised.

"Skunks don't take baths," another contradicted.

"Hey, there's a rope hangin' down over the water," another shop clerk deputy declared. "Somethin's on the end of it."

Three of Stalker's men rode over to investigate. One dismounted and bent over the bank. He turned back quickly enough, his face a study in queasiness.

" 'Fore God, I hate that Smoke Jensen. He's put three rotten skunks in the water."

"Three skunks?" the sheriff echoed.

"Three *rotten* skunks. Flesh all but washed off of 'em, guts all strung out."

Gagging, retching sounds came from a trio of townies. Faces sickly green, they wobbled off into the meadow to void their stomachs. One finished before the others and turned back to the sheriff, who sat his horse with a puzzled expression.

"We—we drank from that crick not half a mile back. Filled our canteens, too."

A couple of Stalker's hard cases began to puke up their guts. Those affected wasted no time in remounting. They put heels to the flanks of their animals and fogged off down the trail in the direction of Socorro. Sheriff Jake Reno remained gape-mouthed for a moment, the slight wound on his hindside stinging from the sweat that ran down his back, then bellowed in rage. "Goddamn you, Smoke Jensen! I'm gonna kill you, you hear me? I'm gonna kill you dead, dead, dead, Smoke Jensen!"

* * *

While Smoke Jensen frazzled the nerves of the posse, five hard-faced men paid a visit to the Widow Tucker and her three small children. Their leader, Forrest Gore, had been barely able to stay in the saddle on the long ride out from Socorro. Jimmy Tucker saw them first, and the smooth, hard-callused soles of his bare feet raised clouds as he darted from the barn to the rear of the house.

"Some more bad guys comin', Maw," he shouted as he banged through the back door.

Martha Tucker looked up from the pie crust she had been rolling out, and wiped a stray lock of hair from her damp forehead with the back of one hand. The effort left a white streak. "You know what to do, Jimmy."

"Yes, ma'am," the boy replied.

He stepped to the kitchen door, put his little fingers between full lips, and blew out a shrill whistle. Rose and Tommy Tucker came scampering from where they had been playing under a huge alamogordo. A stray breeze rattled the heart-shaped, pale green leaves of the old cottonwood as they deserted it.

"Into the loft," their mother instructed.

Without a protest or question, the smaller children climbed the ladder to where all three youngsters slept. Rose covered her head with a goose-down quilt. Big-eyed, Tommy watched what went on downstairs.

"Hello the house," Forrest Gore called in a bored tone. "We mean you no harm. They's five of us. May we come up and take water for our horses?"

"You can go to the barn for that," Martha said from the protection of a shuttered window.

"Thank ye, kindly. Though it's scant hospitable of ye."

"Hospitality is somewhat short around here of late. If yer of a mind to be friendly, when you come back, I'll have my son set out a jug of spring water for your own thirst, and a pan of spoon bread."

"Now, that's a whole lot nicer. We're beholden."

When the five returned, Jimmy had placed the offered refreshments on the small front porch and withdrawn behind the door. The hard-faced men ate hungrily of the slightly sweet bread, and drank down the water to the last drop. When the last crumb of spoon bread had been disposed of, Forrest Gore glanced up to the window; he knew he was being watched.

"Mighty tasty. Say, be you Miz Tucker?"

"I am." Curt answers had become stock in trade for Martha Tucker.

"Then I have a message for you. You've forty-eight hours to pack up and get off the place."

"I thought I'd made it plain enough before. We are not leaving."

"Oh, but you got to now, Miz Tucker. Ya see, yer late husband, rest his soul, sold the ranch the day he was murdered by that back-shootin' scum, Smoke Jensen. No doubt he was killed for the money he carried."

"I don't believe you." Martha Tucker had opened the door and stepped across the threshold.

" 'Fraid you're gonna have to, Miz Tucker," Forrest Gore replied with a polite tip of his hat in acknowledgement.

"Not without proof. Lawrence didn't take the title deed with him to town. He couldn't have sold, and he didn't have any intention of doing so. Now please leave."

"Sorry you see it that way, Miz Tucker. But we got our orders. Forty-eight hours, not a second more. Pack what you can, and get out. The new owner will be movin' in direc'ly."

"We won't budge until I see the bill of sale and a transfer of title."

Gore's face stiffened woodenly and his eyes slitted. "That's mighty uppity lawyer talk, comin' from a woman. A woman's place is to do as she's told. Might be your health would remain a whole lot better, if you'd do just that."

"Meaning what?" Frost edged her words.

"Your husband's done already got hisself killed over this place. Could be it might happen to you next."

"Jimmy." Tension crackled in the single word, as Martha reached back through the open door.

Her son handed her a Greener shotgun, which she leveled on the center of Forrest Gore's chest. Deftly, she eared back both hammers. "Get the hell off our land. And tell whoever sent you that next time, I'll shoot first and ask questions after. My oldest son's a crack shot, too. So there'll be plenty of empty saddles."

Gore blanched white in mingled fear and rage. "You'll wish you'd done what's right . . . while you still had the chance." He mounted with his gaze fixed on the barrels of the scattergun. Nothing worser than a woman with a gun, he reminded himself in a sudden sweat. Astride his horse he cut his eyes to his men. "Let's ride."

Smoke Jensen knew a man could not drive a bear. Not even a big old brown, if one could be found in these desert mountains. But antelope and deer could be herded, if a fellow took his time about it. Through all the days of his travels in the Cibola Range, Smoke had often cut sign of deer. Now he set out seriously to locate a suitable gathering.

His search took only three hours in the early morning. He counted some thirty adult animals, a dozen yearlings, and a scattering of fawns. They would do well for what he had in mind. Slowly he closed on the herd, got them ambling the way he wanted.

It took all the skill Smoke Jensen possessed not to spook the deer and set them off in a wild stampede. A little nudge here, another there, then ease off for a while. So long as they only felt a bit uncomfortable grazing where they stood, they would remain tractable. By noon he had them out of the small gorge where he had found them.

"Easy goes," he reminded his mount and himself.

By putting more pressure on the herd leader, he got them lined out up a sloping game trail toward the crest. That, Smoke knew, overlooked the main trail. And that's where he wanted them any time now. The wary animals heard the approach of other humans before Smoke did. He nudged the creatures out into a line near the top of the ridge, then left the rest in the hands of Lady Luck.

With a whoop, Smoke set the deer into a panicked run. They boiled over the rim and thundered down the reverse slope. Alerted by the pound of many small hooves, the posse halted and looked upward. Dust boiled up through the piñon boughs, and a forest of antlers jinked one way, then the other.

Before they could recover their wits, the outlaws and

townsmen who made up Sheriff Reno's posse became inundated by the frightened animals. The stricken beasts bowled several men off their horses, set other mounts into terrorized flight. Four townies wailed in helpless alarm, and abandoned the search for Smoke Jensen right there and now.

"Aaaawh . . . shiiiii-it!" Sheriff Reno howled in frustration, as a huge stag fixed his antlers on the lawman's cavorting pony and made a spraddle-legged advance.

Seven

Sheriff Jake Reno's eyes bulged, unable to cut away from that magnificent twelve-point rack. Somehow, he knew Smoke Jensen had been behind the appearance of the deer. The grand stag pawed the ground again and snorted, hindquarters flexed for a lunge. Sensing the menace, Sheriff Reno's mount reared, forehooves lashing in defensive fury. It spilled the lawman out of the saddle.

He landed heavily on the sorest part of his posterior, and howled like a banshee. Alarmed, the stag lurched to one side and joined its harem in wild flight. An echo of mocking laughter bounded down from above. Sheriff Reno looked around to find that fully half of the remaining posse had deserted him. That left him with little choice.

He pulled in his horns.

Only eleven men remained with the posse when the corrupt lawman gave up his search for Smoke Jensen and turned back toward Socorro. Smoke watched them go. Faint signs of amusement lightened Smoke's face as he gazed down a long slope at the retreating backs. One leg cocked over the pommel of his saddle, he reached into a shirt pocket for a slender, rock-hard cigar, and struck a lucifer on the silver chasing of his saddlehorn.

A thin, blue-white stream of aromatic smoke wreathed the head of Smoke Jensen as he puffed contentedly. Walt Reardon had thoughtfully provided the cigars among the other supplies the hands had obtained when they planned to get Smoke out of the Socorro jail. These were of Italian origin and strong enough to stagger a bull buffalo.

Not exactly Smoke's brand of choice, it would have to do, he reckoned. And he would have to make tracks soon. South and west would best suit. That would put him closer to Arizona, when Ty Hardy and Walt Reardon brought word from Jeff York.

Smoke Jensen had met Jeff York a number of years ago. The young Arizona Ranger had been working undercover against the gang and outlaw stronghold of Rex Davidson, same as Smoke. When each learned the identity of the other, they joined their lots to bring down the walls of every building in Davidson's outlaw town of Dead River, and exterminate the vermin that lived there. As he rode down out of the northern reaches of the Cibola Range, Smoke Jensen recalled that day, long past . . .

Their pockets bulging with extra cartridges, York carrying a Henry and Smoke carrying the sawed-off express gun, they looked at each other.

"You ready to strike up the band, Ranger?"

"Damn right!" York said with a grin.

"Let's do it."

The men slipped the thongs off their six-guns and eased them out of leather a time or two, making certain the oiled interiors of the holsters were free.

York eased back the hammer on his Henry, and Smoke jacked back the hammers on the express gun.

They stepped inside the noisy and beer-stinking saloon. The piano player noticed them first. He stopped playing and singing and stared at them, his face chalk-white. Then he scrambled under the lip of the piano.

"Well, well!" an outlaw said, laughing. "Would you boys just take a look at Shirley. [Smoke had been using the outrageous moniker of Shirley DeBeers, a sissyfied portrait painter, for his penetration of the outlaw stronghold.] *He's done shaven offen his beard and taken to packin' iron. Boy, you bes' git shut of them guns, 'fore you hurt yourself."*

Gridley stood up from a table where he'd been drinking and playing poker—and losing. "Or I decide to take 'em off you and shove 'em up your butt, lead and all, pretty-boy. Matter of fact, I think I'll jist do that, right now."

"The name isn't pretty-boy, Gridley," Smoke informed him.

"Oh, yeah? Well, mayhaps you right. I'll jist call you shit! How about that?"

"Why don't you call him by his real name?" York said, a smile on his lips.

"And what might that be, punk?" Gridley sneered the question. "Alice?"

"First off," York said, "I'll tell you I'm an Arizona Ranger. Note the badges we're wearing? And his name, you blow-holes, is Smoke Jensen!"

The name dropped like a bomb. The outlaws in the room sat stunned, their eyes finally observing the gold badges on the chests of the men.

Smoke and York both knew one thing for an ironclad fact: The men in the room might all be scoundrels and thieves and murderers, and some might be bullies and cowards, but when it came down to it, they were going to fight.

"Then draw, you son of a bitch!" Gridley hollered, his hands dropping to his guns.

Smoke pulled the trigger on the express gun. From a distance of no more than twenty feet, the buckshot almost tore the outlaw in two.

York leveled the Henry and dusted an outlaw from side to side. Dropping to one knee, he levered the empty out and a fresh round in, and shot a fat punk in the belly.

Shifting the sawed-off shotgun, Smoke blew the head off another outlaw. The force of the buckshot lifted the headless outlaw out of one boot and flung him to the sawdust-covered floor.

York and his Henry had put half a dozen outlaws on the floor, dead, dying, or badly hurt.

The huge saloon was filled with gunsmoke, the crying and moaning of the wounded, and the stink of relaxed bladders from the dead. Dark gray smoke from the black powder cartridges stung the eyes and obscured the vision of all in the room . . .

Oh, that had been a high old time all right, Smoke reflected. But it hadn't ended there. Smoke had gone on back East to reclaim his beloved wife, Sally, who was busy being delivered of twins in the home of her parents in Keene, New Hampshire. Jeff York and Louis Longmont had accompanied him. And a good thing, too. Rex Davidson and his demented followers had carried the fight to Smoke. And it finally ended in the streets of Keene, with Rex Davidson's guts spilled on the ground.

The twins, Louis Arthur and Denise Nichole, were near to full grown now. They lived and studied in Europe. But that was another story, Smoke reminded himself as he gazed upon a smoky smudge on the horizon, far out on a wide mountain vale, vast enough to be called a plain.

Smoke Jensen rode into Horse Springs quietly. He attracted little attention from the locals, mostly simple farmers of Mexican origin. *Ollas de los Caballos,* the place had been called before the white man came. Near the center of town was a rock basin, fed by cold, crystal-clear, deep mountain springs. This natural formation provided drinking water for everyone in town. Fortunately for the farmers, a wide, shallow stream also meandered through the valley and allowed for irrigation of crops of corn, beans, squash, chili peppers, and other staples.

Smoke splashed through it at a rail-guarded ford and saw at once that it also accommodated as a place of entertainment. Small, brown-skinned boys, naked as the day they had been born, frolicked in the water, the sun striking highlights off their wet skin. Clearly, they lacked any knowledge of the body taboo that afflicted most whites Smoke knew. For, when they took notice of the stranger among them, they broke off their play to stand facing him, giggle like a flock of magpies, and make shy, though friendly waves of their hands.

Returning their greetings, Smoke rode on to the center of town. On the Plaza de Armas, he located what passed for a hotel in Horse Springs. *POSADA DEL NORTE*—Inn of the North—had been hand-lettered in red, now faded pink, and outlined in white and green over the arch in an adobe block wall that guarded the building front.

He dismounted and walked his horse through the tall, double-hung, plank gates into a tree-shaded courtyard. A barefoot little lad, who most likely would have preferred to be out at the creek with his friends, took the reins and led Smoke's big-chested roan toward a stable. Smoke entered a high-ceilinged remarkably cool hallway. To his right, a sign, likewise in Spanish, with black letters on white tile, advised; *OFICINA*.

Smoke stepped through into the office and had to work mightily to conceal his reaction. Behind a small counter he saw one of the most strikingly beautiful young women he had ever encountered. Her skin, which showed in a generous, square-cut yolk, a graceful stalk of neck and intriguing, heart-shaped face, was flawless. A light cast of olive added a healthy glow to the faintest of *cafe au lait* complexions. Her dress had puffy sleeves, with lace at the edges, and around the open bodice, also in tiers over her ample bosom, and in ruffled falls down to a narrow waist. There, what could be seen of the skirt flared in horizontal gathers that reminded Smoke of a cascade.

Her youthful lips had been touched with a light application of ruby rouge, and were full and promised mysteries unknown to other women. For a moment, raw desire flamed in the last mountain man. Then, reason—

and his unwavering dedication to his lovely and beloved Sally—prevailed. Those sweet lips twitched in a teasing smile as the vision behind the registration desk acknowledged his admiring stare.

"Yes, *Señor?* Do you desire a room for the night?"

Her voice, Smoke Jensen thought, sounded like little tinkling bells in a field of daisies. "Uh . . . ummm, yes. For a week, at least."

"We are happy to be able to accommodate you, *Señor.* If you will please to sign the book?" When Smoke had done so, she continued her familiar routine of hospitality. "The rooms down here are much cooler, but the second floor offers privacy."

Accustomed to the refreshingly cool summer days in the High Lonesome, Smoke Jensen opted for a first-floor room. The beautiful desk clerk nodded approvingly and selected a key. She turned back to Smoke and extended a hand comprised of a small, childlike palm and slender, graceful fingers.

"When Felipe returns with your saddlebags, he will show you to your room."

"I think I can manage on my own."

Her smile could charm the birds from the trees. "It is a courtesy of the Posada del Norte. We wish that our guests feel they are our special friends."

"I'm sure they do. I know that I—ah—ummm—do." Silently, Smoke cursed himself for sounding like an adolescent boy in the presence of his first real woman. He was spared further awkwardness by the return of the little boy, Felipe.

"Come with me, *Señor,*" the youngster said with a dignity beyond his nine or ten years.

After Felipe had unlocked the door to No. 12 with a flourish and ushered him inside, Smoke pressed a silver dime into the boy's warm, moist palm. Although fond of children, Smoke Jensen preferred to watch them from a distance; he recalled his first impression of this little lad and curiosity prompted him to speak.

"Do you work here every day?"

"Oh, *sí, Señor,* after school is over at *media dia.* It is my father's *posada."*

"Wouldn't you rather be out swimming with your friends at the creek?"

An impish grin lighted Felipe's face. "After my early chores, I get to go for a while. Until the people come for rooms, and my father rings the bell to call me back. Sometimes . . . when I'm supposed to be cleaning the stable, I slip away and also go on adventures."

Smoke had to smile. "You remind me of my sons when they were your age."

Felipe blinked at him. "Did you run a *posada?* And were your sons Mexican?"

A chuckle rumbled in Smoke's chest. "No to both questions. But they were every bit as ornery as you. Now, get along with you."

After Smoke had settled in, he strolled out to the central courtyard. The corridor that served the second floor overhung the edges of the patio, to form alcoves where tables were being set for the evening meal. More pretty Mexican girls draped snowy linen cloths at just the proper angle, while others put in place napkins, eating utensils, and terracotta cups and goblets. Next came clay pitchers that beaded on the outside from the chill spring water they held, and bowls of fiery Southwestern salsa picante. Experience in Arizona, Texas, and Mexico had taught Smoke that prudent use of the condiment added a pleasant flavor to a man's food.

Beyond the alfresco dining arrangements, a fountain splashed musically in the center of the courtyard. Desert greenery had been arranged in profusion, in rock gardens that broke up the open space and gave an illusion of privacy. On the fourth side of the patio, opposite his room, Smoke found a small cantina. Tiny round tables extended onto the flagstone flooring outside its door. Smoke entered and ordered a beer.

It came in a large, cool, dark brown bottle. Smoke flipped the hinged metal contraption that held a ceramic stopper in place, and a loud *pop* sounded. Hops-scented blue smoke rose from the interior. Smoke took his first swallow straight from the bottle, then poured the remainder into a schooner offered by the *cantinero*.

"You are new in town," the tavern keeper observed.

"Yep. Just rode in today."

"If you have been on the trail a while, *Señor,* perhaps you are hungry for word of what is happening in the world. I will bring you a newspaper."

"Thank you," Smoke responded, surprised and pleased by this shower of conviviality.

It turned out to be a week-old copy of the Albuquerque *Territorial Sentinel.* Most of the front page articles had to do with the financial panic back East, and events in and around the largest city in the territory. Smoke read on. The second page provided at least part of the answer to his dilemma, although he did not realize it at the time.

SURVEYORS
TO LAY OUT
WESTWARD ROUTE

Bold black letters spelled out the caption of the story. Smoke Jensen scanned it with mild interest. It revealed that survey crews would soon arrive to begin laying out the right of way for a new spur of the Southern Pacific Railroad. It would pass through Socorro and head westward to connect with Springerville, Arizona, Winslow, and the copper smelters being built south and west of Show Low.

Interesting, Smoke considered. If one had stock in the railroad, or the right copper works. But it didn't seem nearly as relevant as the small article on the third page, which featured an artist's sketch of Smoke's own likeness, and a story about the supposed murder of Mr. Lawrence Tucker.

From it, he gleaned that Tucker had been a long and respected resident of the Socorro area, with a large ranch on the eastern slopes of the Cibola foothills. He was survived by a wife, Martha, and three children, boys aged thirteen and seven and a girl nine. Tucker had been outspoken about the prospects of dry land farming, and used the techniques of the Mexican and Indian farmers, long time residents of the area. He also advocated the protection of those fields by the use of barbed wire.

Not a very popular position for a rancher to take,

Smoke mused. It had been enough to get more than half a hundred men killed over the past decade. Maybe Mr. Tucker had enemies no one knew of? Maybe someone, like Sheriff Reno, knew only too damn well who those enemies might be? Smoke put his speculations aside, along with the paper, and finished his beer. Leaving money on the mahogany for the barkeep, he left to stroll the streets and get a feel for the town.

It might be well to have a hidey-hole. The inn seemed a good one. Although, Smoke allowed, with his face in the newspapers, and no doubt on wanted posters by now, it would be better to lay low in Arizona, until he could piece together more information. He had done well to scatter that posse. And it might be necessary to go back and scatter another, if he were to have that time of peace.

Early on the afternoon of the third day in Horse Springs, Smoke began to feel uneasy. A week had gone by since they had ridden out of Socorro. By now he should have heard from Walt Reardon and Ty Hardy. He would give them a couple of more days and then head west. With that settled, he turned in through the open doorway of a squat, square building with a white-painted, stuccoed exterior.

The odor of stale beer and whiskey fumes tingled his nose. No matter where in the world, or what it was called, Smoke mused, a saloon was a saloon. A chubby, mustachioed Mexican stood behind the bar, a once-white apron tight around his appreciable girth. Two white-haired, retired caballeros sat at a table, drinking tequila and playing dominoes. Smoke Jensen relaxed in this congenial atmosphere and eased up to the bar.

"Do you have any rye?" he asked.

"Bourbon or tequila."

"Beer then."

A large, foam-capped schooner appeared before him a few seconds later. The glass felt pleasantly cool to the touch. Smoke had grown to understand the inestimable value of the icy deep rock springs that had named the town. Smoke drank deeply of the cold beer, and a rumble from his stomach reminded him that he hadn't eaten since early that morning. He'd finish this and find a place to have a meal.

"Jeremy, you don't have the sense God gave a goose." The loud voice drew Smoke's attention to the entrance.

"There you go again, Zack, bad-mouthin' me. I tell you, that feller made it sound so downright good, I jist had to trade horses with him."

"Only it done turned out that he had *two* gray horses, the other one all swaybacked and spavined. Which he hung around your dumb neck."

"Awh, Zack, tain't fair you go bully-raggin' me about that all the time. Hell, cousin, it happened a month ago! That's old news."

"It's an old bunko game, too," Zack replied dryly.

Smoke Jensen marked them to be local range riders. But with a few differences, that could make them dangerous. For instance, the way they wore their six-guns, slung low on their legs, holsters tied down with a leather thong. The safety loops had been slipped free of the hammers. The weapons were clean and lightly oiled, all the cartridges in their loops shiny bright. No doubt, they fancied themselves good with their guns, Smoke surmised. They had silver conchos around the sweat bands of their hats, sewn on their vests, and down the outside seam of their left trouser legs.

A regretful sigh broke from Smoke's lips. Almost a uniform in the Southwest for young, tough-guy punks. Smoke faced the bar, head lowered, and tried not to draw their attention. The one called Zack looked hard at the big-shouldered man at the bar and turned away. Smoke finished his beer, the taste nowhere near as pleasant as it had been, and pushed off from the bar.

Outside, he headed toward an eatery he had seen earlier. He had noticed a sign, hand-lettered on a chalkboard, that advertised HOY CARNITAS. His limited Spanish told him that meant they were serving carnitas today. He had become acquainted with the savory dish while in Mexico to help two of his old gunfighter friends, Miguel Martine and Esteban Carbone. Thought of the succulent cubes of pork shoulder, deep fried over an open, smokey fire, brightened Smoke's outlook considerably.

He had finished off a huge platter of the "little meats," with plenty of tortillas and condiments, and another beer, when he looked up from wiping the grease from his face and saw the same pair of salty young studs again. They stood in the middle of the street, hands on the butts of their six-guns, eyes fixed on the doorway of the bean emporium.

At first, Smoke didn't know if they had gotten so drunk that they couldn't figure how to get in the eatery. But when he rose from his table, paid the tab, and stepped out under the palm frond *palapa* that shaded the front, he soon learned that not to be the case.

"B'god, yer right, Zack. It's him, all right."

"Yeah, Smoke Jensen," Zack sighed out. "An' we've got us a tidy little re-ward comin', Jeremy."

Eight

Seems these boys had read the same newspaper he had seen, Smoke surmised. The reward was something new. Too bad about that. He spoke to them through a sigh.

"Don't believe everything you read, fellers."

"We believe this right enough. You're Smoke Jensen, and they's a thousand dollars on yer head."

"Not by the law. So there's no guarantee you'd *get* the reward, if you lived to collect it."

"What you mean by that?"

Smoke sighed again. "If I *am* Smoke Jensen, there's not the likes of you two who can take me. Not in a face-on fight."

"I ain't no back-shooter, an' I think we can," Zack blurted.

Smoke let Zack and Jeremy get their hands on their irons, before he hauled his .44 clear of leather. Jeremy's eyes widened; it caused him to falter, and he didn't have his weapon leveled when he pulled the trigger.

A spout of muddy street fountained up a yard in front of Jeremy's boot toe. Although a hard, violent man when he need be, Smoke Jensen took pity on the young gunny. He shot him in the hip. Jeremy went down with a yowl, the streamlined Merwin and Hulbert flew from his hand, and he clutched his wound with desperation. Smoke shifted his attention to Zack.

Zack's jaw sagged in disbelief. He hadn't even seen Jensen draw, and already the gunfighter had let 'er bang. Shot Jeremy, too, and he was rattlesnake fast. His consternation held Zack for a fraction of a second, during which he saw eternity beckoning to him from the black muzzle of Smoke Jensen's Colt.

"Nooooo!" he wailed and tried feverishly to trigger a round.

For this one, Smoke Jensen had no mercy. He had taken note earlier of the notches carved in the walnut grip of Zack's six-gun. That told a lot about Zack. No real gunhawk notched his grips to keep score. Killing men was not a game. They didn't give prizes for the one with the most chips whittled out. The only thing that came from winning was the chance to live a little longer. Smoke Jensen knew that well. He'd been taught by an expert. So, he let fly with a .44 slug that punched a new belly button in Zack's vulnerable flesh.

Shock, and the impact, knocked Zack off his boots. He hit hard on his butt in the middle of the street. He had somehow managed to hold onto his Smith American, and let roar a .44 round that cracked past the left shoulder of Smoke Jensen. New pain exploded in the right side of Zack's shoulder, as Smoke answered in kind with his Peacemaker.

"Damn you to hell, Smoke Jensen." Bitter pain tears welled up in Zack's eyes and Smoke Jensen seemed to waver before him like a cattail in a stiff breeze. Supported on one elbow, he tried again to raise his weapon into position. His hand would not obey. It drooped at the wrist, the barrel of the Smith and Wesson canted toward the ground.

"Y-you done killt me, Jensen," he gasped past the agony that broiled his body.

"It was your choice, Zack."

"I—I know." Zack sucked in a deep breath and new energy surged through him.

His gun hand responded this time, and he willed his finger to squeeze the trigger. The loud bang that followed came before his hammer had fallen. Zack couldn't figure that one out. He understood better an instant later, when incredible anguish blossomed in his chest and a huge, black cavern opened up to engulf him.

"You di'n't have to kill him," Jeremy sobbed from his place on the ground.

"The way I see it, he pushed, I pushed back." Smoke made a tight-lipped answer.

Despite his misery, Jeremy had managed to work free his sheath knife. He held it now by the blade. A quick flick of his right arm as Smoke Jensen turned in his direction, and the wicked blade sped on its way. It caught Smoke low. The tip slid through the thick leather of his cartridge belt and penetrated a stinging inch into meat. Smoke's .44 blasted reflexively.

From less than three feet away, hot lead punched a thumb-sized hole between Jeremy's eyebrows, mushroomed, and blew off the back of his head. Smoke eased up, let his shoulders sag. A sudden voice from behind him charged Smoke with new energy.

"¡Tien cuidado, Señor! They have a frien'." Black pencil line of mustache writhing on his brown upper lip, the owner and cook of the cafe where Smoke had eaten, stood in the doorway. He pointed a trembling finger toward the balcony of the saloon across the street. Smoke followed the gesture and saw a man kneeling behind the big wooden sign, a rifle to his shoulder.

Fool, Smoke thought. If he thinks that sign will stop a bullet, he's in for a surprise. The Winchester cracked once, and cut the hat from Smoke's head as he returned the favor. Two fast shots from the pistol in the hand of Smoke Jensen put a small figure-eight hole in the sign and the chest of the sniper. With a clatter, the hidden assassin sprawled backward on the floor planks of the balcony.

In the silence that followed, Smoke Jensen surveyed the carnage he had created. Damnit, he didn't need to be caught knee-deep in corpses. This spelled more complications than he wanted to think about. He reloaded swiftly.

"No question of it, I'm in more trouble than before," he muttered to himself. To the Mexican cook, he added, "The law will be coming soon. Tell them the man who did this is long gone."

The smiling man shrugged. "There is very little law in this town, *Señor.* Only the *alcalde*—the mayor—who is also the *jefe*—the marshal, an' also the *juez . . . el magistrado, ¿comprende?"*

"I reckon I do. You're saying you have a one-man city administration?"

"Seguro, sí." In his excitement over the confrontation in the street, the man had forgotten most of his English.

"Where do I find this feller?"

A broad, warm smile bloomed on the man's face. He

tapped his chest with a brown, chili-stained finger. "It is I, *Señor*."

That made matters considerably less complicated for Smoke Jensen. Smoke recounted where he had first seen the would-be hard cases, and gave his opinion of what had sparked the attempt on his life. The mayor-police-chief-judge, his name turned out to be Raphael Figuroa, didn't even ask if they had the right man. He looked at the human garbage in the street and shrugged.

"They are no loss. This is not the first time they have provoked trouble. Usually with tragic consequences for the other party. This is the first time they have been on the receiving end. You are free to go, or stay as long as you wish, *Señor*."

"I'm fixin' to pull out tomorrow morning," Smoke informed him. He did not give a destination.

Forty-six miles into Arizona, Smoke Jensen discovered why he had not been joined by his companions. Walt and Ty waited for him in Show Low, along with Jeff York. Smoke and the Arizona Ranger had a rousing, back-pounding reunion, and the four men retired to the saloon made famous by the poker game that had given the new name to what had once been Copper Gulch.

A drifter had played cards all through one night with the local gambler and owner of the town. His luck had run well and, on the turn of a card in a game of Low Ball, he had won title to Copper Gulch, which he promptly renamed Show Low in honor of his accomplishment. Or so the story goes.

"What's this about you being wanted for killing a man,

Smoke?" Jeff inquired, his pale bluish gray eyes alight with interest. "Don't sound like the Smoke Jensen I know."

"It's a long story, Jeff. Just yesterday, I found out there's a price on my head. A big one." Smoke went on to explain what he faced. He concluded with, "So with a reward out, I had to figure that sheriff would be out hunting me again, and decided Arizona would be a safer place to stay while I worked it all out."

Jeff York sat in silence a moment before responding to all Smoke had told him. "I'll cover for you here in Arizona, of course. And I'd like to help. As much as I can."

"How's that? The governor got his hand cinched up to your belt?"

"Not so's it chafes. I was up this way to check out something when Walt and Ty came along. So far it's only rumors. Still an' all, the ones puttin' them around are considered reliable men. 'Pears there's some scallywags that have their eyes on a land grab on the White Mountain Apache reservation."

"Do tell," Smoke prompted.

"The word is that some high-rollers are fixin' to bring a number of the big tickets in Washington out to be wined and dined—and bribed—to get them to cut a big chunk out of the res for the benefit of those same local money men."

"Why in the world would anyone want to move in next door to the Apaches?"

Jeff gave Smoke a bleak smile. "Perhaps it's because Chief Cuchillo Negro and some of his braves have found gold on that land. And, of course, it might be that these good ol' boys has gotten a serious dose of religion, and only want to make better the lot of their less fortunate red brothers."

"I'll believe that when pigs fly," Smoke grunted.

Smoke Jensen had fought and killed any number of Indians over the years, and he was not considered one to stomp lace-edged hankies into the mud over the wretched plight of the Noble Red Men. Yet, he respected them as brave men and fierce fighters. The Apaches most of all. He acknowledged the Indians' right to a place in this world. After all, it was Indian land before the white man came to take it away from them. Indians and the white men had different ways, neither one better than the other, to Smoke's way of seeing things. Truth to tell, he sometimes thought the Indian way came out a bit on top. They sure had more respect for nature and the land. And they used to live in harmony with all its creatures.

It wasn't the coming of the white man that spoiled all that, Smoke acknowledged. It was too *many* of them coming, too fast and too soon. Set in their own ways, and pig-head stubborn against change, they never considered the differences beyond the Big Muddy. Civilization ended at the Mississippi, and white folks stupidly refused to admit that.

Sharing that all too human trait, most of the Indians would not make any effort to accommodate to white ways. They preferred to fight a losing battle to preserve their way of life. Those tribes lost, too. Now only the Apaches and a passel of Sioux and Cheyenne remained any sort of threat to the tens of thousands of white men overwhelming the vast frontier. Smoke Jensen shook his head, saddened by his sour reflections. "There's six more

Rangers headed this way. I'm supposed to direct it all, and also get a man inside this consortium," Jeff went on.

"You wouldn't be electin' me to that position, would you, Jeff?"

"No," Jeff York shrugged. As tall as Smoke and nearly as broad, that gesture moved a lot of hard-muscled flesh. His big hands spread on the table, and thick fingers reached for a fish-eye whiskey glass. "I reckoned to do that myself."

"I recall the last time I knew you went under cover."

York smiled at Smoke's remark. "We sure shot hell out of Rex Davidson's Dead River, didn't we."

"And you damned near got yourself killed, before you could get to the doin'," Smoke reminded him.

"Water under the bridge. We're still here, both of us. Now, maybe I had oughtta make myself useful," York changed the subject. "First off, I'll fill you in on who is who around Socorro."

"You Rangers keep an eye on folks from another territory?" Smoke asked.

"Good practice to know the influential folks. Also the bad hombres and riffraff—all part of the job."

"Then tell me about them," Smoke prompted.

"First off, there's the Culverts and the Mendozas. About the richest ranchers around. Old Myron Culvert's son is mayor." He went on to list the power structure of Socorro, New Mexico. Then Jeff's voice changed, took on a tightness. "Then there's some who are sort of on the edge. There's an Englishman, folks say he's a lord or something. They call him Sir Geoffrey Benton-Howell. He owns a couple of large ranches, two saloons, a women's millinery store, and a number of houses he rents out to the Mexican workers. He's partnered up with Miguel Selleres. Selleres looks like one of those bull-fighter fellers. Neat and trim, a handsome dog. But we've heard word he's got a mean streak."

"What about hard cases?"

"Comin' to that, Smoke. Big frog in the pond over that way is Quint Stalker. Supposed to be a gunfighter from Nevada."

"I've heard of him. He crossed my path one time. I should have killed him then."

"He's for sure bad news, then?"

"Bet on it, Jeff."

"All right. He's got a gang of maybe thirty fast guns. There's talk he takes his pay from Benton-Howell. If that's so, we could be in heavy trouble. The lord and Selleres have been buying up parcels of land in New Mexico and Arizona for some time now. Most of them are out in the middle of nowhere. With the money, land, and the guns to back them up, they could become a power to reckon with. Only, why pick such remote spots?"

Smoke recalled the article he had read about surveyors for the Southern Pacific. "Would those parcels be any-where near the proposed right of way of the new South-ern Pacific spur line?"

It was as though a lamp had been lit behind the eyes of Jeff York. "They sure would."

"Water and coaling stops make great places for towns to be built," Smoke pointed out. "The man or men who own one—or in this case, *all* of those—will get mighty rich."

"Where did you come up with that?"

"I read about it in the Albuquerque newspaper,"

Smoke told him. "I wonder now, if the railroad intends to cross land owned by the late Mr. Tucker?"

"I wouldn't doubt it any. I think you waiting out more developments here might be a mistake, Smoke."

"I'm way ahead of you. I reckon we should all head back to Socorro and dig into the affairs of Sir Geoffrey Benton-Howell."

"Maw, there's someone movin' around out there," Jimmy Tucker informed his mother from the small, circular window in the loft.

"Can you make out who?" Martha Tucker asked her son, as she climbed from the bed in the room off the central part of the house.

"No, ma'am." Jimmy had a cold chill down his spine, though, that told him the mysterious figures were up to no good. He had an itch, too, that made him want to snug the butt-plate of his little Stevens .30-30 up against his right shoulder.

Martha crossed the living-dining area of her home in darkness, every inch familiar to her. She took up the Greener and slung a leather bag of shot shells over one shoulder. She reached a window just as a yellow-orange brightness flared in the barnyard. Jimmy also saw it, and the mop of snowy hair fairly rose straight up on his head.

He propelled himself off the pallet that served as a bed and flew down the ladder, his bare feet flashing below the hem of his nightshirt. He, too, went unerringly to the gunrack on the near wall. Martha saw the movement and gasped. She almost blurted out a refusal, then drew her lips into a thin line.

"You be careful, son," she urged him.

"Yes, ma'am."

Jimmy took his rifle and a spare box of shells and went back to the loft. The window that overlooked the barnyard had been installed on a pivot, with latches to both sides. Jimmy undid them and turned the sash sideways. Slowly he eased the barrel of his Stevens out into the night. Then he remembered his father's training. He stuck a small finger in the loading gate and felt the base of a cartridge. Satisfied, he slowly worked the action, to keep as quiet as he could.

Three more torches burned now, and so far none of the nightriders had noticed anything happening in the house. At a muffled grunt of command, the torchbearers started toward the barn. By the light of the firebrands, Martha and Jimmy saw that they wore hoods that covered their entire heads. When they reached a point fifty feet from the barn, the shotgun boomed, with the bright crack of the Stevens right behind.

One arsonist yowled and pitched off his mount, one arm and shoulder peppered with No. 2 goose shot. Another grunted softly, swayed in his saddle a moment, then sank forward to lay along the neck of his horse. For some unexplainable reason, Jimmy Tucker found his breath awfully short and tears filled his eyes. He had to swallow hard to drive down the sour bile that rose in his throat.

He took one deep gulp of breath and levered another round into the .30-30. Good thing he did, because a second later two of the hooded thugs turned toward the house and fired at the ground-floor windows. Jimmy shot one of them through the shoulder, and heard a thin wail answer his defense. From downstairs, he heard his Maw's shotgun belch in anger.

"I'm hit! Oh, God, I'm hit, Smoke," one of the outlaws sobbed.

The use of that name had been a clever contribution by Quint Stalker. He figured it would direct any suspicion away from him, and particularly his bosses. Unseen by the hard cases in the yard, it had the intended effect, as Martha Tucker's face hardened and she swiftly reloaded the shotgun.

"Fire that barn, goddamnit! You boys, go after the corral. Turn out that livestock."

"We're bein' shot at," another thug complained.

"I'll take care of that," the leader responded.

He turned toward the house in time to catch the side edge of a column of shot in his left biceps and shoulder. Grunting, he fired his six-gun dry and wheeled away. Another man took his place and got blown out of the saddle for his determination.

Flames began to flicker in the barn.

Jimmy brushed more tears from his big, blue eyes and sighted in on another man with a torch. At the last moment, the outlaw darted forward and to his left, the .30-30 round shattered his hand. It sent the blazing torch flying from his grasp to land harmlessly on the ground. A dozen young heifers bellowed in terror from the corral, then made thunder with their hooves as others of the nightriders swung open the gate and ran them off.

"We've done enough for now. Let's pull out," came the command.

While they raced off into the darkness, mother and son discharged several rounds each to give wings to their flight. Several ranch hands, who had been held impotent at gunpoint, rushed out and began hurling buckets of water on the blazing barn. But Martha knew it would do no good. A fine, beautiful building, destroyed by that bastard Smoke Jensen.

Then a smile broke through her outrage. At least she'd gotten some pellets in him. He'd be bandaged up after this, and not so cocky anymore. Next time she saw him, she'd kill Smoke Jensen, she swore.

Nine

A hot, dry wind blew steadily across the mesa even at this early hour. A low pole frame sat well back from the rim, protected from the view of unwelcome eyes. It consisted of a lattice framework covered with the thick, green leaves of the agave, what the whites called the century plant. Already five of the lesser chiefs of the White Mountain Apaches had gathered. They waited in patient silence for the arrival of their principal chief, Cuchillo Negro—Black Knife.

Long before their composure had been well tested, ten of the best warriors among the Tinde approached soundlessly from as many directions. At last, when the sun rode high overhead, Cuchillo Negro appeared. With him was Ho-tan, his most trusted advisor. He greeted the assembled council in the harsh gutturals of their language.

"Why do the white men come into our land?" Broken Horn asked of the chief.

Cuchillo Negro considered the question in silence a long time before he made answer. "It is true that many *Pend-dik-olyeh* come to our mountains. Words spoken on the winds say that they covet what little they left to us."

"That could be true," Ho-tan mused aloud. "It is the best of any of our agencies."

"The whites, who are always greedy, must think it is too good for us," Spirit Walker observed with tart humor. "They seek to send us back to San Carlos."

Angry mutters rose over that. Black Knife silenced them with a stern look. The breeze fluttered the long, obsidian wings of his hair, held in place by a calico headband. He rose to his moccasins from where he squatted on a blanket.

"You are right to be angry, my brothers. But we must be cautious, while we go about finding out what is behind this."

"No," Bright Lance, one of the senior warriors growled. "I say we drive them off the agency. I say we follow those who survive and take the warpath to all whites."

"Like Geronimo?" Cuchillo Negro asked sarcastically.

They all knew the fate of the famed and feared warrior chief. He was said to be rotting in a stinking, white man's prison in a far-off land called Florida. Obsidian eyes cut from one face to another. Broken Horn rose to speak.

"I am of a mind with Bright Lance. For us to meekly let the whites push us out, to be returned to San Carlos, is to die. Sickness will waste away our women and children, and we will catch the mosquito fever and die slaving in bean fields. I hate bean fields."

A loud murmur of agreement ran through the assembled council. Cuchillo Negro made a quick evaluation of the change in heart. "No. We cannot do that. I, too, hate bean fields, my old friend," he admitted with warm humor in his voice. "We must not take the fight to the whites off the reservation. That will bring the pony soldiers as certainly as Father Sun follows the night."

Clever man that he had to be to have achieved his paramount position, Cuchillo Negro shifted gears and spoke in laudatory tones of conciliation. "Yet, our good brother, Bright Lance, has some wisdom in what he says. If we hope to keep in our beloved mountains, we must not anger the soldiers. We must not leave the agency to fight." A beaming smile lighted the face of Cuchillo Negro, and his eyes sparkled with mischief. "But Bright Lance speaks well when he says we must punish those who trespass on our land. For now, we must satisfy ourselves with that."

To his surprise and satisfaction, he had no trouble achieving a consensus. The war societies of the White Mountain Apaches would soon ride to take retribution on the interlopers.

Smoke Jensen raised a hand to signal a halt. Ahead, a huge dust cloud rose beyond a swell in the red-brown desert country. Smoke and Jeff studied it a moment.

"Think it could be a posse?" Jeff asked.

"Too much dust for men on horseback. I'd say it's a trail drive."

Jeff cut his eyes to his friend. "Here? Headed this way?"

Smoke broke a grin. "I didn't say it made sense. What say we slip over and get a look?"

Dismounted, Smoke Jensen and Jeff York advanced, crouched low to avoid showing on the skyline. Both men bellied down near the crest of the rise and removed their hats. Jeff put a brass-tubed spyglass to one eye, and Smoke studied the distance with a pair of field glasses.

In the lead were three men, coiled lariats held loosely in their right hands. Behind, blurred by the reddish haze, they made out the horns of some fifty head of cattle. Smoke and Jeff exchanged a glance.

"Looks like you were right," York acknowledged. "Only I can't figure why they're headed toward Arizona."

"Better crossing places into Mexico, I'd reckon." Smoke Jensen took another look at the slow-moving cattle. "The border is less settled in Arizona than New Mexico or Texas. Even I know that. If someone had cattle that didn't belong to him, and wanted to dispose of them at a profit, that would be the way to go about it."

Ranger York didn't buy it entirely. "You think these cattle have been rustled?"

Smoke turned his attention to the men bearing down on them. "From the looks of those boys out there, they aren't regular hands. Not by the way they're dressed, or the way they wear their guns."

Jeff York's eyebrows rose. "If we're fixin' to do anything, we'd better know how many they have on flank and drag first."

"My thinkin' exactly," Smoke agreed. "We'll split up for a while. You take Reardon, I'll take Hardy. Let's ride around this gather and see what we can."

They joined up half an hour later, behind the herd. Jeff York wore a scowl. "Those beeves are wearin' the Tucker brand. I recognized it right off."

"The same Tucker I'm supposed to have killed?"

"Right, Smoke. Only those drovers aren't the sort Lawrence Tucker would have hired. Funny thing is, none of their horses are wearing the Tucker brand."

"What say we swing in for a little talk?" Smoke's suggestion met with ready agreement.

One man rode around the herd, which had been turned in on itself for the night. Five more squatted around a hat-sized fire topped by a coffeepot. A larger blaze had been started to cook on. All six looked up as strangers rode toward the camp.

"Hello, the fire," Smoke hailed. "I thought I smelled coffee."

"Yep," came an answer from a thick-set man with small, piggish eyes. "But we didn't brew up any extra."

Smoke pulled a face. "Now, that's mighty inhospitable in these parts, Mister. Mind if we ride up a piece?"

The gunhawk's eyes shot anger at Smoke Jensen, which didn't match his words. "It's a free country."

Once in by the fire, Smoke and his companions dismounted. They made no move to tie the horses off to the picket line, dropping the reins to the ground. Smoke nodded to the cattle.

"You're a far piece from the Tucker spread," he observed.

The proddy one's eyes narrowed. "Who says we ride for that brand? Truth is, we bought these steers off him three days ago."

"That would be kind of hard, wouldn't it? Considering that he's been dead better than a week."

Smoke's words were all it took. Without knowing who they might be facing off against, the edgy rustler dropped his hand to the gun at his side. At once, the other four did the same. Smoke, Jeff, and Walt beat them all out. For a moment, they had a standoff.

Then the herd guard, a long, lean character with frizzy yellow hair, pounded toward them, his hand clawing at the butt of a Colt on his left hip. Six against four apparently seemed mighty good odds to the argumentative one. He canted the muzzle of his six-gun downward slightly. Smoke Jensen shot him through the chest, before his hammer could fall. Startled into panic, the cattle exploded in every direction. Jeff York put a bullet through the side of another rustler.

He went down with a soft grunt, but kept hold of his revolver, which he aimed at Jeff York a moment before Walt Reardon plunked a round into the gunhawk's forehead and ended his career. Ty Hardy had joined the dance. Hot lead from his .45 Colt snatched the hat off the head of another hard case, who had made a dash to his horse. Dazed by the close brush with a bullet, the rustler fell out of his saddle and rolled into some brush.

Half a dozen head of wall-eyed steers thundered over his body and trampled him into an unrecognizable mess. Smoke Jensen had not been standing still, both literally and figuratively. He had jumped to one side and went to a knee for his second round, which trashed the kneecap of another cow thief. Squalling, the man flopped to the ground, clawed at his waistband for a second six-gun, and hauled it clear.

Jeff York was busy with another gunny, and did not see the swing of the barrel to his midsection. Smoke Jensen did, and dumped the tough shooter into hell with a fast bullet that sliced through the left collarbone, lung, and the edge of his heart. A slug cracked past Smoke's ear, and he moved again.

Snatching at the horn of one steer, Smoke used the animal as cover and transportation. He heard fat splats as bullets smacked into the slab-sided creature. It bellowed in pain and stumbled. It had served its purpose, though. Smoke Jensen let go, and lowered his feet to the ground in a shuffling run. The maneuver had put him behind the last gunhawk.

Surprise registered as the man turned to find himself facing Smoke Jensen. He eared back the hammer and let fly wildly. Smoke, always calm and cool in the heat of battle, had better aim. His bullet found a home in the right shoulder of the hard case. The six-gun he had been holding flew high and came down hard. It discharged the last round of the brief, fierce fight. Slowly, he raised his good left arm.

"Okay, okay. Ease up. I'm done. I ain't never seed anyone so almighty fast. Who are you?"

"You wouldn't want to know," Smoke Jensen told him. "Sit down over there, and I'll patch you up while the rest round up these cattle."

Jeff, Walt, and Ty set off to gather in the stampeded beeves. It was a task that would take them the rest of daylight and part of the next day. From the moment Jeff York had revealed the identity of the owner of the cattle, Smoke Jensen had an idea start to grow. It would be, he decided by the time the shooting was over, a good gesture to return the cattle to the widow of Lawrence Tucker. It might even go some way toward convincing her that he had nothing to do with the death of her husband. A few answers from the survivor of the shoot-out might prove useful, he also decided. So, while he prodded the wound, cleaned it, and poured raw, stinging horse medicine in the hole, he probed for information as well.

"I don't know why I should tell you anything," came the surly answer. "I don't even know who you are."

"I'm the man who let you live, instead of killing you like the rest."

"You gonna give 'em proper Christian burial?"

"There isn't a proper minister among us, but we'll dig a shallow hole and put some rocks on top of them."

Smoke's harsh plans for the dead outlaws seemed to upset the wounded gunman. "You're gonna put my friends in the ground all together?"

"Unless you figure on digging separate graves. Now, where were you taking those cattle?"

"Far as I can tell, it's none of your business."

"They hang cattle rustlers." Smoke's voice had a heavy tone of doom.

Ty Hardy rode up then and waved his hat over his head. "Hey, Smoke, we got twenty-three head rounded up down by the creek."

"Good. Jeff can hold them. You and Walt find the others."

Icy fear touched the voice of the wounded outlaw. "He called you Smoke. What's your other name?"

"Jensen."

"Oh Jesus! Smoke Jensen. I heard you was fast, but that—that weren't human. You gonna kill me, Jensen?"

"If I had that in mind, you'd already be stretched out there with your friends. Let's get back to the point. What about those cows?"

"W-we were takin' them into Arizona, and then into Mexico. The boss had a buyer all lined up."

"This boss have a name?"

"Uh—sure . . . only, I'd get myself killed for sure if I gave it to you."

"Like I said, I could give you to Jeff York, he's an Arizona Ranger, and see you hang."

"Jeez, Mr. Jensen, I don't want to hang!"

"Then give."

His face a lined mask of conflicting terrors, he shook his head. "Quint Stalker. He ramrods the outfit."

"And Stalker works for Benton-Howell," Smoke related later to Jeff York.

A week and a half had passed since the morning when the terrible news of her husband's death had been brought to Martha Tucker. At the time, she believed that nothing could dampen the awful grief she felt. Then the pressure had begun to force her and the children off the land.

She could not believe Lawrence had actually sold the ranch. Adding strength to that conviction had been that none of those who came would reveal the name of the person to whom he supposedly sold. Then the veiled threats took on substance; shots in the night, the attempt to burn the barn, cattle rustled.

Oh, she had been frightened all right. Yet that only served to strengthen her determination. Now she didn't know what to make of this latest development. Part of her wanted to believe. Another portion of her mind urged caution. It could be some sort of trick. The two young men, one slightly older than the other, who stood before her, could be seeking to gain her trust, catch her off guard, drive them from the ranch entirely. She cut her sky blue eyes to her eldest son.

"I believe them, Momma," Jimmy responded, as though reading her thoughts.

The older man cleared his throat as though preparing to repeat his remarks. Martha spoke over them. "Tell me again how you came upon our cattle."

"Well, ma'am, we were ridin' this way from over in Arizona. We came upon these six men workin' some fifty or so head of cattle. One of the men with us, an Arizona Ranger, recognized your brand. Also that none of the drovers was the sort your hus—er—late husband would have hired."

"So we questioned them," Ty Hardy took up for Walt Reardon. "They lied to us, said they'd bought the cattle offin your husband only three days before that."

"How did you know that to be a lie?"

"We—ah—well, ma'am, we were over Socorro way when it happened, him gettin' shot." Ty Hardy looked uncomfortable with the situation.

"Are you men employed somewhere?" Martha asked, liking the cut of them, more than half-convinced they spoke the truth.

Walt Reardon took over. "Yes, ma'am. We are. Our boss was along with us. It was him said we should bring back your livestock."

Thinking to thank whichever of her neighbors had been so considerate, Martha asked, "Who is it you work for?"

"Well—ah—it's . . . Smoke Jensen," Walt reluctantly told her.

Fury burned in those cobalt eyes. "I don't believe it! Not that murdering, back-shooting bastard!" Face pinched with her outrage, she demanded further, "Were you with him last week when he tried to burn down our barn?"

"Ma'am, please listen to me. Mr. Smoke didn't kill your husband. He'd never shoot a man in the back, no-how. And he wasn't within thirty miles of this ranch any time last week. We was all up in the Cibola Range, dodging a posse," Ty Hardy pressed urgently.

"Smoke Jensen is the finest man I know," Walt Reardon added his endorsement. "He—he saved me from a life of crime and evil. I swear it, ma'am. I was a gunfighter an'—and an outlaw. Smoke Jensen reformed me, an' that's God's own truth."

Doubting, but moved, Martha asked, "How'd he do that?"

A rueful grin spread Walt's lips, and he flushed with embarrassed recollection. "First he beat the livin' hell out of me. Only that wasn't enough, so later on he shot me. Said he spared my life because he saw a glimmer of good in me. So, I'm askin' you, not to think harsh of Smoke Jensen. He could never kill a man in cold blood, believe me."

Flustered by this, Martha ran the back of one hand across her brow. "I'll consider what you've both said. The return of our cattle, I must say, adds credence to your story. I'll thank you for that again. And thank your Mr. Jensen for me, also. I'll have to think over what I have learned. Good day, gentlemen."

* * *

Sheriff Jake Reno wanted to hit the man more than he'd ever wanted to hit anyone. Mash those pursed, disapproving, aristocratic lips into bloody pulp. Who was this Fancy Dan to talk down to him. Hell, this limey-talkin' pig probably didn't even carry a gun. Fat lot he knew about facing down Smoke Jensen. The lawman turned his face away to hide the fury that burned there.

"You are to raise another posse and go back into those mountains and track down Smoke Jensen. Is that perfectly clear, Sheriff Reno?" Geoffrey Benton-Howell accentuated each word with a jab of an extended index finger.

"Who am I gonna get? Those that were with me have been talkin' around town. Not a soul will volunteer. They got the idee that Smoke Jensen is ten foot tall, can shoot a mile with his six-guns, and disappear in a cloud."

"Quint Stalker will provide you ample men, Sheriff."

Reno glowered at the expensively dressed Englishman. "Then why the hell don't he jist go out after Jensen his-self?"

"Because we want this done all legally and proper. You are a lawman. Stalker is . . . just my ranch foreman."

"He's a gunfighter and an outlaw, is more near the truth," Reno snapped.

To the lawman's surprise, Benton-Howell chuckled softly. "He is that all right." Then the ice returned to his voice. "And the reason he is not out openly hunting for

Smoke Jensen is because everyone else knows it, too. So, use his men, Sheriff Reno, and bring me back the head of Smoke Jensen."

Ten

At first, Giuseppi Boldoni could not believe his good fortune. Only a month after he, his wife, and three children had gotten off the boat from Napoli, he had become the proud owner of a truly magnificent tract of land in the Far West. Not even the richest vine grower of his native Calabria claimed so many hectares. The nice man who had sold him the land, Dalton Wade, had also made arrangements for two wagons and all of the equipment Giuseppi would need to build his home. He had picked it up in St. Louis. All paid for, part of the—what had *Signore* Wade called it?—the package, that was it.

What Giuseppi Boldoni learned when he arrived in the White Mountains gave his shrewd Italian mind much food for thought. Small wonder the land sale presentation had offered such generous terms. No one had told Giuseppi that his neighbors would all be red Indians. From the start, they had not gotten on all that well. Now, as he faced a dozen hard-faced Apaches, every one of them abristle with weapons, Giuseppi came to the conclusion that his neighbors were down right hostile.

"You will leave our land now," the big one in the middle demanded in mangled English, which Giuseppi understood only poorly. "Take what you can put in your rolling wikiups and go."

"Perche?"

"It is our land." It sounded enough like *porque,* so the leader answered the "why" in Spanish, and Giuseppi could make out most of the words.

"But I bought it," Giuseppi protested in Italian.

"It was not for sale," came the Spanish answer. "Go now." The eyes turned to chips of obsidian. "Or you die."

Giuseppi went. His wife and daughter in tears, his sons blinking unspoken questions at him, they loaded the wagons and drove off with only some clothing, food, and the rifle Giuseppi had purchased in St. Louis.

The two salty prospectors danced wildly in the icy, rushing water of the stream on the White Mountain reservation. They had actually found color. And not flake gold, either. Nuggets the size of a man's thumb! Some even bigger. The man who had hired them to search had promised them a share. But what counted was who's name was on the claim form.

"We done it, Burk. We sure-nuff did. They's plenty here to share," one bearded sourdough went on. "But what says we got to divvy up with that feller with the double last name?"

"Yer right, Fred. There ain't nothin' writ on paper to say we had us a deal. We done the work, took the risk, we should get the reward."

Neither Burk nor Fred got the prize they anticipated. What they got was their last reward. An Apache arrow cut deeply into Burk's back, quickly followed by another.

CUNNING OF THE MOUNTAIN MAN   119

He hadn't even time for a scream, when the third fletched shaft was embedded in his left kidney. He sank to his knees in the stream, eyes glazing on the shocked expression of his partner.

Fred didn't fare any better. A ball from a big, old .64 caliber trade musket punched through his chest and shattered his right shoulder blade. Two arrows festooned his belly and he wobbled obscenely as he gasped for his last breath.

Cuchillo Negro and three Apache warriors appeared before Fred's dying eyes. "You steal the yellow rocks," the war chief stated flatly. "It is said they make you feel good. Let us see if you can eat them."

He motioned to two of his braves, who took Fred by the arms. Cuchillo Negro yanked on the small leather pouch around Fred's neck. He opened it and extracted two of the large nuggets. One by one he shoved them down Fred's throat. Three more followed, before the last caught and set the white prospector to choking.

"It is enough," Cuchillo Negro said in his own tongue. "Let him die like that."

Smoke Jensen and Jeff York were about to discover that Quint Stalker was nowhere to be found. To keep his face out of Socorro during this phase of the take-over, Benton-Howell had dispatched Stalker and three of the outlaw leader's men to the White Mountain reservation. Under a morning sun, already made hot by the sere desert terrain, they busily occupied themselves pounding claiming stakes into the ground.

Stalker knew enough of the general plan to understand

that this land would be taken from the Apaches and given over to white settlement. The first claims filed on it would be those of his bosses. A neat little scheme, he considered it, as he began to collect stones for a boundary marker.

"Sure's hell's lonely up here, Quint," Randy Sturgis announced. "I thought there was supposed to be 'Paches around."

"They're around," his boss replied. "Only we just don't see 'em. Apaches don't usual get seen unless they wants to."

"Gol-ly, Quint, what if they's warriors?"

Stalker paused to give Randy a cold grin. "Then, I'd reckon as how we'd already be missin' our hair."

Half an hour later, Quint Stalker rounded a bend in the creek with an armload of stones for the last marker. He came face-to-face with two startled Apache boys about thirteen or fourteen years of age. The rocks clattered to the ground, and the youths bolted like frightened deer. Quint knew he dare not let the boys get back to their village with news of the presence of white men. His hand found the butt of his Merwin and Hulbert, as he shouted a warning to his followers.

"Heads up, boys. We got us a couple of rabbit-sized bucks headed your way."

A pistol shot cracked loudly a moment later, followed by a thin wail. Quint pushed himself to a lumbering run and caught up to the surviving Apache boy in time to put a bullet through the youngster's right knee. Eyes wide with pain, the youth fell down, lips closed against any show of pain. Stalker shot him in the other leg.

"Never could abide a damn Apache brat."

"Why's that, Quint?"

"They turn into growed-up Apaches, Randy."

"I can fix that quick enough," Randy offered, and shot the boy in the groin.

Intense pain and the horror caused by the nature of the wound brought a howl of agony from the little lad. "He sure ain't gonna have any git of his own," Randy laughed.

"Awh, hell, finish him off," Marv Fletcher encouraged. "Plum cruel geldin' even an Injun."

Quint Stalker turned away indifferently. "You want to do it, go ahead. I'd as leave play with him a little more."

The fatal round sounded a second later. It presented another surprise to the outlaws. A high, thin gasp, followed by a sob, drew their attention to a clump of deer berries on the bank of the creek. Quint Stalker walked to the screen of vegetation and reached in. He yanked out an Apache girl, of an age with the dead boys, her slim forearm firmly in his big-handed grasp.

"Well, lookie here," Randy Sturgis gloated, advancing on the terrified child. "We got us some rec-re-a-tion."

"I get seconds," Marv Fletcher blurted.

Sky Flower had never known such intense pain in all her life. She knew, of course, what men and women did together. Had known for a long time. Only there was no pleasure for her in what was happening. Tears streamed from her eyes, and she felt like being sick.

Her thought became the deed. It earned her a fist to the jaw, when she vomited on the bared chest of the *Pen-*

dik-olye who rode her. With all the pain within her, she never noticed the new source.

"Little bitch, puked all over me," Randy complained.

"No more'n' you take a bath, we'd never notice, Randy," Quint Stalker jibed.

"Go to hell, Quint."

They had all visited her body twice. This one, called Randy by his fellows, had come back for a third encounter. It went on forever before the youthful white outlaw finished.

"Anybody else?"

"Naw," Stalker answered for the others. "Finish her off."

Sky Flower did not hear the gunshot that robbed her of her life.

Walt Reardon and Ty Hardy rode into the small valley with important news. They joined Smoke Jensen and Jeff York at a small, smokeless fire, and eagerly accepted tin cups of steaming coffee.

"The Widow Tucker was mighty grateful for the return of her cattle," Walt drawled.

"Walt told her we worked for you, Smoke. She flew off the handle at first, but calmed down some when Walt an' me explained how you had taken the stock from rustlers and sent us to bring them back."

Walt offered a new possibility. "Way I see it, she might even be willin' to consider the chance you didn't kill her husband."

Jeff York reacted to it first. "I think that's something worth looking into, Smoke."

"When I can prove who *did* kill her husband, then I'll be glad to talk to the woman," Smoke replied stubbornly.

"Wait a minute, now," Jeff urged. "You need a secure place to operate from, right? My reading of our Sheriff Jake Reno tells me that when brains were being passed out, he was behind the door. When we start stirring things up around Socorro, there's bound to be some real serious hunting around for you. The last place Reno would think to look for you, has to be the ranch of the man you're accused of murdering."

Jeff's words received careful consideration. "You may have a point, Jeff," Smoke allowed. "At least it might be worth looking into."

"If a lawman vouches for you, and a famous Arizona Ranger at that," Jeff added with a mischievous twinkle in his eyes, "it might get the widow to see you in a different light."

"You reckon to handle this yourself?"

"Why not, Smoke? It's the strongest card we've got to play right now."

Smoke Jensen took a final sip of coffee. "Walt and Ty are going to poke around a little, see if they can get a line on Stalker. I'm headed south of Socorro. We'll meet in San Antonio three days from now. Between now and then, Jeff, see what you can set up."

Martha Tucker studied the silver badge pinned on the vest of Jeff York. He wore clothes a cut above the average range hand, was well-spoken, and no doubt was who he claimed to be. Still, she considered his proposal outlandish.

"I'm not certain I'm ready for what you have told me, Ranger York."

"Mrs. Tucker, I've known Smoke Jensen for years. In all that time I've never known him to do a dishonorable thing. What motive would he have to kill a total stranger?"

"But he was found beside my husband's bod—body."

"Unconscious, as I understand it. Tell me everything you know about . . . what happened."

For the next ten minutes, Martha Tucker related all that she had been told about her husband's death. Jeff York listened with intense interest. When she had finished, Jeff pondered for a moment before speaking.

"Taken with what Smoke told me, there's no doubt that someone arranged things to make him look guilty. For one thing, your husband was shot with a .45. Smoke carries twin .44s. Always has."

Martha nodded. "Go on."

"Smoke was found with the single holster strapped around his waist. Yet, when he escaped from the jail, his own guns and their holsters were found in the sheriff's desk. How would you suppose they got there?"

"I have no idea." Martha sighed heavily. "It doesn't appear that the sheriff, or the man he sent out here to tell me about it, has been entirely honest with me."

Jeff grinned in anticipation of success. "Not in the least."

"But why would you come over here from Arizona to look into it?"

"Like I told you before, Mrs. Tucker, Smoke Jensen is my friend. We've fought together before. And he's always stood up for what's right. At least, couldn't you hear him out? Give him an opportunity to tell you what he knows."

Martha Tucker's face lightened, and a soft smile of acquiescence lifted the corners of her mouth. "Yes. I suppose it's the least I can do."

Cuchillo Negro's face darkened with the fury of his outrage. They had been running off the *Pen-dik-olye* for three suns now. But to come upon such a scene as this threatened to make him break his resolve to keep their actions on the reservation. Three children, killed without reason, the girl ravaged before she died. He looked up sharply as Tall Hat spoke.

"I know their village, their families."

"You will carry the message to them?"

"Yes. They will want to come and care for their children."

"We will find the white men who did this. Their end will not be easy," the war chief declared flatly.

He sent men out looking for signs. They soon found plenty in the cairns of stones and stakes that marked the boundary of a claim. At the direction of Cuchillo Negro, the warriors scattered these items over a wide area. Faint traces of shod hoofprints pointed the way the interlopers had left the creek bank.

"Follow the trail," Cuchillo Negro ordered two skilled trackers. "We will come along behind."

"If they leave the reservation?" Ho-tan asked.

Black Knife looked back at the ruined face of the little girl. "We will go after them."

The sign left by the white men meandered through the White Mountains, roughly eastward, and downhill toward the land of the Zuni and Tuwa people. Diligently, the Apaches followed. They came upon the site of a carefully disrupted night camp. When Cuchillo Negro saw it, he spoke his thoughts aloud.

"These men know us well. They took care to see that no sign of their camp could be noted. Your eyes are clever, *Waplanowi*. Now see if you can bring me to them before this day is over."

White Eagle beamed with pride at the chief's compliment. "*Zigosti* is wiser than I. He says their fire burned two sleeps ago. We will not find them before *nolcha* sleeps."

Cuchillo Negro frowned. "We travel together from now on. The *Pen-dik-olye* seem in no hurry. By tomorrow we might catch them."

Wink Winkler mopped his brow with a large bandanna. "I'm shore glad we're shut of them mountains. I began to see an Apache behind every tree."

"There ain't that many Apaches around these parts, Wink," Randy Sturgis replied. "Though I'll admit I'm glad they prob'ly not follow us into New Mexico."

The two hard cases sat on a red-orange mesa that overlooked the Rio San Francisco outside Apache Creek, New Mexico. Randy, who could read on only a third-grade level and had quit school at the age of ten, was fortunate not to know how the small community had acquired its name. If he had, he would not have been nearly so confident. Quint Stalker stood with them, giving his horse a blow and considering their remarkably good luck in escaping the Apaches, who had no doubt set out after them.

"We're not out of it yet, boys. We'd best put more miles between us and the White Mountains."

"Awh, we're safe enough here, Quint," Randy protested. "These critters is near to run into the ground. They gotta have a rest. Us, too. From up here, you can see for miles. No way any Injuns could sneak up on us."

Quint worried that around awhile, then nodded, his mind changed. "Right. We can rest the horses and catch our breath. But no fires after dark, hear? Be sure what you do build is small and smokeless."

For all their precautions, Quint Stalker and the three members of his gang learned the extent of their error in judgement shortly before midnight. A dozen Apache warriors rose up in the darkness and fired a shower of arrows into their camp. The first volley failed to find flesh, but awakened two of the targets.

"What the hell?" Randy Sturgis blurted. Then by weak starlight, he made out the familiar silhouette of an Apache. "Ohmygod! It's Apaches, Quint, it's Injuns!"

"I know that, damnit. Make a run for the horses."

"Injuns ain't supposed to fight at night," Randy wailed.

Quint Stalker's .44 Merwin and Hulbert barked and produced a flare of yellow-orange that illuminated more of the warriors. "Someone forgot to tell that to these bucks."

By then the other pair had been roused. They added to the volume of fire and momentarily held the Apaches in check. Another volley of arrows hissed and moaned through the air. Wink Winkler howled and came to his bare feet.

"My arm! There's an arrow shot clean through it."

Quint Stalker put a bullet in the chest of the Apache nearest him, snatched up his bridle, and ran for the horses. If they lived through this, he reckoned, they'd face a lot more hell, being barefoot and without saddles, food, or a change of clothing. Another Apache materialized out of the gloom at the picket line. Quint coolly pumped a .44 round through the warrior's heart. Low, menacing whoops and the soft rustle of moccasins added haste to his fumbling efforts to slip the headstall over the twitching ears of his horse, and shove the bit between fear-clamped teeth.

Randy Sturgis appeared at his side. "Wink's bad hurt. There's three Apaches jumped him."

"I'll fix your bridle, go back and help him."

Doubt and fear registered clearly in the dim light. "That's a hell of a lot of Injuns back there."

"Do it anyway. I never leave a man who ain't dead," Stalker snarled.

"Might be that's already the case," Randy opined.

Gunfire erupted from two locations on the small mesa, which disproved for the moment Randy's expectation. A hard shove from Quint Stalker sent him back to the melee. Halfway there, he encountered Wink Winkler and Vern Draper.

The arrow still protruded from both sides of Wink's left forearm. He had been cut across the chest and a chunk of meat was missing from his right shoulder, where a war hawk had bitten deeply. Vern cut wild, glazed eyes to Randy, and gestured over his shoulder.

"Damn near got myself punctured back there," he panted. "But I freed Randy from those devils."

"Let's make tracks," Randy urged.

Quickly they rejoined Quint Stalker. Bridles fitted in place, the outlaws made ready to mount. Randy and Vern lifted Wink astride his mount. Then Vern gave Randy a leg up. Quint Stalker got Vern Draper on his horse, then vaulted to the back of his own. By then the Apaches had maneuvered into position close enough to see their targets in the dark.

More arrows sung their deadly songs as the white men rode fearfully away toward the trail that led off the mesa. Cuchillo Negro raised his trade musket to his shoulder and squeezed off a round that ended the evil career of the first to violate little Sky Flower. The big .64 caliber ball drove a hand-width chunk of shattered spine through the lungs and heart of Randy Sturgis.

Back arched suddenly, Randy did a back flip over his mount's rump. He landed hard on the reddish soil of the nameless butte that overlooked the San Francisco River at Apache Creek.

Eleven

Five of Quint Stalker's ne'er-do-well hard cases lounged in front of the Tio Pepe cantina in the little town of San Antonio, New Mexico. They listlessly passed a bottle of tequila from hand to hand, drank, spat tobacco juice, or rolled smokes. One of them, Charlie Bascomb, perked up somewhat when a stranger rode into town on a big-chested roan.

"Hey, don't he look like that feller we's supposed to be huntin' down?" Bascomb asked his companions.

Weak-eyed Aaron Sneed squinted and dug a grimy knuckle into one pale blue orb. "Nuh-uh. Don't think so. Last I heard, he was supposed to be up north a ways, in the Cibolas."

"I for one," barrel-chested Buck Ropon declared, "am glad to hear that, Aaron. After I heard what happened to them boys that went along with the sheriff, I'm not so certain I want to tangle with the likes of Smoke Jensen."

"Turnin' yeller, Buck?" Charlie taunted. " 'Sides, them boys was alone most times. They's *five* of us. I say us five can take any Smoke Jensen, or the devil hisself if it came to that."

Unwittingly, Charlie Bascomb had cast their fate in a

direction none of them would have wanted, and which none of them later liked in the least.

After the stranger entered the general mercantile across the way, Charlie kept on worrying aloud. Like a big, old tabby will a little, bitty mouse, it finally wore down the caution so wisely held by Buck Ropon. Rising to his boots, Buck adjusted the drape of his cartridge belt across the solid slab of lard on his big belly, and nodded in the direction of the general store.

"I reckon you're gonna keep on about that until we know for certain, ain'tcha?" Buck Ropon groused.

Charlie screwed his mouth into a tight pucker. "Wouldn't do no harm to get a closer look."

"Are you crazy?" a heretofore silent member of the quintet demanded. "What if it *is* Smoke Jensen?"

Charlie grinned widely, his eyebrows and ears rising with the intensity of it all. "Why, then, we've got his butt and a thousand dollars reward!"

Inside the mercantile, Smoke Jensen ducked his head to miss the hanging display of No. 4 galvanized washtubs, buckets, washboards, and various pieces of harness. A wizened old man with a monk's fringe of white hair around a large expanse of bald pate glanced up through wire-rimmed half-glasses, and peered at his customer.

"What'll it be?"

"Howdy," Smoke addressed the man. "I could use some supplies. A slab of fatback, couple of pounds each of beans, flour, sugar, a pound of coffee beans, some 'taters."

"Yessir, right away." The merchant made no move to fill the order.

"Better throw in a can of baking powder, some dry onions, and a box of Winchester .45-70-500's if you've got them."

"Ummm. That's for that new Express Rifle, ain't it? I don't have any."

In a moment of inspiration, Smoke amended his list. "Then throw in a dozen sticks of dynamite. Sixty percent will do."

"Don't stock that, either. You'll have to go to the gunsmith. He's got a powder magazine out back of his place."

"Thank you. Uh . . . I'll take me a couple of sticks of this horehound candy," Smoke added as he reached for the jar.

"You got youngun's?" the seam-faced oldster asked suspiciously.

"No Smoke replied with a smile. Truth was, Smoke Jensen had always been partial to horehound candy.

The storekeeper took in the double-gun rig: the right one slung low, butt to the rear, the left set high, canted so as to present an easy reach for the front-facing grip. A gunfighter. That fact screamed at the merchant. Hastily, to cover the tremor in his hands, he set about packaging Smoke Jensen's supplies. Smoke, meanwhile, rolled the sweets in a sheet of waxed paper and twisted the ends closed. He stuck his prize in his right shirt pocket, under his fringed leather vest.

When the small stack of purchases had been tallied, Smoke paid for them and removed a rolled-up flour sack from a hip pocket. Slowly, carefully, he put each item inside and hefted the load.

The clerk had a dozen questions forming in his mind— but caution kept him silent. He stood behind the counter and watched his customer head for the door. Then he tilted his chin and shot a glance beyond the tall, powerfully built stranger. He saw the five hard cases in the street, facing his store. He gulped forcefully and licked dry lips with a suddenly arid tongue. How he wished he had taken seriously the suggestions of steel shutters for his windows.

Smoke Jensen stepped out onto the abbreviated board-walk that extended porchlike around one side, and along the wider front of the general mercantile. It also fronted the next building on the main street. No doubt the structures had been built at the same time, by the same man. Blazing, afternoon sun came from the right angle to blind the eyes of Smoke Jensen to all but five pairs of legs, stuffed into an equal number of boots, arranged in a semicircle that curved out into the street and blocked all avenues of egress. All that left him was a fight, or a cowardly flight back through the store and out the rear. Through the distortion of heat waves, Smoke heard a hoarse whisper.

"It's him, right enough."

"What we gonna do?"

"Well, for one thing, we won't even have to shoot him. He's got the sun in his eyes. An' he ain't got nowhere to go to get away. Let's jist jump him, boys."

Smoke Jensen sat the sack of his supplies on a bench

in front of one big display window, his vision gradually clearing. He raised his left hand in a cautioning gesture.

"I think both your ideas are wrong," said Smoke blandly.

Suddenly, three of the men launched themselves at him. Smoke stepped in on one with groping arms. He grabbed a wrist and pivoted on powerful legs. His attacker spun away. When Smoke released him, he hurtled sideways into a shower of glass as a display window broke. He landed in the midst of a selection of bolts of cloth. Bleats of pain came from him, accompanied by the sustained tinkle of more falling shards. Smoke had already turned to face his next threat.

Two hard cases rammed into him at the same time. For all the tree-trunk strength of Smoke's legs, they bore him off his boots. Smoke managed to turn slightly in the air and take them with him. They toppled through the open space created by the shattered window.

"Ow! Gadang, I'm cut," one outlaw wailed, and released his hold on Smoke Jensen.

Immediately Smoke flexed his right knee and drove it into the belly of the hard case. Forcibly ejected from the display counter, he slammed painfully into a four-by-four upright of the awning over the boardwalk. His ribs could be heard breaking like dry sticks. A painful howl tore from his throat. Before Smoke could get to work on the other, hard hands clamped on his shoulders and strong arms yanked him into the store.

"You're gonna git yours, Jensen," Charlie Bascomb snarled.

"I'm gonna kill him!" the outlaw with the broken ribs shrieked. "Let me at him. I'll kill him." He stumbled through the door, fingers curled around the flashy pearl grips of his six-gun. "Get outta my way, Charlie!"

Charlie got; but before he could fully register what happened, Smoke Jensen had recovered from his man-handling, drew, and fired. Smoking lead pinwheeled the crazed gunman. He dumped over, arms flying wide. His released Colt sped from his hand and broke a glass display case. A wail of protest came from the merchant, now crouched behind his counter. He had cause for further complaint a moment later, when the thug in the window reared up and threw a wild shot at Smoke Jensen.

It spanged off the cast-iron side of a black, pot-bellied stove, richocheted through the ceiling, and left a crack behind. Because Smoke Jensen was no longer where he had been. He moved the instant he fired. Now he swung the hot muzzle of his .44 toward the offensive gunhawk.

Smoke's six-gun spoke, and a yelp of surprise and pain came as shards of wood from the window's inner frame-work showered the gunhawk's face. It was not enough to incapacitate him, Smoke soon learned. Two more rounds barked from the outlaw's .45, as the remaining pair of gunslicks charged through the open doorway.

Another hasty round clipped the thug in the shoulder, a moment before the last mountain man ducked behind a floor island to escape a murderous hail of lead from the newcomers. A soft grunt told him he had scored a hit. Bullets ripped and shredded a rack of black, weather-proofed dusters, searching blindly for Smoke. He easily kept ahead of their advance, then hunkered down and duck-walked back along the section the slugs had chewed through. At the end of the island, the wounded hard case in the window spotted him and blinked in surprise.

"Nobody could live through that," he declared in astonishment a second before he died, a bullet from Smoke Jensen turning his long, sharp nose into an inverted exclamation point.

Smoke immediately reholstered his expended six-gun and cross-drew his backup. A snigger came from Charlie Bascomb. "That's five, iffin' I count right, Jensen. We're comin' after you."

Could this one they called Charlie be so stupid as to not have seen his second six-gun? Or did he forget about it? Smoke let go of the questions as quickly as he had formed them. He ducked low and spotted the boots of his taunter. The big iron barked, and Charlie shrieked as he went to the floor. He found himself staring into the steely gray gaze of Smoke Jensen.

Without visible pause, Charlie began to roll toward the door. He blubbered and sobbed as he called entreaties to his remaining sidekicks. "Go after him, boys. He's right back o' them coats."

Only Smoke was not there any more. One outlaw ankled around the far end of the island to discover that fact. He stared disbelievingly, while his partner emptied another six-gun into the linen dusters and his companion. The thug died without Smoke firing a shot.

The man from the Sugarloaf made up for that quickly enough, though. The last of a trio of fast shots found meat. A grunt and curse preceded a stumbling bootwalk across the plank floor toward the back counter. Smoke had only a single round left. He edged along a wall of shelves loaded with boots and shoes, until he could see the counters at the rear of the store.

From his vantage point, the gunhawk saw Smoke first.

He tripped his trigger on a final round, and immediately abandoned it for a large knife. When the target jinked to Smoke's right, it threw his shot off. Smoke's last slug punched through the outer wall of the store. Only then did Smoke see that the knife was not the usual hog-sticker carried by frontier hard cases. In fact, it looked more like a ground-down sword, with a two-foot blade.

While that registered on Smoke, his adversary gave a roar and leaped at him. The blade swished through the air with a vicious sound. Smoke jumped back and to the side, away from the swing. He instantly stumbled, tripped, and fell into a double row of light farm implements. Their clutter muffled his muttered curse. A second later, the knife-wielder charged Smoke again.

His own coffin-handle Bowie, formidable under any other conditions, would be of little use against this on-slaught. Smoke Jensen knew that in an instant. He bought himself some time by a quick, prone scramble down the aisle. Not quite far enough, as the two-foot blade whirred through the air and clipped a heel from Smoke's boot. While his opponent remained off balance, Smoke thrust upright. He backed away further, both hands groping among the tools.

A snarl of triumph illuminated the contorted face of Buck Ropon. He rushed after Smoke Jensen with his altered sword raised high. He had just begun the down-swing—aimed to split Smoke's head from crown to chin—when Smoke's hands closed on the familiar per-pendicular handle of a scythe. He tightened his grip and jumped backward.

Swiftly, Smoke swung the keen-edged blade like the Grim Reaper. The long handle easily outdistanced the reach of Buck Ropon. The big, curved blade hissed through a short arc. Shock jolted up the handle to Smoke's arms when the edge made contact. With Smoke Jensen's enormous strength, it cut clean through. Buck Ropon had just been decapitated by a scythe.

His headless body did a grotesque quick-time dance, while twin streams of crimson fountained to the ceiling. The head, lips still skinned back in a snarl, hit and rolled on the floor. When the blood geysers diminished, the deflated corpse fell full-length. Smoke Jensen immediately recovered himself.

He set the scythe aside and started to reload both six-guns. Stunned into mindless shock, the merchant stumbled around his business, alternately sobbing and cursing. Bitterness colored his words when he was capable of comprehensible speech.

"Mein Gott! Mein Gott! Look at this. I'm ruined! Who will pay? Who will pay for all this damage?"

By then, Smoke Jensen had finished punching fresh cartridges into both weapons, loading six rounds in each. Seeming to ignore the distressed shopkeeper, he went from corpse to corpse, examining the contents of their pockets. He accumulated a considerable amount of paper currency and coins. Then, with the merchant looking on in horror, he stripped the boots from them and recovered even more.

It totaled about two hundred dollars and change. He handed it to the horrified man. "This should help. And that scythe is like brand new. All you need do is clean it up, and sell it to someone."

"Never! No one would want it. I'll never be able to sell it."

Smoke delved into one of his own pockets and brought out a three-dollar gold piece. "Then I'll buy it."

"That's it, *Mench?* You are going to hand me money and walk out of here like nothing happened?"

"You saw it all. You can tell the law what happened. They attacked me, right? I only protected myself."

"Wh-who . . . are you?"

"Smoke Jensen."

A sudden greenness crept into the existing pallor of the merchant's face. *"Ach du lieber Gott!"* he wailed, as he tottered toward the cash drawer with the money clutched in one hand.

Smoke Jensen retrieved his supplies and assessed his own damage. He found the worst that had happened was that his horehound candy sticks had been broken. He left San Antonio without a backward glance.

Smoke camped a hundred yards off the only road he figured Jeff and his hands would use coming to San Antonio through this sparsely settled country. Sure enough, early the next evening, while coffee brewed and he tended a hat-sized fire over which biscuits baked in a covered skillet, he heard the thunder of the hooves; he made it out to be three horses in a brisk canter. Smoke kept a careful eye to the north, as the sound grew louder. He had the polished metal shaving mirror from his personal kit cupped in one hand, and when the riders came close enough to recognize, he signaled them by a series of flashes.

"You could have took that damn thing out of my eyes a little sooner," Jeff York complained, as he rode up to where Smoke bent over to add more fatback to a second skillet.

"Wanted to make sure you knew it was me. Might have been you Arizona boys don't know that trick," Smoke teased.

"Hell, the Apaches have been usin' mirrors to signal with since the Spanish brought them way back. That smells good."

"Step down and pour coffee. You two as well. What's the news?"

"We can't find anything of Sheriff Reno or Quint Stalker, nor any of Stalker's hard cases," Jeff declared.

"Everything is set up with the widder for two nights from now," Walt added his good news.

Smoke nodded. "Small wonder you didn't see any of Stalker's men. I had a run-in with five of them yesterday in San Antonio. That's why I'm out here waiting for you."

Jeff snorted and ran a hand through his sandy blond locks. "Did you stick around to explain to the local law?"

Smoke gave him a blank look of innocence. "I didn't know there was any. Didn't overstay my welcome by finding out. Not when one of them got away. My guess, our friend Sheriff Reno is in charge around here anyway."

"Losing five of his prize possemen will sure enough make his day for him," Walt said drolly. "Uh . . . one thing we did find out, the sheriff is usin' Stalker's outlaws on the posse. There's some folk around Socorro don't take too fondly to that. Includin' the Widow Tucker."

"Then I am even more inclined to meet with the good woman." Smoke's eyes twinkled with suppressed merriment, as he continued, "I seem to recall you mentioned she was some looker, Walt. There any chance of you making a place for yourself?"

"You hurt me to the core, Smoke. You know I ride for the Sugarloaf an' no one else."

"Sometimes the heart has a way of changing the mind. Whatever," Smoke summed up, "eat hearty and sleep with a packed outfit. Tomorrow we ride to the Tucker ranch."

Twelve

Smoke Jensen stared down into the black pool in his coffee cup. It struck him powerfully to realize how long it had been since he had last drank strong, dark brew from a delicate china cup like this. Of course, it had been back home, on the Sugarloaf. For all her ability to rough it like a man, Sally Jensen insisted on her finery in the large, log building that housed the headquarters of Smoke's horse-breeding ranch. Only there, he noted, the tension didn't grow so thick it could be felt and tasted.

After Jeff York had made the introductions, Martha Tucker sat across from Smoke Jensen, at the core of that tension. From her viewpoint, Smoke allowed, she had ample cause to radiate so much distrust and suspicion. Might as well get on with it and see how much of that he could boil away. Sighing, Smoke cut his eyes to the woman across the table. His eyes locked with her sky blue ones. In a soft, steady voice, pitched low, Smoke described what he knew of events surrounding the death of Lawrence Tucker.

She listened, hands in her lap, palms up, like opening flowers. Her face remained impassive, until he recounted the discovery of their cattle on the trail outside of Datil. Suddenly strained muscles tightened her face into deep, shadowed lines. She drew a sharp breath, recalling when and how the livestock had been driven off the ranch.

"Those cattle were stolen more than a week ago," she stated in a hollow voice. "The men who did it called their leader Smoke."

Smoke Jensen looked sharply at her. "Someone was being cute. My guess, based on what the survivor of that encounter told us, is that Quint Stalker thought that one up." He sighed and paused. "It couldn't have been Stalker. He's not been seen around Socorro for a good two weeks."

"Where might he be?" Martha asked.

"We . . . don't know," Jeff York inserted.

"Wherever he is, he'll be up to no good, you can be sure of that."

Smoke first picked up on this change in Martha's attitude. "Pardon me, Mrs. Tucker, but could you tell us more about what has happened here, to you and your children? Jeff has filled me in on part of it, though surely not everything."

Smoke's prompting opened the flood gates. "First, a man came from town, Elert Cousins it was, to tell me tha—that Lawrence had been killed. He said the sheriff had caught the man who had done it. That it was . . ." Her voice faltered, lowered, "Smoke Jensen."

"And now, maybe you're not so sure?" Smoke urged.

"You can count on what Smoke told you," Jeff York jumped in. "Like I said before, Smoke is on the right side of the law, a straight shooter." A sudden pained expression of embarrassment twisted the Arizona Ranger's handsome features. "Sorry. Poor choice of words."

"I understand," Martha said softly. Then she continued

to recount the efforts to force her and the children to abandon the ranch. When she had ended her account, she added, "At first they claimed that you had taken the money and bill of sale when you killed Larry. After that, when I insisted on seeing the transfer of title and sale bill, they stopped even mentioning that.

"Lately, I've been giving it some thought," Martha continued. "Especially after talking with your hands, who were quite gentlemanly, though with a few rough edges. Then, Ranger York, who spoke on your behalf. I got to wondering how it could be that you were found unconscious, beside my hus—beside his body, and they didn't find the money and bill of sale on your person?"

Smoke Jensen studied her calm demeanor. Certainly a powerfully attractive woman. Her heart-shaped face revealed a firm, though not stern mouth, wide-set, clear, blue eyes, and a high brow. Her hands, worn by years at the washboard and cookstove, still retained a semblance of youthful elegance. Carried herself well, too. Even the hostility she had directed toward him at the outset had been muted by an inner disposition toward true justice, rather than revenge. Her children, quiet and polite, showed good upbringing. They had been clean and wore neat clothing. They had gone off to their loft beds shortly after Smoke and Jeff arrived.

Most of all, as he had just discovered, her mind worked rather well. No one else had come up with that particular question, let alone an explanation.

"Score one for the lady," Smoke announced to break his contemplation. "I asked the sheriff that very question when he came into my cell to—ah—arrange a confession. He didn't have an answer."

"Neither do I," Martha allowed. "That's what perplexes me."

Much as she disliked the direction of her thoughts, Martha Tucker had to admit that this trim-waisted, broad-shouldered man was far more handsome than either of his hands. His hair, cut a bit longish for current fashion, had a natural curl in the ends, that turned inward to brush at his earlobes. His eyes had turned a soft, comforting gray. Martha had no way of knowing that they could take on the color of glacial ice when angered. To her dismay, Martha Tucker found herself comparing him with her husband, with Smoke Jensen coming out ahead in most attributes. She chastised herself for the strong, though unwanted attraction she felt toward the rugged mountain man-gunfighter.

Although, to give herself credit, she also felt repelled by his reputation. There! She had said it all. Yet, he seemed sincere in what he said. What with Ranger York to vouch for him, what reason did she have to distrust Smoke Jensen? She suddenly realized that she had been asked a question, when Smoke repeated it.

"How do you mean, Miz Tucker?"

"Why, simply that there have been rumors about our Sheriff Reno. It's said that he's lazy, which I can vouch for. Also that to make work easy, he's sent more than one innocent man to the gallows."

"That's not true, ma'am," Jeff York interjected. "The law don't have anything to do with convictions and sentencing. That's up to the judge and jury."

Martha's eyes held a heretofore unseen twinkle. "Don't their decisions rely a great deal on a lawman's evidence and testimony?"

Jeff knew when he had been bested. A light pink flush colored his fair cheeks. "You got me there, ma'am."

"I see that I haven't been entirely clear. What I was getting at, is that Sheriff Reno is supposed to have created evidence out of whole cloth several times before, also withheld evidence or suppressed testimony that would have favored the accused person."

"Fits with the way he handled this case," Smoke Jensen provided. "Last thing I remember, I was wearing my own guns. Then they showed up in Reno's desk drawer. And I was supposed to be packin' some hand-me-down, castoff, conversion Remington. And if I had the money I was supposed to have taken, he would have bragged that up to me, too."

Martha, who had cast a nervous glance up at the loft, cut her eyes back to Smoke. "Of course, it would be argued that the sheriff, or that sticky-fingered jailer of his, could have relieved you of it while you were unconscious. For my part, I think there never was any money. Because I know that Larry had no intention of ever selling this ranch."

"So then, that's what led you to believe me?" Smoke prodded.

Martha took a deep breath, sighed it out. "Yes. At least enough to ask you, what do you intend to do about it?"

"I intend to find the one who did it and why. That'll clear my name."

"Then the next question has to be, what can I do to help?" It had taken Martha considerable effort to frame those words, yet the strain did not show on her lovely face.

Smoke and Jeff exchanged smiles. "Well, Miz Tucker,

I need a place to operate out of. Somewhere the sheriff and Quint Stalker's men would never believe me to be."

"I can let you and your two hands and Ranger York move onto the ranch. They've tried so hard to make me believe you are guilty, no one would ever suspect you to be here."

Smoke beamed at her. "We'll be settled in by morning. Then I'll come let you know where we set up."

"Why, in the bunkhouse, of course. I read somewhere that if one wanted to hide something important, the best place would be in plain sight."

"Poe, I think," Smoke offered. *"The Purloined Letter."*

More of her heavy mood sloughed off, and Martha clapped her hands together in delight. "I am impressed, Mr. Jensen. I never expected—"

"A gunfighter to be well read? I had a good teacher."

"Who was that, Mr. Jensen?"

"A man they called Preacher. He raised me up from about the age of your oldest. Taught me things that would astound a body. Some of 'em I never believed until I'd gotten around a bit. Walt and Ty are close at hand. We should be moved into the bunkhouse before midnight."

"Fine." Martha rose, extended a hand in courteous fashion. "Then I'll see you for breakfast at first light. We can start laying plans on how to expose the truth."

Geoffrey Benton-Howell set aside the sheet of thick, creamy, off-white linen stationery. He could not restrain the smile of triumph that lighted his face, all except his malevolent, deep-set, blue eyes. He rose to his highly polished boots from behind the cherry wood secretary desk, and crossed the room to the tall, drape-framed window that overlooked the main street of Socorro. Backlighted by the searing sun, he struck a familiar pose, proud of his lean, hard body for all his fifty-one years.

"They will be here, as expected. Train to Albuquerque, then on by carriage. I suggest we send one of ours. It will make a good impression. These politicians of yours seem to dote on such privileges."

Miguel Selleres took a deep sip from a glass of excellent port wine. "They are not *my* politicians, my friend. I am a citizen of Mexico."

"New Mexico, to be precise," Benton-Howell thrust a sharp barb. "The country of your adopted nationality lost this territory to the United States in the Treaty of Guadalupe Hidalgo. That was long before you were born."

"No, *amigo,* I was born in this part of Mexico in 1845, and to me and my family, the distinction of which country has claim to it on paper is not in dispute. It is a part of Mexico. It always will be. The day will come when we cast off the foreign occupation of our lands."

Lordy, Quint Stalker thought as he stared at Miguel Selleres in disbelief, this boy's wagon's got a busted wheel. One good thing—so far no one had asked him why they had come runnin' back to Socorro with their tails between their legs. A moment later Benton-Howell destroyed Stalker's sense of relief.

"They will be entertained as planned. Now, tell me, Stalker, what brings you so hastily back to Socorro?"

A pained expression preceded Stalker's words. "Truth to tell, Mr. Benton-Howell, the Apaches runned us clear the hell an' gone out of them mountains."

Benton-Howell's tone mirrored his disbelief. "A few scruffy savages with bows and arrows? Surely you had enough firepower?"

"Not for more 'an a dozen of them. Those Apaches is tough fighters, Sir Geoffrey." Try a little flattery, Stalker told himself.

"Perhaps your men have lost their *cojones, ¿es verdad?*" Miguel Selleres sneered.

"Don't you get on my case, *Señor.*" Quint pronounced it *sayn-yor.* "What is it your people call them?"

"Ah, yes," Selleres replied, recalling. *"La raza bronce que sabe morir.* The bronze race that knows how to die. But they *do* die."

"Eventual." To Benton-Howell, Stalker explained, "Oftentimes, their raiding parties are no more than five, six men. But they can tie up a platoon-sized army patrol for weeks at a time. All the while, they're killin', burnin', an' running off stock. Those stinkin' Injuns kilt one of my boys, stuck arrows in three more. We was lucky to get out of it with our hair."

"Yes, I can appreciate that. The fact remains that we must keep control of those claims. I want you to gather in all of your men and head back to the White Mountains. This time, make certain you can hold off every red nigger there, man or boy."

"Mr. Benton—Sir Geoffrey," Stalker protested through a series of gulps. "Thing is, we take in too many, and it attracts the attention of the soldier-boys an' the Arizona Rangers. We can't fight all of that at once. Besides, I need to leave a few men here, keep a lid on things."

"Very well, those who are out with Sheriff Reno on

the posse can remain here to handle local matters. Take the rest and leave by noon tomorrow."

Chastened, Quint Stalker came to his boots, his head hung, and started for the door. "Yes, sir, if that's what you want." At the door he asked, "Does that mean you're givin' up the hunt for Smoke Jensen?"

"Oh, no, my dear boy. Not at all. We have some other plans for your Mr. Smoke Jensen. Plans I'm sure he will find most unpleasant."

They had left the Tucker ranch after this admonition: "Jeff, I want you and Walt to ride into Socorro. Hang around the saloons, the barber shop, and livery. I'm sure you know why," he added, cutting his eyes to Jeff.

"Any lawman knows that's where you hear all the gossip," Jeff replied with a grin.

"Right. Go soak up all you can get on Quint Stalker, this Benton-Howell you mentioned in Show Low, and his partner, Selleres. Find out about the sheriff, too."

Jeff and Walt reached town as the swampers were dumping their mop buckets and tossing out the dirty sawdust from the previous day. Jeff, who sported a clean-shaven face and fresh haircut, opted for the livery. Walt ambled his mount down the street to the barbershop.

He entered and settled himself in a chair. "Trim and shave. Trim the mustache, too."

"Right away, sir," a mousey, pigeon-breasted individual with a pince-nez squeaked.

"Hear there's been some excitement in town since I left?" Walt probed gently.

"Oh, yes, yes indeed. Were you here when Mr. Lawrence Tucker was murdered?"

"Yep. Rode out the next day."

"Well, then, you don't know about the jailbreak!"

"What jailbreak?"

"Three desperadoes broke that Smoke Jensen out of the jail."

Walt noted that the barber—Tweedy was the name on the fancy diploma above the sideboard, bevel-edged mirror—omitted to mention the lynch mob in his colorful rendition of Smoke's escape. When he at last wound down, Walt remarked dryly, "That sounds like quite a tale, right enough. Are you sure those desperadoes weren't part of the Stalker gang?"

"Oh, no, not at all. Mr. Stalker lent his foreman and some of his hands to the posse the sheriff took out. He's got more out with him now."

"Then . . . this Jensen is still on the loose?"

"From what we've heard. Hold still now, I have to shear over your ears."

Scissorlike sounds came from the mechanical clippers in the hand of Tweedy. He shaped and trimmed in silence for a while, then bent Walt's head the other direction. "One more now, and we're almost through."

Two men entered and peered curiously at Walt. Under normal circumstances this constituted a serious insult to any man on the frontier. Well accustomed by his years on the dodge, Walt Reardon showed not a flicker of annoyance at the scrutiny. As it continued, though, another idea occurred to him.

"You—ah—lookin' for somebody you know, Mister?" he gravel-voiced at the nearer of the pair.

"No—no, just thought I'd seen you around."

"Maybe you have, but what business is it of yours?"

Tweedy, a nervous, flighty type, dithered in agitation. "Now, now, gentlemen. I'm sure these fellows meant no disrespect, sir."

"I ain't heard from the other one yet," Walt growled.

A long second ticked by, then the smaller of the pair cut his eyes away from Walt Reardon's riveting stare. "No offense, Mister. We was lookin' for a friend."

"That's right," the other one blurted hastily, suddenly nervously conscious of the miles-long, gunfighter stare of Walt Reardon. "We expected him to be here ahead of us."

Walt sensed a pair of easy marks here, and produced a smile. "No offense taken, then. Tell you what. I'll buy you a drink when we get through."

"That's mighty white of you, Mister—ah?"

"Walt—" He cut it off, well aware that the name Reardon still meant gunfighter to many. "Kruger."

"I'm Sam Furgeson. This is Gus Ehrhardt. We'll just take you up on that drink, Walt. Say at the Hang Dog?"

"I know where it is. I'll be waitin' for you there."

Hands still shaking, barber Tweedy knicked Walt's left cheek with the straight razor. Wincing as though he had cut himself, the short, slender tonsorialist quickly dabbed with a towel and applied a piece of tissue paper to the tiny wound. "Sorry, there. Just a little slip."

"Make certain you don't slip like that when you get to my neck."

"Oh, no! Why, I'd never—" Tweedy caught a glimpse of those gunfighter eyes in the mirror, and choked off his protest.

* * *

Three riders, looking the part of ranch hands, rode into the livery stable shortly after Jeff York arrived there. Jeff knew they were not wranglers when they turned their mounts into nearby stalls and called to the old codger who ran the place to take care of them, then walked down the alternating stretches of boardwalk and hard-pounded pathway into the center of town. A lifetime of observation had told Jeff York that *real* cowboys would never walk anywhere. They would straddle their horses to go from one saloon to another, even if only two doors apart.

Jeff stood in the shade of the big livery barn and watched them ankle down the street. He marked the saloon they entered, then turned back to the liveryman. "They come in often?" he asked.

"Right as rain." He added a wink, a nod, and a sharp elbow in Jeff's ribs. "Some of Quint Stalker's randy crew. Real hard cases. Looks like they don't bother you none."

"Oh, they do. It's just I don't show it all that much," Jeff told him lightly.

"There's some things a feller could say about them, sure enough. The breed, if not them in partic'lar."

"Oh?" Jeff prompted gently.

"Them three do their best work on wimmin an' kids, way I hear it. Right tough hombres, when it comes to scarin' the bejazus outta some ten-year-old."

"Sounds like you don't hold them in great esteem?"

"Nawsir. They're lowlife trash, an' that's for sure."

Jeff gathered a few more tidbits and then made his way to the saloon the men had entered. The Blue Lantern turned out to be a dive. Hardly more than a road ranch, Jeff York evaluated it, as he pushed through the hanging glass bead curtain that screened the interior from passersby. He had barely turned left toward the bar, when one of the trio spun around, his fingers closed on the butt of a big Colt in a left-hand holster.

"You followin' us, Mister?" Apparently with odds of three to one, they had no qualms about bracing a full-grown man.

"No, not at all," Jeff responded in his calming voice. "I only got in town a bit ahead of you."

"An' waited all this time to come in here, huh?" The taunting tone turned to vicious challenge. "I say you're snoopin' around where you don't belong. You smell of lawdog to me. You want to prove otherwise, you'll have to do it with an iron in your hand."

Well, crap, Jeff York thought. Not in town a quarter hour, and already he had a gunfight on his hands.

Thirteen

In the split second that passed after Jeff York's recognition of the situation facing him, he made a quick decision to follow a maxim of Smoke Jensen. "Let speed work for you, but remain in control," the savvy gunfighter had advised Jeff during their sojourn in Mexico with Carbone and Martin. So, Jeff followed that suggestion now.

Jeff's Colt appeared in his hand in a blur. The sound of the hammer ratcheting back made a loud metallic clatter. Jaws sagged on the three gunnies, which drew their mouths into gaping ovals. They had not even made a move. The one with his hand on the grip of his six-gun released his hold instantly, his arm rising up and away from his body.

"Did any of you ever see a lawdog haul iron that fast?" Jeff asked in a sneer.

All three shook their heads in a negative gesture. Then the mouthy one recovered enough aplomb to get in a word or two. "Well, there is Elfego Baca."

"He don't count," one of his companions nervously blurted. "He's over Texas way right now. Besides, Baca's about half-outlaw anyway."

"Right. An' Sheriff Reno runned him out of town after

that dustup with McCarty an' his crew down in Frisco," the third hard case added.

"So what will it be, fellers?" Jeff demanded.

"Awh, hell, we was just a little proddy. We been out chasin' some jackass who killed a rancher here-about."

Jeff recalled that Stalker's men were serving with the posse. If he could completely defuse this situation, he might learn something useful, he surmised. "All right by me. I'm just gonna ease this hammer back down, and then I'll join you for a drink."

"Shore enough, Mister. Say, you got a name?"

"It's Jeff."

"Good enough for me." He made the introductions of his companions and the palpable tension in the room bled off in a relieved sigh from the bartender.

Walt Reardon had gone on ahead to the Hang Dog Saloon, where the two rough-edged ranglers from the barbershop joined him half an hour later. A short while before they arrived, a conversation at the bar drew his interest.

"Say, I sure wouldn't mind workin' for the B-Bar-H right about now," one obvious cowhand advised his friends.

"Why's that?" one of the latter asked.

"Ain't you heard, Yancy? That English feller that owns the place is fixin' to throw a real fiesta. Gonna be the get-together of the season, from what some of his hands have been sayin'."

"What's the occasion? He gettin' hitched?" another one asked.

"Maybe he found a place to sell beeves for more than twenty dollars a head," suggested a third with a snorting laugh.

"Way I got it, this here Benton-Howell is doin' it to honor some big shot politicians from Washington."

Mighty interesting, Walt thought to himself as he took another swig of beer. Might be we'll hear more about that, he speculated hopefully. The gossipy one continued.

"Gonna be in three days. Even the hands is invited. At least after the high mucky-mucks git their fill of vittles. They're roastin' a whole steer, doin' some *cabrito,* too. There'll be likker and music and dancing. Those are lucky boys to be workin' for that English dude."

Yancy had another question. "What's these politicians done to be honored for, Hank?"

Hank smirked. "Don't mean they done anything . . . yet. The way it is, politicians are always lookin' for a little somethin' extra, if you get my drift. So, it don't harm nothin' to have 'em in yer pocket, *before* you want a favor done."

Walt's new, slightly nervous friends banged through the door at that point, and the interesting revelations got tuned out.

Smoke Jensen spent the day in a fruitless search for any sign that could lead him to the men who had been pestering the Tucker family. From the confession he had gotten out of the wounded rustler, he knew that Quint Stalker and his gang were involved in that job. Could he be responsible for all the other harassment?

More than likely, Smoke considered as he headed his

big roan back to the ranch headquarters. Ty Hardy cut his trail some ten minutes later.

"What did you find?" Hardy asked Smoke.

"From the look on your face, the same as you."

Hardy grunted. "A whole lot of nothin'."

"Too much time has gone by. We can't sift any strange tracks from those of the hands. I've been hearin' about a lot of little incidents around the valley from Mar—ah—Miz Tucker. One of them is a trading post owner who got himself killed back a couple of weeks. From what I figure, it happened the same day I got away from that lynch mob. I know this might be just chasin' another whirlwind, but I'd like you to ride over that way and find out what you can."

The younger man nodded. "I can do that, Smoke. What was the man's name, and where do I find this trading post?"

"Ezekial Dillon. He ran his outpost at the far side of the valley, north and east of Socorro."

"I'll set off first thing in the morning."

When they returned to the barnyard, Jimmy Tucker met them with an enthusiastic welcome. "Mom says we got fried chicken, smashed taters an' gravy, an' cole slaw for supper. An' a pie. She also said that if it holds off hot like this after, Tommy an' me can go down to the crick for a swim. You want to come along?"

Grinning in recollection of his own sons' boyish exuberance, Smoke Jensen declined. Still close enough in age to be vulnerable to the call of such youthful enticements, Ty Hardy agreed to accompany the boys.

After a sumptuous spread of savory food, Smoke Jensen took his last cup of coffee out onto the porch and lit up a cigar. Pale, blue-white spirals rose from the glowing tip. The rich tobacco perfumed the air. Sniffing appreciatively, Martha Tucker joined him a short while later.

"My father smoked cigars. I always liked the aroma. I suppose that's one reason I married a cigar smoker," she informed Smoke in an unexpected burst of candor. "Have you been married long, Mr. Jensen?"

Smoke flushed slightly. "Many years," he answered. "How'd you reckon I was a married man?"

Martha did not need to think about her answer. "The way you are with the children; affectionate, but not overbearing. Also, I might add, the remarkable restraint you show in my presence." She blushed furiously.

Half-amused, and uncomfortably aware of her alluring presence, Smoke answered with some evasion. "Not long ago you believed I had murdered your husband. But, I'll thank you for considering a more noble motive. Yes, Sally has been my treasure for most of my grown life. We have a daughter of marrying age and three younger."

"You must miss them?"

"I do. This is a far piece from the High Lonesome," Smoke admitted.

"The High—? Oh, I understand," Martha went on quickly. "Your hands said your ranch was in the heart of the Rockies. It must be beautiful. So much variety, compared to the desert sameness everywhere one looks around here."

"You're right about that." Smoke took a long draw on the dark brown tobacco roll.

For all her determination, and her grief, Martha could not help herself, she realized. She found herself strongly attracted to the big, handsome, soft-spoken man from the mountains. He's as closedmouthed as he is strong, she mused, then put her thoughts to words.

"You're not very talkative, Mr. Jensen. Don't take that as a criticism. What I mean is, that you may not say a lot, but your words are filled with meaning. It takes a wise man to conduct himself like that."

"I'm flattered," Smoke said, finishing his coffee. He came to his boots. "I'll be headin' to the bunkhouse now. Ty's headin' out early in the morning, and I want a few words with him before he turns in. Provided, of course, your boys don't drown him down there at the creek."

Martha laughed with an ease that surprised her. "Good night, Mr. Jensen."

By nightfall, liquor had loosened plenty of tongues in the saloons of Socorro. Jeff York and Walt Reardon had each obtained several independent confirmations of the big fiesta to be held at the B-Bar-H. When they met in the *Comidas La Jolla* for a meal of *carne con chili verde,* they quickly discovered this.

"I'd say Smoke would be mighty interested," Walt opined after they had exchanged information.

"What I think he'd be most likely to want to know, is what's behind the festivities. I'm going to try to wangle you and me an invitation."

"You think you can do it?" Walt sounded doubtful.

"Should be easy. A rich, Arizona cattleman, interested in buying the seed bull I saw advertised at the feed mill. Inquiries to be addressed to Mr. Geoffrey Benton-Howell, of the B-Bar-H."

Walt Reardon gave him a blank look. "I'll be damned. I missed that one entire."

Jeff York gave him a friendly chuckle. "You've got to have a lawman's eye for small details, Walt. We'd best head for the Tucker place and fill in Smoke. Then I'll outfit myself in expensive clothes, do up a flash-roll of currency, and head for the office of Benton-Howell. Might be we'll find out what's behind all this without any effort at all."

Late the next afternoon, Geoffrey Benton-Howell effusively welcomed Steven J. York, of Flagstaff, Arizona, into his office. He ushered his visitor to a plush chair beside the huge cherrywood desk, and crossed to a sideboard where he poured brandy for two.

"This is the first personal inquiry I've received from such a distance," the Englishman informed Jeff in dulcet tones. "May I ask what excited you sufficiently about Herefordshire Grand Expositor to pay me this visit?"

Jeff York leaned back in the chair with a comfortable slouch, conveying his ease to an attentive Geoffrey Benton-Howell. "I know it's common practice, and I don't want you to take offense," he drawled. "But I've learned that in horse trading and cattle buying, it's best not to purchase sight unseen." He chuckled softly and sipped the brandy to soften the implication of distrust.

"A wise man, indeed," Benton-Howell responded as he clapped one big hand on a thigh. "Of course, before any transaction was completed, I would urge the buyer to make a personal inspection of Expositor. He's a fine Hereford bull, and I'm justifiably proud of him."

He studied his visitor, while the Arizona cattleman framed a response. Geoffrey saw a well-dressed man, turned out in dustless boots. A hand-tooled, concho-decorated cartridge belt, of Mexican origin no doubt, fitted snugly around a lean waist. A shaft of magenta sunlight put a soft glow to well-cared-for gun metal in the leather pocket. The suit had a flavor of Mexico in its cut, sort of the *haciendado* style favored by Miguel Selleres. The flat-crowned Cordovan sombrero clinched it for Benton-Howell. He bought the man as genuine.

"I've heard good things about crossing these new, short-horn, polled Herefords with range cattle. Improves the stock remarkably," Jeff spieled off from memory of conversations with the more progressive ranchers in Arizona Territory.

"More meat, more pounds, with less size. They're all the rage back East."

"Not many willin' to take the risk out here, I'll bet."

Benton-Howell nodded agreeably. "Not so far. Tunstil tried it, and some say that's what got him in the Lincoln County War. Some people are slow to accept any change. Take barbed wire."

Jeff made the expected nasty face at mention of the often lethal barriers. That encouraged Benton-Howell to risk planting yet another false lead to Smoke Jensen. "We had a fellow around here who loudly advocated the use of barbed wire. Said all the small Mexican farmers around Socorro needed it, to keep range cattle out of their fields. There's some say that's why a gunfighter named Smoke Jensen was hired to get rid of him."

"Smoke . . . Jensen? I've heard of him. Did this happen recently?"

"Only a couple of weeks ago. Rancher's name was Lawrence Tucker. He was thrown out of the Cattlemen's Association because of his stand on barbed wire." Benton-Howell chuckled lightly and took Jeff's glass for a refill. "Might be someone took the whole matter a bit more personally than others. For my own part, I say live and let live. God knows there's plenty of rocks around here. If the Mexicans want to protect their fields, let them busy themselves building stone walls. They've worked well enough in jolly old England, I dare say."

"Quite," Jeff responded, well aware of the irony of his sally. "Aah, thank you," he acknowledged the excellent brandy handed to him. "Now, when can I get to examine Expositor?"

"How long did you intend to stay in Socorro?" Benton-Howell inquired.

"Two or three days. As long as it took to see this championship animal of yours."

Benton-Howell thought for a long moment. "I'm having a rather gala soirée at the ranch two days hence. I would be honored, if you would attend. You can see Expositor, and I can introduce you to some gentlemen who might be of some benefit to you over in Arizona."

"Sounds good to me. I've always liked nice parties— enjoy good grub, good whiskey, and interesting company." Jeff was enjoying himself, playing the role to the hilt.

"You're staying at the hotel?" At Jeff's nod, Benton-Howell went on. "I'll have one of my hands meet you there tomorrow, escort you to the ranch."

"Much obliged, Mr. Benton-Howell. It's sure nice doin' business with a gentleman like yourself." Jeff finished off the brandy and rose to his boots to leave. "Oh, I have my foreman along with me. He's a better judge of prime cattle than I am. Would you mind, if I bring him along?"

"Oh, not at all. He'll be most welcome. Until tomorrow, then, Mr. York?"

"Hasta la vista."

Down on the street, as Jeff York strode away from the brick bank building, he congratulated himself on catching a mighty big fish. That, or he'd gotten himself into one damn dangerous situation.

Out at the Tucker ranch, Smoke Jensen made his own plans for the day of Benton-Howell's big fiesta. He wanted to be on hand to inspect the layout firsthand. To do so, he would have to make a scout of the place. And that night seemed ideally suited to his needs. He asked Martha Tucker for directions and rode out an hour before sundown.

While midnight beckoned with stygian darkness, Smoke Jensen crested a piñon-studded ridge and started down the back slope. Only the scant, frosty light of stars illuminated his surroundings. Well and good, Smoke thought to himself. If Benton-Howell had night riders posted, he had a better chance of eluding them this night. What he had in mind could all go up in a flash, if some nighthawk stumbled on him prematurely.

Might be he was overcautious, Smoke decided, as he descended the eastern grade that formed the bowl valley which housed the B-Bar-H. The thicket of trees grew denser the further he drifted toward the distant ranch house. He wanted to check out sites within long-rifle range of the area where the fiesta would be held, in the event he needed to make use of them.

Smoke had used this tactic with telling effect in earlier confrontations with some of the evil trash that infested the frontier. Not one to discard a useful strategy, he always considered employing it when presented the opportunity. Preacher had seen to it that a much younger Smoke Jensen had learned to be an effective fighter, even when entirely alone. Yet, he didn't like being out of contact with Jeff York. No idea what might develop there. He had to live with it, though.

The widespread nature of this sinister business made it necessary to go at it from more than one direction at a time. He recalled situations in the past when it would have been convenient to be able to divide himself in two or even three parts. A sudden flare of yellow light alerted Smoke that Benton-Howell had put out sentries.

Not very smart ones, at that. The flare of a match not only gave away the position of a guard, but destroyed his night vision long enough for him to lose his hair, if there were Indians about. One of the first lessons Preacher had taught him, Smoke thought grimly. Now he would have to find out how many there might be, and where.

Smoke combined his missions. He worked his way with great caution around the crescent face of the ridge through the long hours of early morning. A thin line of gray brightened the eastern horizon when he finished scouting the ranch. Another hour on foot took him away from the area far enough so that he could risk mounting and riding off toward the Tucker spread.

It would take some doing, but he could spoil Benton-

Howell's little party right easily. "And that's the way I like it," Smoke said aloud to himself.

"Viejo Dillon come to these mountains long time ago," the wrinkle-faced, Tuwa grandfather related to Ty Hardy, both men seated outside his summer brush lodge.

"I hear he was killed recently," Ty prodded.

A curt nod answered him. The old man looked off a moment, then spoke in his lilting manner. "It's supposed to look like a thief took things. But this one's eyes saw the men who came."

"Do you know them?" Ty hadn't thought of getting this much so fast.

"Oh, yes. Very bad men—*malos hombres.* The big one . . . their chief . . . this one has seen him before. He is called Stalker."

Ty's eyes widened, and he fought to keep his expression calm. "You are sure of this? Did you tell the law about it?"

The Tuwa shrugged. "Why do this? This Stalker and the *Jefe* Reno are like two beans in a pod, this one is thinking."

How many other unexposed secrets lay buried in this old gray head? And those of others like him. Ty had learned much about respect for Indians from Smoke Jensen. And, Ty considered, the old man sure had the sheriff down right.

"Thank you, Hears Wind. I will hold your words close to me."

"You tell the *Jefe* Reno?" Anxiety lighted the obsidian eyes.

"I don't think so. I work for another man. Smoke Jensen."

Hear Wind's expression changed to one of pleasure. "His name is known to our people. That one walks tall with honor. You are fortunate to be one of his warriors. Go with the sun at your back."

Ty Hardy left with the certain knowledge that he had learned something important, and also that he had been honored simply for being one of Smoke Jensen's hands. Powerful medicine, as the Injuns said.

Fourteen

Still done up as a wealthy rancher, Jeff York, along with Walt Reardon, arrived at the B-Bar-H mid-afternoon the next day. Not a lot of originality in that name, Jeff thought for the tenth time since discovering the notice of sale in the feed mill office. He was greeted by Geoffrey Benton-Howell in person; he had come out the day of their meeting to oversee final preparations.

"Glad you came," the Englishman remarked abruptly. "I'll introduce you to some of the other guests who journeyed out early. Then I'll show you Expositor."

"That's my main interest," Jeff replied.

On a wide, flagstone veranda, several portly men, dressed in the typical garb of Washington politicians, lounged in large wicker chairs. All had drinks in their hands, and it was obvious to Jeff York that these were not their first for the day.

Benton-Howell ushered Jeff and Walt from one to the next, making acquaintances. Uniformly, their handshakes were weak, soft, and insincere. Not a one of them has done a day's work in his life, thought the Arizona Ranger. A white-jacketed servant shoved a cut crystal glass of bourbon into Jeff's hand, and he took an obligatory pull.

After their first drinks had been drained, Walt acknowledged a signal from Jeff and excused himself. He wanted a good look around the ranch. Most of the next half-hour conversation centered around competing accounts of the importance of each man to the smooth functioning of the federal government. Jeff York endured it with less than complete patience. He felt genuine relief and expectation, when Benton-Howell announced that he intended to show off his prize stud bull.

"What do you think of them?" the corrupt rancher asked, once he and Jeff were out of earshot of the guests.

"They're not long on sparkling conversation," Jeff replied cautiously.

"Boors, the lot of them. Boobies, too," Benton-Howell snapped. "Although, quite necessary, if one is to operate unhindered in your territory or mine. Well, then, here we are," he concluded, directing Jeff into a small barn that contained a single stall.

Expositor had a slat-level back, his face, neck, and chest a creamy white mass of tight curly hair. The rest of him, except for the tip of his tail, was a dark red-brown with similar woolly appearance. The bull had one slab side turned toward them, and he regarded them over a front shoulder with a big, brown eye. Although a lawman, rather than a stockman, Jeff considered him to be a magnificent animal, and said so.

"I thought you'd be impressed. He's barely four years old, and he's already topped over three hundred heifers and cows."

Jeff chuckled. "Wonder he isn't worn down to a nubbin'."

Geoffrey Benton-Howell had been away from England, and on the frontier, long enough to understand. "Oh, there's nothing wrong with his equipment. Far from it. If I had a cow in season, I'd show you."

They talked of the animal's performances for a while, then Jeff moved in close to look at the confirmation of the huge beast. "He's certainly blocky," Jeff observed.

"That's how you get the weight-to-size ratio to work out," Benton-Howell advised. "The bloodline came originally from Herefordshire." Benton-Howell pronounced the county name *Hair-ford-sure.* "They've revolutionized livestock raising back East. Even a man with a small farm can pasture thirty or forty head. Not like out here, where one needs a thousand acres for fifty head."

For a moment, Jeff began to doubt Benton-Howell's involvement in the murder of Lawrence Tucker, or anything else not above board. The man's expert knowledge of animal husbandry, and his obvious rapt interest in it, argued that it must be his main concern. Yet, why the obvious allusions to bribing or otherwise obtaining a favorable connection with the slippery striped-trouser crowd? Jeff would have to wait and see if something important came out at the fiesta the next day.

"What time does this shindig start tomorrow?"

"When the heat breaks over. About four o'clock, I would imagine," Jeff's host responded genially. Then he changed the subject. "Are you ready to buy Expositor right now?"

"He's a handsome critter, I'll allow. A lot bigger than I'd expected from the breed. I'd like to think on it awhile."

Benton-Howell clapped a hard hand on Jeff's firm shoulder. "Sleep on it, if you want. Enjoy what the ranch has for diversions tomorrow, and then give me your answer at the fiesta."

* * *

A festive atmosphere prevailed over the ranch head-quarters the next morning from early on. Two huge, stone-lined pits had been stoked with wood long before dawn. With the contents reduced to glowing coals, half a steer turned slowly over each of them. Whole goats revolved on smaller spits on fires of their own. Ranch hands worked clumsily at unfamiliar tasks, erecting striped canvas awnings to provide shade and a pretense of coolness, setting up tables under them and laying out tableware and napkins. More guests began arriving shortly after an early breakfast. Jeff York took careful note of the occupants of each buggy, and consigned to memory the name and position of each visitor.

"And this is Senator Claypoole," Benton-Howell introduced yet another to York. "He's on the committee for Indian Affairs. Steven York from Arizona," he concluded.

Claypoole had a politician's, glad-hander shake, pale blue eyes dancing with merriment. "A pleasure, sir. Are you a cattle breeder, too?"

"No. I raise cattle for market."

"I see." The good senator cooled off, wondering why a common rancher had been invited. "Sparse vegetation over Arizona way, I'm told. How many hundred head can you feed?"

"Not hundreds," Jeff exaggerated wildly, "thousands. I run five thousand head this time of year. And I hold most of the mountain pasture from Flagstaff to Globe in the Tonto Range."

Claypoole warmed immediately. This was a big rancher. "I—ah—stand corrected. How do you manage such a vast area? Aren't the Indians a constant threat?"

Jeff gave him a warm smile. "Not really. If all the Indians killed in the dime novels had been for real, there wouldn't be an Apache left alive. I've found that the Eastern journalists tend to embellish the truth."

Another carriage, a mud-wagon stage coach hired for the occasion, rumbled in with more politicians. That ended the exchange between Jeff York and Senator Claypoole, much to Jeff's relief. Benton-Howell took him in tow and made him acquainted with the newcomers. From the corner of one eye, Jeff noted that Claypoole made directly for the heavily laden liquor table.

The heavy drinking began around ten-thirty. Jeff held onto a single tumbler of whiskey and took sparing sips from it. He began to wonder what Smoke Jensen had in mind for this gala party. Knowing the gunfighter as he did, Jeff could not see Smoke passing up such an opportunity.

Noontime came, and still no sign of the fine hand of Smoke Jensen. Many of the ranch hands drifted in during the next hour. They all had the look of second-rate gunhawks to Jeff. The rich aromas of cooking meat and pots of beans, field corn, and other delights filled the air. Jeff had emptied his glass and had turned back to the beverage table, when he found himself face-to-face with a man he knew only too well.

"What the hell you doin' here, Ranger?" Concho Jim Packard growled in a low, menacing voice.

"Excuse me? You've got me mixed up with someone else," Jeff tried hard to misdirect the desperado.

"Not a chance. No gawdamned Arizona Ranger kills

three of my best friends and I don't remember him."
Packard turned to search the crowd for his employer.
"Hey, Boss," he shouted over the buzz of conversation.
"You done brought a rattlesnake into your nest."

Geoffrey Benton-Howell came over at once. "What
are you talking about?"

"This one," Concho Jim snarled, pointing at Jeff.

"Why, Mr. York's my guest. He's come to buy Expositor," Benton-Howell spluttered.

"He has like hell! His name's York, right enough, but
it's Jeff York, Arizona Ranger," Concho Jim grated out.

Strong hands closed on Jeff York's arms before he
could react or try to make a break. Benton-Howell gave
him a disbelieving look, then cut his eyes to Concho Jim.
"You're sure of this?"

"Damn right I am. He got me locked up in the territorial
prison for six years, killed three of my partners, too."

Unseen, but witnessing it all, Walt Reardon made a
quick evaluation of the situation. Two guns against all
those present made for poor odds. Better that he get
away from here and find Smoke Jensen. He edged his
way out of the crowd and made for the livery barn and
his horse.

Frowning, Benton-Howell lowered his voice and addressed the gunhands holding Jeff. "Let's not make a
spectacle of this. Take him away quietly. Lock him in the
tool shed. We'll deal with our spy later, after our distin-
guished guests have eaten and drunk enough to forget
about it."

Careful to create the least disturbance possible, the
hard cases lifted Jeff York clear of the ground and carried
him to a shed out of the direct sight of the partying poli-

ticians. There they disarmed him and threw him inside. A drop bar slammed down, and Jeff heard the snick of a padlock.

By three o'clock that afternoon, most of the guests of Geoffrey Benton-Howell had forgotten the small disturbance in the side yard of the ranch house. Great mounds of barbecued beef and goat *(cabrito)* filled the serving tables, where a splendid buffet had been laid out. Laughing and talking familiarly, as colleagues do, they lined up to pile Benton-Howell's largess on their plates. Some tapped a toe to unfamiliar strains of music.

Mariachi musicians played their bass, tenor, and alto guitars, Jaliscan harp, and trumpets with gusto. Songs such as *La Golandrina, Jalisco, Cielo de Sonora,* and *El Niño Perdido,* won applause and praise from the visitors from Washington. Three white-aproned cooks toiled over the pots of beans, bowls of salsa, skillets of rice, platters of corn boiled in its shucks, and, of course, the savory meat, as they ladled and served the festive crowd. Beer, whiskey, and brandy had flowed freely since mid-morning. It kept everyone in a jolly mood.

Yes, his fiesta was going exceedingly well, Geoffrey Benton-Howell thought to himself as he gazed on this industrious activity. It continued to go well until a whole watermelon, taken from among half a dozen of its twins in a tub of icy deep well water, exploded with a wild crack, and showered everyone in the vicinity with sticky, red pulp.

* * *

Smoke Jensen shifted his point of aim and destroyed a line of liquor-filled decanters in a shower of crystal shards that cut and stung the now terrified guests. He levered another .45-70-500 round into the chamber, and blasted a round into a large terracotta bowl of beans, showering more of the politicians with scalding *frijoles*. That made it time to move on to the next position.

Two hours earlier Smoke had met with Walt Reardon. The ex-gunfighter had come upon Smoke with the news of Jeff York's unmasking and capture. Quickly he panted out his account of events. He concluded with, "They put him in a little shed out of the way of the party."

"With the right distraction, do you think you could get in there and get Jeff out?"

Walt grinned. He had a fair idea of what Smoke Jensen considered the "right distraction."

"Damn right."

"Then, let's ride."

They made it back unseen to the ridge overlooking the B-Bar-H headquarters. Walt ambled his mount down a covered route back to the party. He soon found he had not been missed. No one, in fact, paid him the least attention. He took up a position close to the tool shed and waited for Smoke to join the dance.

Smoke Jensen had a clear field of fire over the whole ranch yard. He used it to good advantage, firing four more rounds, then reloading the Express rifle on the move to another choice location. Two of Benton-Howell's hard cases had more of their wits about them than the others. They grabbed up rifles and began firing back.

Their spent rounds kicked up turf a good two hundred yards short of Smoke's last position. Smoke knelt and shouldered the .45-70-500 Express, and squeezed off another shot. The bullet made a meaty smack when it plowed into the chest of one rifleman. The dead man's Winchester went flying, as he catapulted backward and flopped and twitched on the ground. His cohort made a hasty retreat. Then Smoke went to work on the nearest buffet table.

A stack of china plates became a mound of shards as Smoke's rifle spoke again. A short, stout congressman from Maine yelped, and popped up from the far side of the table like a jack-in-the-box. He lost his expensive bowler hat to Smoke's next round. With a banshee wail, the portly politician ran blindly away from the killing ground.

He crashed headlong into a Territorial Federal judge. They rebounded off one another, and the little man wound up on his butt. "I say, Judge, someone is trying to kill us," he bleated.

"Congressman Ives, you are an ass," the judge thundered. "If whoever is out there wanted to kill us, we'd be dead. Like that outlaw thug who returned fire. Now, get ahold of yourself, man, before someone thinks you're a coward."

When another watermelon showered those nearby with wet shrapnel, Walt Reardon considered the confusion to be at maximum. Lips set in a thin, grim line, he made his move. He approached the shed from the rear. Rounding one side Walt placed himself behind a guard posted by Benton-Howell. With a swift, sure move, Walt drew his six-gun and screwed the muzzle into the sentry's right ear.

"I'll have the key to that lock, if you don't mind," Walt growled.

"What the hell—!"

"Do it now, or I'll put your brains all on one side of your head."

"You son of a bitch, you don't have a chance," the gunhawk displayed the last of his rapidly waning bravado.

"I'm talking the outside," Walt snarled, and gave his Colt a nudge.

It took less than a second for the thoroughly cowed hard case to fish a brass key from his vest pocket. His hand trembled, when he raised it above his shoulder. Walt Reardon snatched the key with his left hand.

"Thanks, buddy," he told his prisoner a moment before he clubbed him senseless with the barrel of the Peacemaker.

Walt bent to the lock on the door of the shed, as Smoke shifted his aim to the house. Smoke had already scattered the striped-pants politicians in utter panic. Some had fled to the carriages that had brought them, and driven off in reckless abandon. Others dived into corrals, Smoke noted with amusement, where fresh, still-warm cow pies awaited them.

Now the last mountain man listened to the satisfying tinkle of glass, as he shot out windows and trashed the interior of one room after another. A sudden gout of black soot from a chimney told Smoke a ricochet had hit a stove pipe. Half a dozen females—painted ladies provided by Benton-Howell to entertain the politicians—came shrieking out every door visible from Smoke's position.

While he kept up this long-range destruction, Smoke kept an eye on an unpainted shed, its boards faded gray by the intense New Mexico sun and desiccating effects of the desert. It was there, Walt Reardon had told him, that Geoffrey Benton-Howell had confined Jeff York. Smoke saw the guard stiffen, and a hand appear with a six-gun poked in the hapless fellow's ear. Good work, Smoke mentally complimented Walt. Now it's time to make a stir down there.

When Walt opened the door and Jeff came stumbling out into the light, Smoke shifted his aim once more. Two of the outlaw trash Benton-Howell hired walked rapidly toward Walt, each with a hand on a gun. The third mother of pearl button on one hard case centered on the top of the front post of Smoke's Express rifle. The weapon slammed reassuringly into his shoulder, and a cloud of powder smoke obscured the view. A stiff northwesterly breeze cleared it away in time for Smoke Jensen to see the impact.

Shirt fabric, blood, and tissue flew from the front of the gunhawk's chest in a crimson cloud. It slammed him off his boots, and he hit the ground first with the back of his head. No headache for him, Smoke thought. He shifted his sights to the second saddle tramp in time to see him jackknife over his cartridge belt and pitch headlong into hell. Smoke cut his eyes to where he had last seen Jeff and Walt.

A thread of blue-white smoke streamed from the muzzle of Walt's six-gun. He and Jeff advanced on their challengers, and Jeff stooped to retrieve both of their weapons. Smoke took advantage of the lull to shove more fat rounds in the loading gate of the Winchester Express. Time to move, he decided.

From his fourth location, Smoke had a clear view of the other side of the headquarters house. The windows quickly disappeared in a series of tinkling, sun ray-sparkling showers. Faintly, Smoke Jensen made out the rage-ragged bellow of Benton-Howell.

"Goddamn you, Smoke Jensen!"

At least he knew who had paid him a visit, Smoke allowed with a smile. From his final position, where he had left his roan stallion tied off to a ground anchor, Smoke Jensen gave covering fire, while Walt Reardon and Jeff York burned ground out of the B-Bar-H compound. Smoke chuckled as he mounted and set off obliquely to join them, well out of range and sight of the terrorized mass of milling men below.

"Smoke Jensen?" The name echoed through the raddled politicos after Geoffrey Benton-Howell's furious bellow.

Livid with outrage, their host stomped around the flagstone veranda of his house, looking bleakly at the broken windows, shredded curtains, the bullet holes in the interior walls. He cursed blackly and balled his fists in impotent wrath.

"Everything is under control, gentlemen. Don't let this act of a mad man interrupt our celebration today. Come, fill your plates, get something to drink. You there, strike up the music." Then Benton-Howell turned away and hid his bitter anger from the still-shaken politicians. "I know it was him," he shouted to the skies as though challenging the Almighty. "It was Smoke Jensen. Somehow . . . he's . . . found . . . out."

Most of those present had no idea of what he meant. Miguel Selleres, who had taken a slight nick in the left shoulder, knew only too well. He hastened to the side of his co-conspirator. "Softly, *amigo,* softly! It would not do to bring up such unpleasant matters in the presence of our guests. You have suffered enough loss today."

"How do you mean?" Benton-Howell demanded.

"When the shooting stopped, all but two of your working hands rolled their blankets and departed. They don't like being shot at."

Benton-Howell blanched. "Damn them! Cowards, the lot. Oh, well, they were only fit for nursing cows anyway."

"One does not run a ranch without someone to nurse the cows, *¿como no?*" Selleres softened his chiding tone to add, "I can lend you some men, until you can hire more. Or clear up this difficulty with Smoke Jensen."

"Thank you, my friend." Benton-Howell clapped Selleres on his uninjured shoulder. "Now, I want the—ah—other hands to assemble outside the bunkhouse. Tell those hired guns of Quint Stalker's to hunt down Smoke Jensen and *kill* him, or don't come back for their pay!"

Fifteen

Much to his discomfort, Forrest Gore had to deliver orders to the hard cases hired on to do Benton-Howell's dirty work. With the boss gone, leadership devolved on Payne Finney, who had sent him out to take over the boys in the field. Finney was making slow progress in his recovery from the pellet wounds given him by Smoke Jensen. If he could speak honestly, Finney would prefer to have nothing further to do with Smoke Jensen. Absolute candor would reveal that he feared the man terribly.

With good cause, too, Payne Finney told himself as he sat in the study of the B-Bar-H, covering ground already talked out with Geoffrey Benton-Howell. He had never seen a man so skillful that he could divide a shot column between two targets. Benton-Howell's next words jolted him.

"I don't care if you have to use a buggy. I want you out there looking for Smoke Jensen." Half of the influential men he had gathered at the ranch had failed to return after the shooting ended. It put a damper on the conviviality of those who remained. He hadn't even been able to broach the subject of cutting away a portion of the White Mountain Apache reservation.

"I take my orders from Quint, the same as all the

others," Payne began to protest. "I'm still weak from being shot. I doubt the men would do what I told them."

Benton-Howell's fist hit the tabletop like a rifle shot. "They had damned well better! Stalker isn't here now. You give the orders; I'll see they are obeyed."

Payne Finney winced at the pain that shot from the knitting holes in his lower belly as he came to his boots. He accepted the finality of it with bitterness. "I'll do my best."

Half an hour later, Payne Finney rode out of the B-Bar-H on the seat of a buckboard. His face burned with the humiliation of being reduced to such a means of transportation, and for being talked down to like some lackey on the mighty lord's tenant farm. His saddle rested in the back, along with supplies he carried for the men searching for Smoke Jensen. His favorite horse trailed behind, reins tied to the tailgate. With effort, he banished his resentment and thought of other things.

If Finney had his way, Smoke Jensen would be run to ground in no more than two days. After all, the man was flesh and blood, not a ghost. He had to eat and sleep and eliminate like any other man. And Payne Finney had brought along the means of ensuring that Smoke Jensen would be found.

Seated right behind him, tongue lolling, was a big, dark brindle bloodhound. All they would have to do is find a single place Smoke Jensen had made camp, and put the beast on his trail. That's why Finney gave the ambitious estimate of two days. He raised himself slightly off the seat, and his right hand caressed the grip of his .44 Smith and Wesson American.

"Goodbye, Smoke Jensen, your butt is mine," he said

aloud to the twitching ears of the horses drawing the wagon.

Forrest Gore had his own ideas about finding Smoke Jensen. "It's goddamned impossible," he declared to the five men gathered around a small pond in the Cibola Range.

"Smoke Jensen camped here last night. We all know that," Gore lectured to his men. "Then he rode out to the west early this morning."

He was wrong, but he didn't know it yet. Ty Hardy had spent the night there, and ridden back to the Tucker Ranch shortly before first light. Two of the hard cases, suspecting that they chased the wrong will-o'-the-wisp, muttered behind gloved hands. A minute later, Smoke Jensen proved them right.

With startling effect, a bullet cracked over their heads and sent down a shower of leaves. Forrest Gore jumped upright and hugged the bole of a tree, putting its bulk between him and the direction from which the slug came. Then the sound of the shot rippled over the mountain slopes.

"We been set up," another gunhawk announced unnecessarily. "That's Smoke Jensen out there, and he's got us cold."

"I'm gettin' out of here," the fourth man announced.

"No! Wait," Forrest Gore urged. "Keep a sharp eye. When he fires again, we can spot where he is, split up, and close in on him."

Vern Draper snorted in derision. "By the time we get there, he'll be gone."

"Yeah, an' firin' at us from some other place," Pearly Cousins added.

Forrest Gore gave their words careful consideration. They had been hunting Smoke Jensen for the better part of two weeks now. With always the same results. The bastard was never seen, and they got shot at. Maybe it wasn't Smoke Jensen at all? With a troubled frown, Gore worked his idea over out loud.

"What if that's not Jensen at all? What if it's one of those hands of his, who broke up the lynch mob? It ain't possible that he was down in San Antonio and leadin' you fellers around by the nose up here in the Cibolas at the same time."

"I don't think it was him down there," Cousins opined.

"Who else could do in four of our guys, and send Charlie Bascomb runnin' with his tail 'twixt his legs?" Gore challenged. "I say we're lookin' in the wrong place. I say we leave whoever it is up here to hisself, and head south."

"You better clear that with Quint," Vern Draper suggested pointedly.

"Quint's busy elsewhere. Payne sent me out here to help you find Smoke Jensen. I think he's clean out of the area. So, we go where he is."

Another round from the Express rifle of Smoke Jensen convinced the others to follow the rather indistinct orders of Forrest Gore.

Later that day, Smoke Jensen met with Jeff York and the hands from the Sugarloaf. They sat around a table in the bunkhouse at the Tucker ranch, cleaning their weapons and drinking coffee. Smoke made an announcement that caught their immediate attention.

"Looks like the searchers are being pulled out of the mountains. I think it's time to pay another visit to the B-Bar-H."

Jeff produced a broad grin. "I sorta hoped you'd do that. I want to pay my respects to Sir Mucky-muck."

They rode out half an hour later. Ty and Walt went deeper into the Cibolas, to track and harass the hard cases with Gore. Also to determine where they might be headed. Smoke and Jeff covered ground at a steady pace.

An hour before nightfall, they reached the tall, stone columns with the proud sign above that declared this to be the B-Bar-H. Smoke studied the fancy letters a moment. Then he cut his eyes to Jeff.

"I think this is a good place to start," Smoke declared.

He loosed a rope from his saddle, and Jeff did the same. It took them only a minute to climb the stone pillars and affix their lariats to the edges of the sign. Back in the saddle, they made solid dallies around the horns, and walked away from the gateway. When the ropes went taut, the metal frame began to creak and groan. Smoke Jensen touched blunt spurs to the flanks of his roan stallion, and the animal set its haunches and strained forward.

Jeff York did the same, with immediate results. A loud crash signaled the fall of the wrought-iron letters. Badly bent and twisted, the B-Bar-H banner lay in a cloud of dust, blocking the entrance road. Smoke and Jeff retrieved their lassos and chuckled at their mischief, as they cantered off over the lush pasture grass. The rest of Smoke Jensen's plans contained nothing so lighthearted.

* * *

Geoffrey Benton-Howell had learned one thing from the attack on his headquarters. Smoke Jensen located the first night guard while a magenta band still lay on the mountains to the west. He signaled Jeff to ride on to their chosen spot, and put a gloved index finger to one eye to sign to keep a lookout for more sentries. Then he walked his roan right up to the guard.

"Who are you?" the surly hard case asked, a moment before Smoke Jensen drew with blinding speed and smacked the hapless man in the side of his head.

Well, perhaps they weren't all that much smarter than those he had encountered before. At least this one recognized a stranger when he saw one. Smoke dragged the unconscious outlaw from the saddle and trussed him up. He pulled the man's boots off and stuffed a smelly sock in a sagging mouth. Then, with the empty boots fastened in the stirrups, he smacked the rump of the gunhawk's mount and sent it off away from the house.

A short distance further, he found another one, similarly done up by Jeff York. Smoke smiled grimly and rode on. A roving patrol of two came into sight next. Smoke Jensen eased himself out of the saddle and slid through the tall grass. When the horsemen drew nearer, Smoke rose to the side of one silent as a wraith. Sudden movement showed him Jeff York likewise engaged.

One startled yelp came from an unhorsed hard case before Jeff had him on the ground and thoroughly throttled. Smoke's man made not a sound. Smoke came to his boots after tying the sentry, and waggled a finger at Jeff.

"Sloppy. He made a noise."

"Sorry, teacher," Jeff jibed back. "I'll do better next time."

"Might not be a next time before we're in position. I'd like to put them all down, before we start shooting."

"That'll take some time," Jeff observed.

"That's why we came early."

Smoke drifted off to recover his horse. Jeff York swore to himself that he had not even seen his friend start away. For a moment he had a flash of pity for the men they would encounter this night. Then he said softly to himself, "Nawh."

A quarter hour went by before Smoke found another night guard. The man sat with his back to a tree, eyes fixed on the higher ground away from the ranch house. Somewhat brighter than the others, Smoke reasoned. He had no reason to suspect someone coming from behind him. Too bad.

Easing up to the tree, Smoke bent around its rough bark and popped the unaware sentry on the head with a revolver barrel. It took only seconds to secure tight bonds. Then Smoke Jensen slipped on through the night. There would be a moon tonight. Smoke had taken that into consideration.

He and Jeff would fire and move, fire and move, until each had exhausted a full magazine load. Then time to leave, before the silver light of the late-rising half-moon made them too easy to see. All in all, he anticipated making life even more miserable for Geoffrey Benton-Howell.

* * *

Windows had been reglazed in most of the downstairs portion of the two-story frame house. Yellow lamplight spilled from one, as Smoke Jensen eased into a prone firing position on the slope above. He sighted in carefully, with the bright blue-white line of the burning wick resting on the top of his front sight. Slowly he drew a deep breath, let out half, and squeezed the trigger.

With a strong jolt, the steel butt-plate shoved his shoulder as the Winchester Express went off. While Smoke came to his boots, he listened for the tinkle of glass. It came seconds later, followed at once by sudden darkness within the house as the lamp exploded into fragments. An outraged voice wailed after it.

"Goddamnit! Jensen's back," Geoffrey Benton-Howell raged in the darkness.

While Smoke moved to his second location, Jeff let off a round from the opposite side of the house. Yells of consternation came from the bunkhouse, as the thin wall gave little resistance to a .44-40 slug. Grinning in the starlit night, Smoke dropped into a kneeling stance.

"Get in here, somebody! Damnit, this place is on fire," came a yelp from a now frightened Benton-Howell.

"Tien paciencia, amigo," Miguel Selleres called out.

"Have patience, hell! I'll burn up in here."

An eerie new light glowed in the ruined window. It flickered and grew in intensity as Smoke Jensen sighted in once more, this time on the door across the room. He put a round about chest-high through the oak partition. A muffled scream came from the hall beyond. It served to notify Benton-Howell that he had a fat chance of getting out that way.

Smoke Jensen was already at a steady lope through

the trees, when the remaining glass in the sash tinkled and Geoffrey Benton-Howell dived through to escape the flames. Smoke stopped abruptly and fired a round into the pool of darkness directly below the window. A howl that blended into a string of curses told him he had come close, but not close enough. Jeff York shot twice this time, and dumped a man in the doorway of the bunkhouse with a bullet in one leg.

"Don't get overconfident, Jeff," Smoke whispered to himself.

From the position he had selected earlier, Smoke put a .45-70-500 round through a second floor window. At once, he heard the alarmed bellow of a man, nearly drowned out by the terrified shriek of a woman. His shoulder had begun to tingle. He knew from experience that it didn't take too many cartridges run through the big Winchester, to change that sensation to one of numbness. Three rounds left in the magazine tube.

Smoke wanted to make them count, so he swiftly changed positions. On an off chance, he put the next bullet through the outhouse at about what he estimated would be an inch or two above head high on an average man. He was rewarded with a howl of sheer terror as a man burst out the front of the chicksale, his trousers at half-mast. Legs churning, the Levis tripped the hard case and sent him sprawling. Two cartridges to go, then Smoke would meet Jeff where they had left their horses.

Unexpectedly a target presented itself in Smoke's field of fire. A huge man, barrel-chested, thick-shouldered, arms like most men's thighs, hands like hams, barreled around the corner of the house and snapped a Winchester to his shoulder. He fired blindly, the slug nowhere near

Smoke Jensen or Jeff York. Cursing, he worked the lever rapidly and expended all eleven .44-40 rounds.

Sprayed across the hillside, the next to the last found meat in horseflesh. Jeff York's mount squealed in pain and fright, reared, and fell over dead on its side. Anger clouded Smoke Jensen's face.

"Damn, I hate a man who'd needlessly kill a horse," Smoke grunted.

He took aim and, as the last bullet sped from the Winchester in the giant's hand, discharged a 500 grain slug that pinwheeled the shooter and burst his heart. Only twenty yards from his horse, Smoke put out another light in a downstairs window and hurried to the nervous roan.

Jeff York joined him a moment later, and began to strip the saddle off his dead mount. Smoke had the bridle and reins in one hand. "We'll double up," he informed Jeff.

"Make it easier to track and catch us," Jeff complained. "I'll walk out."

"No. I brought you here; I'll get you back. They aren't going anywhere for a while."

Jeff looked back toward the house. A bucket brigade had formed to douse the flames that roared from two rooms of the ranch house. With a whinny, a horse-drawn, two-wheel hand-pumper rolled up from a small carriage house next to the barn. A pair of hard cases ran with a canvas hose to the creek bank, and plunged the screened end into the water. At once four volunteers began to swing the walking arms up and down. An unsteady stream spurted from the nozzle.

"No, I guess you're right," he told Smoke.

Even so, Smoke Jensen wasted no time, nor spared

any caution in departing from the B-Bar-H. He left behind a cursing, shrieking, livid Geoffrey Benton-Howell.

After the large number of recent disasters, Benton-Howell had been forced to send for reinforcements. The nine men who had been patrolling the slope behind the house on the previous night had quit first thing after being found the next morning. Smoke Jensen had nearly succeeded in burning down his house. His study was a ruin. All meals were being prepared in the bunkhouse; the kitchen had burned out completely. Now he confronted one of the men he considered responsible for his current calamity.

Sheriff Jake Reno stood across the cherry wood desk in Benton-Howell's office above the bank. With him was the mayor of Socorro. Both wore sheepish expressions. Benton-Howell had poured copious amounts of his deep-seated vitriol over them. Only now had he begun to wind down.

"I didn't spend the money to get you two elected to hear a constant stream of reports of failure. I expected competence. I expected success. Now, I'm going to get it. I want your full cooperation. No complaints, no excuses, no lectures on why it can't be done. I'm putting out the word for every available gunhand in the Southwest, to come here to put an end to Smoke Jensen."

"I thought you wanted it all done legally," the sheriff protested.

"I wanted results!" Benton-Howell snapped.

Mayor Ruggles looked stricken. "You'll fill the streets of Socorro with saddle tramps and every two-bit gunslick around," he whined. "Think of the good people of the community."

"I am thinking of the good people—Miguel Selleres and myself."

"Why don't you simply offer a larger reward?" Jake Reno suggested.

Too tightfisted to raise the ante on Smoke Jensen's head, Geoffrey Benton-Howell spluttered a minute, then focused his disarrayed thoughts on a new proposition. "Without gunmen to collect it, that would only tie up more of my money. What's going to happen, is that the city is going to add a thousand dollars to the reward."

"What?" the mayor and sheriff echoed together.

"If you think it such a good idea for me to put out more funds for the purpose, then surely it behooves you to do it." To Mayor Ruggles he added, with a roguish wink, "Sort of putting your money where your mouth is, eh, old boy?"

In that quick, pointed thrust, Mayor Ruggles lost his head of steam. "If that's what you want, we'll see about it right away. Only let me appeal to you to keep the gun trash out of town."

"It's your posterior they'll be saving, as well as mine. You and Sheriff Eagle Eye here. Now, get out of here and run your errands like good little lads. I want fifty—no a *hundred* guns in here, and Smoke Jensen stretched over his saddle shortly thereafter."

Sixteen

Socorro became a busy place as the word went out for fast guns. Mayor Ruggles stewed and dithered, his anxious eyes scanning the rough-edged characters who swarmed the streets. The new posters came out with the wording: "$2000 Reward Offered for Capture Dead or Alive of the Killer of Lawrence Tucker." No mention was made of Smoke Jensen. It sounded good that way, all agreed.

Some of the gunfighters and wannabes who came to Socorro to search for the "killer," left suddenly when they learned the identity of the accused. Sheriff Jake Reno noted with some smugness that eleven no-reputation young pretenders departed in a group shortly after the mention of the name Smoke Jensen.

"Perhaps they decided that it was safer to travel in numbers," he confided to Morton Plummer at the Hang Dog shortly after they blew out of town.

"Considerin' who it is they were expected to run to ground, I'd say they're right smart fellers," Mort responded with a grin. He loved to tweak this pompous ass of a sheriff.

Reno scowled. "Watch that lip, Mort." He quickly downed his shot and beer and stormed out of the saloon.

Being on the payroll of Benton-Howell and Selleres had other drawbacks, Sheriff Jake Reno considered as he directed his boots toward the jail. Those politicos who remained behind had been frightened almost witless by that second visit from Smoke Jensen. Only an hour ago, Benton-Howell had summoned him to the office to demand that he put men on the ranch to keep the politicians there, until an agreement could be reached on his White Mountain project.

"Like he'd bought all my deputies, too," Reno complained aloud, as he hurried to round up men to guard the B-Bar-H.

He returned to the world around him in time to meet the cold, hard stare of one of a pair of gaunt- and narrow-faced men with the look of gunfighters about them. Their square chins jutted high in arrogance, and the mean curl of their lips had to come from hours of practice before a mirror. The one with black leather gloves folded over his cartridge belt spoke, revealing yellowed, crooked teeth.

"Sheriff. Just the man we wanted to see. How are we supposed to find this feller done killed your Mr. Tucker, if we don't know his name? Who is he, or do you know?"

"Oh, I know all right. The name is Smoke Jensen."

"Not *the* Smoke Jensen?" the sneering one blurted as his face grew pale.

"The only Smoke Jensen I know," Sheriff Reno replied, as he laughed inwardly at the discomfort his words sparked.

The sneer gone from his face, the gunhawk cut his eyes to his partner. They appeared to reach wordless agreement that concluded with a nod. "Do you happen to have any idea where he might be found?" The question seemed to lack conviction of being acted upon.

"Yep. He's hangin' out in the Cibolas, last I heard."

"Why ain't you got a posse out?" the taller of the two challenged.

"I already lost a dozen good men to that bastard. I don't reckon to reduce the whole population of Socorro to bring him outta there." It was a lie. Smoke Jensen had killed only three of the posse, wounded six or seven more. Also some twenty had quit all together. What Sheriff Reno wouldn't admit was that he couldn't get anyone to go after Smoke Jensen. Not even Quint Stalker's men.

"Bein' we're from Texas, which way is these Cibolas?"

Suspecting what would come next, Sheriff Reno waved his arm expansively. "All around here. To the east, north, and mostly to the west. That's where Smoke Jensen can be found, west of here, I'm certain of it."

"Thank you kindly, Sheriff," the tall one replied.

Together they crossed the boardwalk and mounted their horses, while Sheriff Reno watched in silence. They touched reins to necks and pointed the animals south. Face alight with quivering amusement, Sheriff Reno pointed out their error.

"West's that way, fellers."

"We know it," the second-string hard case with the black gloves replied in a low, gruff voice.

They barely cleared the business district of Socorro, down in its canyonlike draw, before they fogged out of town in a lather. Behind them, Sheriff Jake Reno bent double with a torrent of laughter that rose from deep within. He kept on until the tears ran, then laughed even more . . . until he counted score and realized that that made a record of twenty-two for one day, and left him with that many less to stand between him and Smoke Jensen.

Senator Claypoole examined the certificate authorizing him to draw on the Philadelphia mint for the sum of twenty thousand dollars in gold bullion. Carefully he folded it and placed it reverently in an inside coat pocket. He gave a beatific smile to Geoffrey Benton-Howell, and patted over the spot where he had deposited the draft.

"You are a gentleman and a scholar, Sir Geoffrey. Likewise a man of his word. Nice, anonymous gold has always appealed to me. It can be used anywhere."

Benton-Howell pushed back his castored desk chair and lit a fat cigar. The rich aroma of a Havana Corona-Corona filled the study at the B-Bar-H. "I dare say, if you fail to use your usual, impeccable, diplomatic skill in this, you might have need of somewhere else to spend that."

"I know. My colleagues and I shall invent some sort of reason why that land has to be separated from the reservation. Heaven forbid that we ever mention gold being found there. Too many others would want a piece of the pie, and spoil your project all together."

"You understand only too well, Chester. Now, then, I suggest a small tot of brandy to seal the bargain, and then I have others to see."

"Certainly."

Ten minutes later, Chester Claypoole had departed, and the leather chair opposite Benton-Howell had been occupied by His Honor, Judge Henry Thackery of the Federal District Court for the Territory of Arizona. His Honor didn't seem the least bit pleased. A heavy scowl furrowed his high, shiny forehead.

"You've handled this Smoke Jensen affair miserably, Geoff," he snapped, accustomed to being the ranking person in any gathering.

"I will admit to having erred slightly in regard to the security of my ranch headquarters," Benton-Howell answered with some asperity.

"It's a great deal more than that, Geoff. If it ever comes out that your man, Quint Stalker, arranged the scene of the crime to indicate the guilt of Smoke Jensen, you may find yourself seeking the life of a grandee down in Mexico, or even South America. Or worse still, standing on the gallows in Santa Fe. I certainly do not intend to be there beside you."

Benton-Howell fought to recover some of his sense of well-being. "And you shall not be, my friend. Judge, everything is arranged as you asked. Seven thousand, five hundred in gold coin, mostly fifties and twenties. It is right there in my safe. A like amount to be paid, whenever you are called upon to hear any challenge to our claim of the White Mountain reservation land."

Judge Thackery pondered a moment, pushed thin lips in and out to aid his musing. "That's satisfactory. However, Geoff, I must caution you. Smoke Jensen has to be dealt with swiftly and finally . . . or the consequences will fall on you."

Jeff York and Walt Reardon rode into Socorro with Smoke Jensen. They had come for supplies for the Tucker ranch. Martha's idea of hiding in plain sight seemed to have worked so far. Recently, Smoke began chafing at the inactivity, and expressed a willingness to test how anonymous he had become. Walt halted the buckboard at the rear loading dock of the general mercantile, and dismounted.

"Jeff and I are going to amble over and visit with Mort Plummer at the Hang Dog, while the order is filled."

"Fine with me. I'll meet you there when it's loaded," Smoke replied.

"We'll be waitin', Kirby," Jeff drawled, a light of mischief in his eyes.

Being a purloined letter did not include speaking Smoke's name in public. Jeff had wormed Smoke's given name out of him for just such events as this. From the pained expression on the face of the gunfighter, Jeff gathered that Kirby was not Smoke's favorite handle. Walt untied his saddle horse from the tailgate of the wagon, and stepped into a stirrup. Together, he and Jeff rode to the mouth of the alley and turned left on the main street.

Business was sparse in the saloon at this early hour. Only a handful of barflies lined the mahogany, shaky hands grasping the first eye-opener of the day. Walt and Jeff ordered beers and settled at a table near the banked and cold potbelly stove. Walt started a hand of patience.

"You ever play two-handed pitch?" he asked Jeff.

"Yeah. About as exciting as watching grass grow."

"Now, I don't know about that," Walt defended the game. "If it's four-point, a feller's got a whole lot of guessin' to do to figure out what his opponent is holdin'."

"For me, I like to have all the cards out. Seven players s my sort of game."

"What about that fancy game all the hoity-toity Eastern dudes play—whist?"

"Not for me," Jeff declined. "I'm a five-card-stud man myself."

Walt chuckled. "Now yer talkin'. I ain't had a good hand of poker for nigh onto six months. Nobody on the Sugarloaf will play with me anymore."

"You win too much?"

"You got it, Jeff. And honest, too. No dealing seconds or off the bottom, either. Never stacked a deck in my life."

Two young wranglers stomped into the saloon. They turned to the bar at once, and did not take notice of the pair in conversation at the table. Jeff York had a good look at them, though. He grew visibly tense and sat quite still.

When they had sipped off their first shots and chased them with beer, the tall, lanky blond turned from the bar and peered into the shadowed corner that contained Jeff York and Walt Reardon. His face took on an expression of extreme distaste.

"I'll be goll-damned, Sully. It's that no-account Ranger from back home."

"You're seein' things, Rip. We's in New Mexico now."

"Nawh, I'm right. Turn around an' see for yourself. I know an asshole, when I see one."

Walt Reardon cut his eyes to Jeff York's muscle-tightened face. Jeff knows this pair, that's a fact, he reasoned. This could get deadly in about a split second. He scooted back his chair, came to his boots, and started for the rear.

"Got to hit the outhouse," he announced to Jeff, but cut his eyes toward the location of the general store. Jeff nodded.

"Hey, Rip, you're right," Sully declared as he turned to look Jeff's way. "It's the same lawdog that locked us away in Yuma prison for three years. Like to have kilt me, heavin' all them big rocks onto the levee. Bit far from your stompin' grounds, ain'tcha, Ranger?"

"You're making a mistake, Sullivan," Jeff grated out.

"Nope. Way I sees it, it's you've made a big mistake. They's two of us . . . and this time our backs ain't turned."

Jeff rose slowly, shook his head in sad recollection. "Never could abide a liar, Sully. You two were facing me that day in Tombstone. Didn't either one of you clear leather before I had you cold. I did it then, I can do it now."

"You've got older now, slower, Sergeant York."

"No. It's Captain now, and I'm not getting older . . . only better."

Two more second-rate fast guns stepped through the batwings and took in the action. "Sully, Rip, you got some fun lined up?" the chubby one asked.

"That we have, Pete. Just funnin' with an old acquaintance from Arizona. Ain't that right, Ranger York?"

"Can we get a piece of him, too, Sully?" the skinny teen next to Pete asked eagerly.

"Sorry, Lenny. When I get through, I don't reckon there'll be enough left to go around," Sully refused the offer, a sneer aimed at Jeff York.

"You're forgetting the Ranger here has a friend along," Mort Plummer said from behind the bar. He hoped to delay the inevitable. To at least get the killing started out in the street, not in his bar.

"He run out at the git-go. Plumb yellow," Sully brayed.

"I don't think so," the bar owner countered. "I sort of recognize him from a while back. Never asked him personal, understand? But I figger him to be Walt Reardon, the gunfighter from Montana."

"No wonder he ran. I hear he lost his belly a long while ago."

"Not so's you'd notice," Walt Reardon announced, as he pushed his way between Pete and Lenny. He was followed a second later by Smoke Jensen.

"I'm gonna go get the rest," Lenny declared, as he moved his boots quickly through the door.

Mort Plummer chose that moment to avoid damage to his property. "Get out. The bar's closed."

Sully turned back to him. "I don't think so. Pour me another shot, and set up the boys, too, when they come."

"Get out of my saloon."

"You pushin' for a bullet all your own, barkeep?"

Mort Plummer tried to stare Sully down, but it was Smoke Jensen who answered. "You've got a nasty mouth. Too bad you don't have a brain to go with it."

Two of the town drunks, who blearily recognized Smoke Jensen from the day of the lynch mob, beat a hasty retreat. One literally dived through the space below the spring-hinged batwings. He collided with the legs of five proddy outlaw trash. Lenny led the way as they entered. Mort Plummer had gone white with fear. The hard case quintet spread out and faced off against three coldly professional guns. Eight to three. Pretty good odds, the way Sully figured it.

"You boys have no part of this," Jeff told the new-comers. "Walk out now, and no harm will come of it."

Sully's eyes never left Jeff. "You boys have a drink on me, then I'll open this dance."

"No. I will," Smoke Jensen contradicted. Smoke's .44 leaped into his hand, leveled at Sully's belt buckle, before the wannabe gunhawk's hand could even reach his. Smoke forced a sneer to his lips. "You're too easy."

The humiliation of having been tossed back, like an undersized fish, pushed Sully to unwise desperation. He foolishly completed his draw.

"Goddamn ya, I'll kill ya all."

Smoke Jensen didn't even bother with him. Jeff York had iron in motion, and completed the life of the petty outlaw with a round to the heart. Sullivan never even fired a shot. Three of the gang of outlaws-turned-bounty hunter had their own six-guns in play. Smoke shot one of them in the upper right chest, and put another down with a .44 slug in the thigh.

When that one went down, three of the remaining shooters pounded boots on the floor in an effort to widen the space between them all. Walt Reardon tracked one, and took him off his boots with a bullet in the side. Jeff accounted for another. But the third had disappeared. Sudden motion behind Smoke Jensen's back ripped a warning from Mort Plummer, who had ducked below the thick front of his bar and had seen the reflection in the mirror.

"Look out, Smoke!"

"Smoke Jensen!" Pete and Rip yelled at the same time.

"Oh, my God! I give up," Lenny wailed. "Don't shoot me, Mr. Jensen, please. Ranger," he appealed to Jeff, "I give up." He raised his arms skyward, the Smith American dangling from one finger by the trigger guard.

"Yeller belly," Rip growled at Lenny as he swung his six-gun on Smoke Jensen. "Kiss your butt good—"

Smoke Jensen drove the last word back down Rip's throat with a sizzling .44 slug. Mort Plummer moaned in anguish. Glass exploded outward in a musical shower from one of the paint-decorated front windows, as two of the remaining hard cases dived through it to escape certain death.

Pete found himself alone, facing the guns of Smoke Jensen, Jeff York, and Walt Reardon. Pete's momma had always considered him a bright little boy. He proved her right when his Colt thudded in the sawdust that covered the plank floor. He raised trembling hands above his head.

"All righty, I call it quits. After all, Sully said we was only funnin' with y'all."

Smoke cut his eyes to Jeff. "Do you want him, or shall I?"

"My pleasure," Jeff York announced as he reholstered his .45 Colt.

He took a pair of thin, pigskin leather gloves from his hip pocket and slid them on his hands, his eyes never off of Pete for a second. Slowly he advanced on the frightened two-bit gunhawk.

"Eight to three. Is that the way you boys usually play it? Now it's just one-on-one," Jeff taunted. "You got a choice. You can pick up that gun on the floor and try me . . . or you can use your fists."

"I ain't got no quarrel with you, Ranger. Ain't no fight in me," Pete pleaded.

"No backbone, either," Jeff retorted. "Do something, even if it's wrong. I'm getting tired of waiting."

Pete's eyes widened suddenly, then swiftly narrowed. He lunged at Jeff with a knife that seemed to spring from behind his back. Jeff popped Pete solidly in the mouth. Lips mashed and split, blood sprayed from Pete's face in a rosy halo.

Jeff sidestepped the blade and grabbed the wrist and upper arm of the knife hand. He brought it down, as he quickly raised a knee. The elbow broke with an audible pop. Pete went down, to howl his agony in a fetal position in the spit-and-beer-stained sawdust. Jeff silenced him with a solid kick to the head.

"Sneaky bastard, wasn't he?" Jeff rhetorically asked the silent room.

"The supplies are loaded," Smoke Jensen said dryly.

"Then I suppose we're through in town," Jeff said in an equal tone.

"You weren't never here, Mr. Jensen," Mort Plummer swore from behind his bar. "Wouldn't do to confuse our good sheriff as to who shot up my place."

"Take whatever you can find in their jeans to cover your loss," Smoke suggested.

"Right. And I've never seen you in my borned days. Good luck."

"We'll need that," Smoke advised him. "Used up a bit here today."

Seventeen

He didn't like going to Arizona to take charge of the turnover of the White Mountain land. He felt even worse when the lacquered carriage he rode in jolted to an unexpected halt.

"Woah up, Mabel, woah, Henry, hold in," the driver crooned to his team. "What the hell do we have here?" he asked next.

"Yes," Miguel Selleres called from the interior of the coach. "What do we have? Why did you stop out here in the middle of nowhere?"

"It's—it's . . . I think it's Quint Stalker and some of his boys."

"They are supposed to be in Arizona," Selleres shot back.

"Well, we're here," came the familiar voice of Quint Stalker, noticeably weakened.

Selleres poked a head out of the curtained window. Four men, without horses, all wounded, all dirty and powder-grimed, stood at the side of the road. Astonishment painted Selleres's face. He had never seen the proud, gamecock Stalker so bedraggled. "How did this happen?" Selleres demanded. "Why are you not in Arizona?"

"We were headed there," Stalker related glumly.

"Those damned Apaches waited around and hit us a second time. Killed all but us four. And we're all wearin' fresh wounds."

"You have had a hard time. There are some *tanques* not far ahead. Climb on the top and we'll ride there. After you've cleaned up, you can ride inside with me," Selleres told them grandly.

"Well, thanks so damned much, *Señor* Selleres," the aching Quint Stalker replied sarcastically. "Only we ain't gonna go back out there. No way, no how."

"Oh, I disagree, *Señor* Stalker."

His patience tried beyond any semblance of his usual cool nature, Miguel Selleres reached under his coat and drew out a Mendoza copy of the .45 Colt Peacemaker. Slowly he racked back the hammer, as he leveled the weapon on the tip of Quint Stalker's nose. "You will go back to that Apache reservation with me, or I will shoot you down for the cowardly dog you are."

Nervously, Quint cut his eyes to his three remaining men. Slowly he shrugged and outstretched both hands, palms up. "Who can argue with such logic?"

Martha Tucker looked at the mound of supplies being carted into the kitchen and the bunkhouse with eyes that shined. The ranch had run dangerously low of nearly everything in the three weeks since her husband's murder. She clapped her hands in delight, and made much of the small, tin cylinder cans of cinnamon, ground cloves, allspice, and black pepper.

"Now I can bake pies again! What would you like?" That she directed to Smoke Jensen.

"Anything would be fine. I'm pleased you approve of my shopping. It's not often I do such domestic chores."

"And I'll bet your Sally doesn't have to send along a list," Martha praised him delightedly.

Color rose in the cheeks of Smoke Jensen. "No, Mrs. Tucker, but then, Sally usually comes along with me. Watchin' her is how I learned to pick the best."

They had ambled off during this exchange. Horizontal purple bars filled the western quarter of the sky, layered with pink, orange, and pale blue. At this altitude, stars already twinkled faintly in the east. Martha Tucker led the way to a circular bench, built around the bole of a huge, old cottonwood. There she turned to face Smoke Jensen.

"I feel that Mr. Jensen and Mrs. Tucker are rather stiff after so much time. May I call you Smoke?"

"If you wish, Martha." Smoke produced a rueful grin. "You know, it's funny, but I've been thinking of you by your given name for several days now."

They sat, and each resisted the urge to take the other by the hand. "I don't wish to seem prying, but could you tell me about your life before now," Martha urged.

Smoke sat silent for a while, then sighed, and laced his fingers around his right knee, crossed over the left. "I ran away . . . ah, that's not quite true. My home ran away from me, when I was twelve. I wandered some, and wound up out on the plains. I was about to get my hair lifted by some Pawnee, when this woolly-looking critter out of hell rose up from the tall grass and shot two braves off their horses with a double-shot Hawken rifle. Dumped two more with another of the same, then banged away with a pair of pistols, which I later learned were sixty caliber Prentiss percussion guns, made in Waterbury, Connecticut. That's how I met Preacher."

Smoke went on to relate some of the milder adventures he had encountered as a youth in the keeping of Preacher. Martha listened with rapt attention. When words ran dry for Smoke, she told of her life back East, before she married Lawrence Tucker.

"We had a fine place, right outside Charleston, South Carolina. The War ruined all that, though. I was not yet eighteen, when I met Lawrence. He had come down with the occupation forces of Reconstruction. Like a proper young Southern lady, I hated all Yankees. Yet, Lawrence seemed somehow different.

"He had genuine concern for the well-being of white Southerners. He treated whites and darkies with the same reserve and respect. And I found out later that he didn't profit a penny's worth out of the false tax attachment schemes that deprived so many of their land and property."

"Given the circumstances, I'm surprised you ever got together," Smoke prompted.

"I had little choice. Lawrence and his staff occupied our plantation house. Daddy had lost a leg at Chancellorsville, and been invalided out of the service. Lawrence insisted from the first day his carpetbaggers moved into the main house, that rent be paid. Only, it was him paying that rent.

"He was young, and a lawyer. He'd only served the last year of the War with the Bluebellies." Smoke smiled at the use of that term, while Martha paused to order her recollections. "One night at the dinner table, he absolutely astonished the whole family by stating forcefully that the War had been fought for economic reasons and politics, and had nothing whatsoever to do with slavery."

"Not a popular opinion among our brethren to the north," Smoke observed.

"I'll say not. He and Daddy got along famously after that. One day, one of the vilest of carpetbaggers showed up with those falsified documents about back taxes on Crestmar. Lawrence produced a stack of paid receipts, and said those taxes were not due anymore." A tinkle of laughter brightened her recounter. "He even threatened to have the man run off the plantation by our darkies, who were working then for wages. They were armed with some shotguns and a few Enfield muskets left over from the War. We whites were not permitted to carry arms, even for self-protection, although General Grant said we could."

A profound change had come over Martha Tucker. She talked like a young girl, when she recalled her life in the South. Her mannerisms also revealed the stereotypical Southern belle. Smoke noted this with not a little discomfort. He saw it as though she were two different persons, the lighthearted one hidden under the burdens of the other. He wondered if it was good for her. To make matters worse, he received a strong impression that she was flirting with him.

"I've enjoyed this talk of old times, Martha. No offense, but right now, my stomach thinks my throat's been cut."

"Oh, my! What a ninny," Martha babbled, the Old South sloughing off her speech as she rose. "I'll see to supper right away. The children will be starved, too. And thank you for confiding in me about your past life."

Smoke Jensen heaved a long sigh of relief as Martha Tucker headed toward the kitchen. A soft chuckle came from the far side of the tree trunk, and Jeff York stepped into view. "That one's fallin' in love."

"You can go straight to hell, Jeff York," Smoke growled as he came to his boots.

Awakening at the palest of dawn light, Miguel Selleres drew a deep breath, redolent with sage and yucca blooms. He immediately understood why Benton-Howell coveted this land so much. Very like the valleys of the Sierra Madre Occidental, where he had grown up. A moment later he received a lesson in why it was not wise for white-eyes to desire this vista of piñon-shrouded mesas.

Some twenty-seven Apache warriors—in varying sizes from short and squat to tall and square, painted for war— rose up to fire a volley of arrows into the camp erected by the seven men who had accompanied Miguel Selleres and Quint Stalker's survivors. The whirring messengers of death had barely begun to descend on the unsuspecting white interlopers, when a ragged fusillade of rifle fire erupted, shattering the quiet of early morning.

With grim silence, the Apaches swarmed down into camp on the tail of their surprise opening. Shouts of confusion and alarm came from the sleep-dulled outlaws. Only their leader had the presence of mind to make a positive move. Miguel Selleres unlimbered his Mendoza .45, and shot the nearest Apache through the breastbone. He then came to his boots and made directly for his carriage.

Unlike most of its contemporaries, fashioned by the

skilled wainwrights of Durango, it did not have sides and a roof of thick oak planking. Sandwiched between layers of veneer, strong sheets of steel—fashioned from the boiler plates of a wrecked locomotive on the *Ferocarril de Zacatecas*—made it nearly impregnable. Even the curtained windows had bulletproof shutters. Miguel Selleres reached his goal, along with Quint Stalker, who knew about the construction of the coach. They entered, secured the doors and shutters, and began to pick targets among the attacking Indians.

Durango's coach makers had provided firing ports, not so much for fighting off Apaches, but for bandits. They well knew the requirements of the rich and powerful in their own country. The armored vehicle withstood assaults from arrow, lance, ball, and stone war club. Many who attacked it died for their efforts. A growing volume of firepower drove off the Apaches after a closely fought five minutes.

"Did you think to bring some water and grub?" Quint asked anxiously, when the shooting dwindled to long-range sniping.

"Under the seat. There's extra ammunition, *también.*"

"You think of everything, *Señor* Selleres."

"Not everything, or I would not be in here, with those cursed devils outside."

Quint Stalker actually cracked a smile, and his troubled countenance brightened. "That shines! I like a man with a sense of humor in tough situations."

"You flatter me. Help yourself to my humble repast."

Stalker dug into the wicker hamper inside the hinged rear seat. He pulled out a cloth bag of *machaca*—shredded dry beef, Mexican style—another of parched corn, a tin can of bean paste, and another of peaches. "We're gonna feast like kings," he exclaimed with delight.

"The men won't fare so well, unless they gather up what the *indios* failed to destroy. I suggest you order them to bring everything they can, and form defenses around my carriage. We could use two more guns in here. The rest can form barricades from rocks, saddles and . . ." Selleres winced, "dead horses."

Mid-morning came and the situation had changed little. It had grown blood-boiling hot inside the coach. Great wet patches showed under the arms of the occupants and along their spines. Several of the hard-bitten outlaws had managed to round up enough horses to harness the carriage and provide transportation for the survivors, if some rode double. Miguel Selleres noted that spirits had risen considerably. Then Fate struck them cruelly again.

This time, when the Apaches charged, the solid drum of shod hooves joined in the whisper rush of moccasin soles. A dozen Arizona Rangers, led by Tallpockets Granger, stormed the mesa top and the desperate hard cases who had been trapped there. A steady swath of bullets made a drum of the inside of the carriage.

Desperation added its own brand of discipline to the forlorn outlaw band. When the Apaches crashed into the improvised barricades, the white vermin reversed their rifles and used them for clubs. Winchesters bashed Apache heads, broke ribs, slowed the advance, and low-held six-guns blazed a clear path through the throng.

Miguel Selleres spotted it first. The reins of the team had been threaded through a narrow, hinged slot near the oof of the coach. Selleres handed them to one hard case and shouted through a riskily opened window.

"Get this team going. Surround the coach and ride for it. That's our only chance."

"That was damned Arizona Rangers out there fightin' alongside the Apaches," Quint Stalker observed in a wounded tone. "What they takin' the redskins' side for?"

Miguel Selleres gave him a droll look. "Perhaps our bought politicians have not been able to accomplish all they promised. Or they aren't honest."

"What's a honest politician?" Quint asked, never having known of one.

"One who, when he's been bought, stays bought by the same people," Selleres answered glibly.

"Oooh, hell, here they come again," Stalker groaned as he slammed the shutters tight.

At once the two outlaws at the lead team spurred their mounts and got the armored vehicle in motion. Firing to their sides, they fought clear of the horde that rushed at them. Driving blind, the border trash who held the reins expected at any instant for the carriage to turn over. Bouncing and swaying, he kept erect as the seconds, then the minutes passed.

"Ohmygod!" he gulped in a rush, as the coach canted downward onto the trail off the mesa.

"I think . . . we have . . . made it," Quint Stalker muttered in wonder.

"*¡Gracias a Dios!* I do believe we have," Miguel Selleres breathed out softly.

* * *

Tallpockets Granger watched the heavy carriage lumber down the steeply inclined trail and called in his detachment of Rangers. Most of the tough, Arizona-wise lawmen cautiously eyed the charged-up Apaches, who also broke off pursuit. An explosive situation could erupt at any second, Tallpockets knew, yet he had to fight an amused smirk as he made known his plan. Using the *Tinde* language, which he had learned as a child, he made a stunning announcement to Cuchillo Negro and his warriors.

"Black Knife, I want you and your braves to raise their right hands. Yeah, that's the one. Good. Now, do you swear to uphold the laws of the Territory of Arizona, obey the orders of the law chief over you, and keep the peace as directed? Answer, *enju.*"

"Wadest, what is this you are doing, *shee-kizzen?'* Cuchillo Negro asked, calling Tallpockets White Clay— the name he had earned as a boy when his father was agent to the White Mountain people—and calling him blood brother.

"Why, I'm making you my deputies, *shee-kizzen.*"

Black Knife's reaction began as a grin, grew into a broad smile, and ended in a deep belly laugh. *"Enju-enju*—yes, yes," he responded. "I never believed I'd live to see this day."

Tallpockets, who at six-foot-five truly fit the name, pulled a perplexed expression. "General Crook organized two companies of Apache scouts for the Army, so why can't the Rangers take you on?"

"For what purpose?"

"To track down those white lice and squash them," the long-faced Tallpockets stated levelly, his one brown

nd one blue eye glinting with his anger. He had heard
f what had been done to the Tinde children.

Tension evaporated as the rest of the Tinde offered
heir oaths and went among the Rangers clasping fore-
.rms in the Apache fashion. Tallpockets stood beside his
)lood brother and accepted the fealty of the warriors, all
he while glancing at the fading streamer of dust that
narked the course of the outlaws. At last his patience
vore thin.

"Let's mount up and go after that slime."

Sir Geoffrey Benton-Howell received two pieces of ex-
remely bad news at the same time. The rider from town
)rought him word of the shoot-out in the Hang Dog, and
ι telegram, sent in haste from Springerville, Arizona Ter-
·itory. He listened in a growing storm of rage.

"It was Smoke Jensen, right enough. Enough folks
·ecognized him while the shootin' was goin' on, and
vhen he rode out of town. He was with a buckboard
·rom the Tucker ranch."

"WHAT!" Benton-Howell bellowed.

"He was with some riders who drove a Tucker ranch
)uckboard."

"I heard what you said, fellow, I just could not believe
ιt. We worked so hard to convince that foolish woman
that Smoke Jensen had killed her husband. How could
she do this?"

"He didn't kill Tucker?"

"Of course not, you lout," Benton-Howell snapped, his
control rapidly slipping. "One of Quint Stalker's men,
Forrest Gore, did the job, and bungled it mightily I might

add. Wait here while I read this, then I will have some instructions for you."

Benton-Howell slit the yellow envelope and pulled the message form. His face went crimson with each word that leaped from the page. Miguel Selleres defeated and put to route by a band of Apaches and the Arizona Rangers? His mind refused to accept it. The Arizona Rangers? Impossible. That made it even more important to end this matter with the Tucker woman at once.

"Rocky, I want you to round up five or six men, and ride over to keep a watch on the Tucker ranch. Better take enough to send messages back, for that matter. What you will be looking for is the next time Smoke Jensen leaves there. You are to send word to me, and then go in and apprehend the widow and her children. We're going to make them disappear from the face of the earth, and then take that ranch."

Eighteen

Smoke Jensen turned away from the window that overlooked the dooryard of the Tucker ranch. "I'm not satisfied with the results of the visits to Benton-Howell's ranch. We need to take the fight to what's left of Stalker's men around Socorro. The four of us can get them mightily stirred up."

"How you figure to work it?" Jeff York asked.

"We'll split up, cover more area that way. You and Walt, Ty Hardy and I."

"Must you do this?" Martha Tucker asked with almost wifely concern as she entered the room.

"I'm afraid so. I don't figure this Englishman for being stupid. His partner's smart enough from what I've heard," Smoke explained. "They'll figure out sooner or later that the only place we can be is here. I want to keep the fighting away from you and your youngsters."

"I'm grateful for that, Smoke, but the risk . . . ?"

Smoke gave her a smile just short of indulgent. "I've taken risks before and come out all right." He didn't mention the scars that crisscrossed his body, or the eyes swollen shut and blackened by hard knuckles, the loose teeth and split lips. "We'll head out in half an hour," he told Jeff.

Not unexpectedly, Jimmy Tucker wanted to ride along. When the four gunfighters—Ty Hardy just a beginner—had mounted up, Jimmy came to them and blurted out his wishes. Smoke Jensen looked down at the lad long and hard.

"That's not possible, Jimmy. Although they're hardly the best of a sorry lot, it's no place for you to be. You're good enough with a gun to protect your mother and the other kids, so your place is to stay here and do just that."

Jimmy made a face like he might cry, then turned away. "Awh . . . hell, I never get to do anything," he muttered.

Smoke Jensen withheld his sympathetic chuckle until they had ridden away from the ranch headquarters. When he looked back at the crest of a low rise, Martha and Jimmy were waving at them with equal enthusiasm.

Forrest Gore slid the brass telescope closed and slipped it in the case hung from his saddle horn. "They're long gone, and nothing's stirring around the bunkhouse or corrals. You boys spread out, take your time, so's we can hit them from all sides at once. Today's washday, so the woman'll be out in the yard. If we cut her off from the house, we won't have any troubles at all."

For once it worked exactly like Gore wanted it. He and seven men swarmed down on the Tucker ranch, and caught Martha Tucker at the clothes line. Arms above her head, a sheet flapping in the breeze, she did not have a chance to reach for the rifle that leaned against one upright of the drying rack. Two men literally plucked her off the ground and rode away.

After her first, startled yelp, Martha shouted desperately, "Run, Jimmy!"

Only Jimmy Tucker did not obey. He dived for his own rifle and came up with the lever action cycling. The other five men, led by Forrest Gore, closed in on the children. A slug cracked over Gore's head, close enough to make him cringe. He still smarted from the pellet wounds given him by Smoke Jensen. Three of the Tucker hands got into the fight a moment later.

Outnumbered by the outlaws, one went down almost at once, as Marv Fletcher blasted him in the center of his chest. A second gunhand took a bullet in the leg and lay helplessly under the guns of the Stalker gang. The third hunkered down behind a large water tank and fired at those surrounding his friend.

After Vern Fletcher took a slug in his shoulder, Arlan Grubbs got around behind the wrangler and shot him in the back. Jimmy got off another round before the broad chest of a lathered horse knocked him off his bare feet.

Forrest Gore dismounted swiftly and wrestled the rifle from the boy's grasp. Then he backhanded Jimmy hard enough to loosen teeth. Quickly he tied the boy's hands and feet. With a grunt of effort, he booted the dazed lad onto the crupper of his saddle. Shrieks of fear from Rose and Tommy Tucker cut through the rumble of hooves. Dust swirled in the abandoned yard, as the outlaws rode off with their prisoners.

"What do we do with 'em?" a snaggle-toothed hard case asked.

"We're to take them to the B-Bar-H. Sir Geoffrey wants to entertain them for a while," Forrest Gore replied with a lustful leer.

* * *

Jeff York pointed ahead to what Smoke Jensen had already seen. "Someone's sure foggin' the road this way," the Arizona Ranger stated the obvious.

"Must have come from a long way off," Smoke stated flatly. "I've been watching the dust rise for a good twenty minutes."

"Carbone said you had the eyes of a *halcon*—a hawk," Jeff said softly. "Now I believe him. Who do you think it could be?"

Smoke studied the growing column of red-brown dust, and the thin line far behind. "Not someone we're going to enjoy meeting."

"Quint Stalker and his gang?" Jeff suggested.

"It could be, Jeff. Right funny if we set out hunting them and they find us first."

"I'd maybe see the fun in it, if we still had Walt and Ty along," came Jeff's glum reply.

Smoke looked around the barren desert terrain. "There's nowhere to hide out here."

"There'd be plenty, if you were an Apache."

Smoke cut his eyes sharply to Jeff. "Think like an Indian. That's a shinin' idea, Jeff. Let's get busy."

A quick coursing of the ground located a shallow gully. Smoke and Jeff rode into it and dismounted. At Smoke's direction, they stripped the saddlebags from their mounts and put the animals down on their sides. With stones from the bottom of the wash, they reinforced the lip of the draw in two places and set out rifles and ammunition.

"Nothing left to do but wait," Jeff spoke out of nervousness.

"Not for long, either." Smoke had already picked up the distant, growing rumble of wheels that moved fast and carried a heavy burden.

They had a good view down the reverse slope of the elongated ridge where they had found the gully. Only thing, the road curved out of sight against the swell of the land, a scant three hundred yards away. Outriders came into view first.

Smoke caught sight of the heads of their horses, then the forward-bent outlines of three men, riding abreast. Behind them came a six-up team, hauling a lumbering coach. The men to the rear of the carriage had their weapons out and ready, and kept casting glances behind them.

"Whoever it is, looks like they're in some sort of trouble."

"I reckon, Jeff. Only, which side do we pick?" At Jeff's droll expression, Smoke went on. "Reckon we let them get in close enough to see if we recognize any of them."

"Not too close, I hope," Jeff suggested. "I count nine men, plus whoever is in that coach."

"Funny there's no one up on that box to drive." Jeff nodded understanding at Smoke's observation.

By then the lead riders had come well within field glass range. Smoke studied the faces, and his full lips thinned into a grim line. He put the binoculars aside and levered a round into the chamber of his Winchester.

"One of them is Quint Stalker," Jeff advised a moment later.

"Well, we know which side we're on," Smoke tossed back as he made ready for a fight.

Quint Stalker had obtained a horse at the first homestead they came upon after escaping from the White Mountains. He used the simple expedient of stealing it. He had so far ridden two mounts into the ground, and the team hauling that armor-plated carriage had been replaced three times. The cause of their unseemly haste hovered tauntingly on the western horizon.

Contrary to the assurances of Miguel Selleres, the Apaches had continued in pursuit, and by all appearances, the Arizona Rangers rode with them. Try as he might, Quint Stalker could not visualize those two traditional enemies as allies. Yet they had joined against him and the eight men who remained. That conclusion had been reached in the moment Quint swerved his mount to the left to avoid a large rock in the trail.

That movement put the bullet meant for his heart in the eye of his horse, and killed the animal instantly. When the dead beast's foreknees hit the hard, red-brown soil, Quint Stalker catapulted out of the saddle. He hit hard, the air driven from his lungs, and rolled along in the sharp-edged gravel that lay in his path.

His chin took a lot of punishment, and wound up bleeding profusely when he sprawled to a halt. What the hell? Those Injuns couldn't have gotten ahead of them. After his ordeal, thoughts didn't stick too well in Quint's mind. He tried to see to his left, from where the shot came, only everything looked fuzzy. Then his blood turned to ice.

From behind, he heard the coach bearing down on him.

He'd be squashed into a red pulp by two dozen hooves. To say nothing of those wheels! Squalling, Quint lurched upward and threw himself to one side. He could see the hooves of the horses up close, and feel the heat of their bodies as they thundered past. The swaying carriage halted directly beside him.

"Get in here, you idiot!" Miguel Selleres growled from the open doorway.

Grateful for the protection of those armored walls, Quint Stalker did so with alacrity. Once secure, he found himself the target of unanswerable questions.

"What happened out there?"

Quint Stalker gaped at Miguel Selleres. "I . . . don't know. Someone shot my horse out from under me."

"Who? How many? I don't see anyone," Selleres rattled off, while squinting out the firing loop of one window. "It can't be *los indios*," he added to himself.

"That's what I thought, and you're right. It can't be."

"Then who?"

Stalker's first attempt at an answer got drowned out by the loud slam of bullets into the side of the coach. In a brief lull, he tried again. "Smoke Jensen."

"*¡Bastante, no mas!*" Selleres barked. "We have enough men to finish him for all time."

He came to his feet and leaned over the seated outlaw. A hinged panel in the back of the coach opened, and Selleres shouted through it. "Get over there and find who's shooting at us."

At once the gunmen spread out, and jumped their horses toward the lip of the ravine. Withering fire challenged them, yet they pushed on. One hard case yowled and clutched at his arm, where a bloodstain began to spread. Another doubled over, lips to the neck of his mount, as though kissing it. The remainder drew off, seeking cover behind the carriage.

"*¡Cobardes! ¡Pendejos!* Get out there and kill those men! I see only two guns against you. *¡Adalante, pronto!*"

With obvious reluctance, the outlaws charged again. This time they fired steadily at the noted gun positions. Their heavy volume of fire forced Smoke and Jeff to pull down below the lip of the bank. Selleres watched with growing satisfaction. The riders reached the edge of the gully.

Then a gunhawk from Albuquerque threw up his hands and fell backward off his horse. Smoke Jensen had switched to his .44 and blasted upward into the man's face. Jeff York opened up also. Bullets gouged the ground and cracked through the air. Another gunhawk grunted in pain, as one of Smoke's slugs pierced his left leg, front to rear, right below the knee. Suddenly they had had enough.

Huddling behind the armored coach, they heard a muffled string of curses from inside. The shutters opened on one window, and they saw the face of Quint Stalker. "Get over there and finish it, you sonsabitches."

"Give us some covering fire, damn you," Charlie Bascomb snarled.

"Yeah—yeah, good idea. Spread out, hit them from two sides. We'll keep their heads down."

It worked even better than Miguel Selleres expected from the thoroughly demoralized gunmen. He and Quint Stalker opened fire first, the riders charged out from behind the carriage, and streaked for the arroyo ahead of and behind the position of the ambushers. Victory lay only fractions of a second away.

Then Selleres and Stalker learned how deceptive the desert terrain could be to eyes accustomed to a fifteen-mile horizon. Around the bend in the road that masked the back trail, swarmed some twenty Apache warriors and a dozen Arizona Rangers. Rapidly closing ground, they opened fire immediately. Miguel Selleres weighed the outcome quickly and accurately.

"Get us out of here," he snapped to the driver at his side.

Tallpockets Granger saw the coach stopped in the road ahead. A dead horse lay on its side behind the armor-plated vehicle. Someone had ambushed them. He knew that someone had to be Capt. Jeff York. At once he turned in the saddle, waved an arm over his head, and pointed forward.

"Unlimber your irons, boys. It looks like ol' Jeff's bit a bear in the butt."

They crashed into the nearer trio of outlaws with rifles and six-guns blazing. One man fell without a sound, shot through the head. Another took two bullets in his side and dropped from the saddle. The last threw up his hands. The Apaches accompanying the Rangers streamed on by, intent on taking on the child-killers beyond the coach. Suddenly the vehicle bolted forward, the horses straining to pull the heavy load.

Terror blanched the faces of the *Pen-dik-olye* as Cuchillo Negro and his warriors raced toward them. One had self-control enough to steady his mount and take careful aim. Smoke Jensen rose up slightly and put a slug through his chest. The gunhawk made a gurgling cry as he fell sideways off his saddle.

His companions started dying seconds later, hard and slowly, as the Apaches swarmed over them. It took some time to stop them. While the Rangers did what they could to drag the vengeful warriors off the outlaws, Tallpockets Granger pounded boots to the edge of the draw.

"Thought it might be you, Cap'n," he drawled through a grin. A nod toward Smoke. "Mr. Jensen, good to see you again. Them horses you brought us worked real good. Let us run the hell out of those *ladrónes.*"

Smoke came up onto the level. "Glad you like them. What brings you over this way?"

"We decided to wipe out that Stalker gang once and for all. Besides, I sort of figgered ol' Jeff here might need some help."

"And the Apaches?" Jeff asked with a nod toward Cuchillo Negro.

"They're my deputies." At Jeff's astonished gape, he added, "We're after the same enemy, Cap'n."

Smoke clapped a hand on one shoulder of Granger. "Then they are as welcome as can be. Only thing that bothers me, is that coach got away. I thought we'd shot it to doll rags."

"Wouldn't have done no good," Tallpockets informed Smoke. "That belongs to Miguel Selleres. It's all made of boiler plate under thin wood."

"That ties everything together," Smoke allowed, after hearing an account of the battle in the White Mountains. "I think the time has come to move directly on Benton-Howell and his partner."

* * *

Tallpockets Granger volunteered his posse of deputy Arizona Rangers. That gave them an effective force of fifteen. To Smoke's surprise, the Apaches led by Cuchillo Negro offered to continue as deputies to Tallpockets. At the suggestion of Smoke Jensen, they rode first to the Tucker ranch to enlist any others who wanted to join the fight.

"A good place to start is in Socorro. We can clean out the trash that Benton-Howell has been gathering, then close in on the ranch," Smoke declared.

When they reached the Tucker ranch two hours later, a wounded hand, Sean Quade, gave them the bad news. "They killed Hub and Carter," he concluded, "and took Miz Tucker and the kids."

"Who?"

"Don't know all of them. Some of the trash that's been showin' up in town. Forrest Gore led them. I saw him clear."

"Which way did they go?" Smoke asked with winter in his voice.

Quade scratched an isolated circle of sandy hair that hung down his forehead. "Southwest, toward Socorro."

Shock at learning of the abduction had turned to cold, controlled anger in Smoke Jensen. "Then that's the way we're going. We'll send a doctor out to take care of that leg, Sean," Smoke advised the wounded man.

"Damned right," Jeff agreed.

"I'm goin', too," Sean Quade stated flatly.

Jeff York tried to reason with Quade. "You wouldn't be much use with a bullet in your leg."

"I can sit on my butt in a buckboard, and use a shotgun," Sean defended his decision.

"You've lost a lot of blood," Smoke Jensen told the man. "The ride in could knock you out, or worse."

Quade could not argue with that. "All right. I'll stay here and wait for the doc. Good luck . . . and keep your heads down."

Nineteen

Socorro literally burst at the seams with gunfighters and wannabes. From beyond rifle range, Smoke Jensen studied the crowded streets through field glasses. When he had worked out in his mind how it should be done, he turned to Cuchillo Negro and spoke, with Tallpockets translating.

"I want to save you as a nasty surprise for the gunhawks in there."

The Apache chief pulled his full lips into a grim smile. "These white men will have no heart for the fight when we attack."

"That's what I'm thinking. They won't think much of the rest of us riding in. We can take a few by surprise. But the best of them will fort up somewhere. When that happens, and we get bogged down, you hit them from the far side of town."

Cuchillo Negro cut his eyes to Tallpockets. "This one thinks like a *Tinde.*"

Tallpockets rendered it in English. Smoke nodded in acceptance of the compliment. "I learned most of my fighting skills from a man named Preacher."

Eyes widened, Cuchillo Negro grunted harshly. "My father knew such a man and spoke of him often. We

Tinde called him Gray Wolf. No other man could move so silently, or fight so ferociously. I do not say that lightly."

"He'd be proud to know you folks thought so highly of him," Smoke returned.

Black Knife smiled around his eyes. "Many *Chiricahua, Mescaleros,* and *Tinde* died before we learned to respect him."

That could go on Preacher's headstone, if he had one, Smoke thought. "They had plenty company," he told the Apache chief.

A second later, the Apaches left for their position. They seemed to dissolve into the empty terrain. One moment they were in plain view, the next, only faint puffs of dust showed where their horses had walked. And *they* had this great respect for his mentor. For perhaps the thousandth time, Smoke saw Preacher in yet a new light.

"We'll give them half an hour, then ride in," Smoke informed the others.

Two second-rate hard cases sat their horses at a point where wood rail fences and a cattle guard kept livestock from wandering the streets of Socorro. One of them jolted out of a doze at the sound of approaching riders. He tipped up the brim of his hat and peered into the wavery heat shimmer of midday.

"More guns on the way," he remarked to his companion. "You'd think we were going after an army."

"Hell, Mike, for twenty dollars a day I'd take on ol' Gen'ral Sherman hisself."

"No denyin' the money's good." Suddenly Mike's

spine stiffened him upright, and his hand went to his gun.

"Damn! That one in front's Smoke Jensen!"

"Yer seein' things," his partner contradicted. He just knew Smoke Jensen would never be within ten miles of Socorro.

Mike whipped his six-gun clear of leather. In the time it took for him to reach the hammer, his intended target had spoken and drawn his gun.

"Your friend's right, you know."

"Awh, hell."

The last thing Mike saw was the beginning of a spurt of smoke from the barrel of the .44 aimed at him. He died so quickly, he didn't fall off his horse. Smoke Jensen's second bullet hit the other would-be gunfighter somewhat lower. It ruined his liver and spine on the way out. He pitched to one side and landed with a heavy *plop.*

"So much for taking anyone by surprise," Smoke complained, as he and the Rangers rode past the dead men.

Halfway down the block, a trio of lean, gaunt-faced men stepped into the street to block the way. "That something personal between you an' Mike?" the one in the middle asked. Then he saw the silver badge on the vest of Jeff York. "Awh, damnitall," he bemoaned his fate as he drew against the Arizona Ranger.

Jeff shot him with the Winchester in his right hand. The other two scattered. They threw wild rounds behind them, as they made for the nearest saloon. Jeff grunted and put his free hand to his left shoulder. It came away bloody-fingered. Jeff brought the rifle to his right shoulder then, and took careful aim. His bullet shattered the offender's ankle and put him on the ground.

Smoke's second slug shattered a kerosene lamp beside the door through which the last gunman dodged. The Rangers spread out, weapons at the ready. Smoke and Jeff continued toward the barroom. Jeff York stuffed a neckerchief under his shirt front, to sop up the blood from the deep gouge cut in the meat of his shoulder point. Glass crunched under their boot soles, when they dismounted and stepped up on the boardwalk. Smoke and Jeff entered through the batwings together. They found themselves facing nine outlaw guns.

Five of those roared at once. Showers of splinters erupted from the door frame and lintel. One bullet went by so close to the ear of Smoke Jensen, that it made more of a hum than a crack. Smoke already had one of the shooters on the floor, doubled over the hole in his belly. Jeff York had a second gunhand down, crying really sincere tears over his ruined left hip. Then the remaining four six-guns exploded into life.

Smoke Jensen had dived to one side and flattened a felt-covered poker table, scattering chips, cards, and players in all directions. He did a forward roll before the table came to rest, then bounced to one knee, flame spitting from the muzzle of his six-gun. At short range, a .44 slug does truly awful damage to human flesh. Smoke's round hit a thick, hard-muscled belly, with a *splat* like a baseball bat striking a whole ham.

His target gave a hard grunt and looked down stupidly at the hole where his fifth shirt button used to be. "Jeez, Mister, who is it killed me?" he asked weakly.

"Smoke Jensen," the owner of the name told him.

Then Smoke was on the move again. He jumped over a man who had only then come off the sawdust from his upset chair. The move saved his life. The hard case they had chased into the saloon leveled a round at where Smoke had knelt. All it killed was a fly on the faded, pale green wall. The gunhawk gaped at his act of minor mayhem, and paid for it with his life as Jeff York shot him down.

One of his comrades in murder reeled backward into the bar, blood gushing from a neck wound he had received courtesy of Smoke Jensen. The bodies continued to pile up at an incredible rate, the bartender, Diego Sanchez, noted. He sat on the floor behind two full beer barrels, and watched the slaughter in reverse through the mirror. It was a technique barkeeps learned early on in their profession, or they didn't have long careers.

A stray slug shattered a decanter and sent shards of thick crystal shrapnel flying. They in turn broke half a dozen cheaper bottles, and inundated the bartender's apron with bourbon, rye, and tequila. Taking a bath in booze came with the territory also, Diego Sanchez knew from experience. *¡Por Dios!* His Conchita would make him sleep in the hammock between the palo verdes again.

Suddenly it got eerily silent in the saloon. Not a boot sole scraped the floor. No one could be heard breathing. No glass shards tinkled. Even the echoes of gunshots had died out. Slowly, Diego Sanchez sucked in air. He raised himself slowly until his eyeballs came above the top of the bar. Four men faced one another from opposite ends of the mahogany. Two he knew; Logan and Sloane, gunfighter trash that had drifted into town three days ago.

The other pair wore badges, a U.S. Marshal and an Arizona Ranger.

"It's your choice," the Marshal said tightly.

Jesus, Maria y Jóse, he was a big one. Diego moved back from the bar, until he pressed against the shelf behind.

"You ran that thing dry," Logan drawled nastily. "Now I'm gonna ventilate that tin star of yours."

"You know, I think you're right," Smoke Jensen told him, as he threw the .44 in the air and instantly snatched the second one from its left-hand holster. The hammer dropped on the primer before Logan could react and yank his trigger. Smoke caught the flying six-gun left-handed, at the same moment his bullet punched a hole through Logan's chest. The gun in the Ranger's hand blasted a second later and downed his man.

"Jesus, Smoke, I didn't think anyone could do that," Jeff York said in awed tones.

Smoke? Smoke Jensen? Diego Sanchez sucked in air and crossed himself. Then he slowly lowered his head below the bar. As though spoken from far away, his words reached the ears of Smoke Jensen.

"Vereso nada, Señor Jensen."

"He said, 'I saw nothing,'" Jeff translated.

"Yeah. I caught that. I think we're through here, Jeff." Then, with a chuckle, *"Adios, Señor cantinero."*

"Conosco nada, nada," came a weak reply.

Diego Sanchez might have been willing to see and know nothing, but that didn't go for the swarm of hard cases and two-bit gunslingers who thronged the streets of town. They damn well wanted to know what was going on in the *Cantina La Merced*. They didn't like what they found when the batwings swung outward. Smoke Jensen and Jeff York had reloaded, and met the gathered gun-slicks with six-guns roaring.

"This town is out of bounds for your kind from this minute on," Jeff York bellowed over the sound of gunmen panicking. Half a dozen of them were foolhardy enough to resist. Two of them died instantly. One of them shot the hat off Smoke Jensen's head and bought an early grave for his efforts.

"On the balcony over there, Smoke," Jeff shouted.

Smoke pivoted to his left and sent another wannabe gunfighter off to hell. The gunman staggered forward and tripped over the railing. He did a perfect roll in the air on the way down. The other lawmen had spread out along the main street, and began herding surprised hard cases off benches and out of saloons, prodding them toward the jail. By that time, Jeff had drilled a second resister in the shoulder.

"Jeff, drop!" Smoke shouted the warning as a gunhand popped up from behind a rail barrel and aimed at Jeff York's back.

Jeff went down, and the bullet fanned air where he had been standing. A fraction of a second later, a .44 slug from Smoke Jensen's iron flattened the back-shooter against the wall of the Mercy Cantina. The corpse left a long, red smear down the whitewashed stucco, as he slumped beside a cactus in a large terracotta pot.

Hot lead cracked through the air around Smoke then. He moved swiftly across the street, charging the shooter instead of fleeing. The mountain man's six-gun bucked one. The gunslinger stiffened, then his knees buckled. Smoke had already turned away.

None of the original, six foolish gunslingers remained on their feet. Smoke cut his eyes to Jeff and nodded down the block to where the volume of fire had increased noticeably. "I think Tallpockets and the boys could use some help," Smoke suggested.

"Then, let's go see," Jeff agreed, shoving fresh cartridges into his still-hot Colt.

Some twenty gunfighters and assorted saddle trash had banded together and taken over a bank building. Its thick fieldstone walls made it into a fortress. The structure stood alone, an island at an intersection, which allowed the Rangers to completely surround it. When Smoke Jensen and Jeff York arrived, the occupants hotly exchanged shots with those outside.

"I reckon they have the Tuckers in there," Smoke allowed.

"Won't they be in danger?" Jeff asked.

"Most likely they'll be somewhere safe. Probably in the cellar, if there is one. Dead hostages don't make good bargaining chips."

On the roof, the head and shoulders of a hard case appeared. He apparently wore all black, and had a full-flowing walrus mustache in matching color. He put a Ranger down with a bullet in the side. While he ducked down behind the stone verge and cycled the action of his rifle, Smoke Jensen didn't even break stride. His hand dropped smoothly to the .44 at his side, which came free of leather with a soft whisper. When his left boot sole next struck the street, the weapon barked in Smoke's hand.

Above, behind the low stone parapet, the gunman's hat took sudden flight, along with a gout of blood and brains. Jeff York stared at his friend in open amazement. Smoke pointed with the smoking barrel of his Peacemaker.

"There's a narrow crack right . . . there. I just waited until his black hat blotted out the light."

"That was one steady-handed shot," Jeff complimented. Smoke merely shrugged and sought another target. When the volume of fire increased even more, Jeff looked toward the north end of town. "Any time now," he observed.

"Them damn Rangers ain't even supposed to be over here," one lanky gunfighter from Arizona declared, as he fired an unaimed shot into the street. "They ain't got no juri—jures—they ain't the law in New Mexico!"

"You see that slowin' down the lead they're punching at us?" growled an exceptionally short, bushy-headed gunslick with thick, gold-rimmed glasses.

"Shut up, Bob," the Arizonan snapped.

Glass tinkled like chimes as more windows took fire from the Rangers. Gradually, over the roar of gunfire from both sides, the men inside the bank heard the rumble of hooves and thin, high-pitched yelps. Bob cut his eyes upward at the slender Arizonan.

"What the hell's that?"

"Sounds . . ." The gunfighter cocked his head and concentrated. "Sounds like Injuns."

"What Injuns would that be?" Bob challenged.

"By god, it sounds like Apaches. I've heard enough of them to last a lifetime."

"What are *they* doing over here?" Bob gulped. "Are they attacking the town?"

Arizona Slim edged to a window on the north side of the bank lobby and peered out. "No. Oh, hell no! I can't believe this. They—they've joined the damned Rangers. They're comin' after us!"

Outside, the Rangers checked their fire as the Apaches swarmed through their cordon and flung themselves directly at the shot-out windows of the bank. The Arizona lawmen began reloading, while the men led by Cuchillo Negro raced closer, firing bent low over the necks of their mounts. Three dived through shattered sashes with stone-headed war clubs held high.

Muffled gunshots came from inside, and the screams of dying men. A second wave hit the stone building, and a lance hurtled through an opening to pin Bob to a desktop; bloody froth accompanied his screech of agony. With the Apaches rampaging inside, the Arizona Rangers charged the building.

Once the lawmen got in close and mixed it up with the gunhawks, all resistance ended quickly. When the survivors had been rounded up and secured in manacles, Smoke Jensen and Jeff York made a thorough search of the cellar. They came up with no sign of the Tucker family. But Smoke did find Payne Finney, hiding in a coal bunker.

"The Tuckers? Where are they?" he demanded of the thoroughly demoralized Finney.

"They aren't here. Never have been. I don't know where Stalker told Gore to take them," Finney lied smoothly.

Smoke clasped Finney by one shoulder, his thumb boring into the entry wound from a .44-40 round. Finney squirmed and grunted. "You wouldn't figure to try to run a lie past me now, would you?" he asked Finney in a calm, level tone.

"No—no. I'm serious. I don't know where they took them. I've been here all the time."

"He's right," a surly member of the Stalker gang supported Finney. "He's been in town like the rest of us. We never heard anything about the Tuckers."

Smoke cut his eyes from Payne Finney to Jeff York. "Case of the right hand not lettin' the left know?" he asked.

"Could be. Where do we start from here?"

"Back at the ranch." Jeff groaned as Smoke went on. "The trackers I set out should have something by now. It's not your fault, Jeff. I figured, too, that they'd want to take 'em to some neutral ground to arrange terms."

Jeff brightened. "There's only one place makes sense. We can save a lot of time, if we ride direct for the B-Bar-H."

"That fits. But I want to hear what the trackers say first. And we do have these prisoners to take care of. After that, we'll ride."

Twenty

Half a dozen hard cases had ridden out of Socorro as the Rangers thundered into town. From a safe distance they had watched the roundup develop, heard the gunfire raise to a crescendo, and then watched in horror as a horde of Apaches swarmed into town. Then they lit out for the B-Bar-H.

They arrived on lathered, winded horses that trembled and walked weak-kneed to turns at the water trough. Charlie Bascomb, the nominal leader of the contingent that had escaped, reported to Quint Stalker and Geoffrey Benton-Howell. What he had to tell them did not get a warm reception.

"It's the truth, Sir Geoffrey. I tell ya, the Apaches sided with those Arizona lawmen. My guess is they'll be headed this way before long."

Quint Stalker swore and smacked a balled fist into the opposite palm. "That's the same lawmen that came after us. But they ain't got authority in New Mexico."

Frowning, Benton-Howell answered him, "I'm afraid they do. It's called hot pursuit. If you are right, then they can keep coming until you are caught."

"You ain't gonna let them, are you?" Stalker all but pleaded.

"Of course not. You've served me well and faithfully—ah—with a few recent exceptions. I think it expedient to bid my friends from Washington and Santa Fe a fond *adieu*. We can hold off any force here, until the governor learns of my plight. I'm sure he can get the interloping Arizona lawmen out of his territory."

"Hummm. That could be," Stalker caught at the thin strand of hope.

"Meanwhile, I want you to organize the men we have here. Fortify the headquarters, and prepare to stand off a siege."

"Do we got supplies for that?"

"Oh, my, yes. Ample food and ammunition, even some dynamite. Water might become a problem, if this becomes protracted."

Stalker raised a brow. He knew the absolute importance of water in a desert. "Like how long?"

"Four or five days. All of the wells are out in the open. A marksman's delight, don't you know?"

"What about the Tucker woman? Can't we use her and the brats to bargain with?"

Benton-Howell considered Stalker's words a moment. "That was my intention, if the situation required it. More to the point, I want her signature on a bill of sale. That must come first. I'm going to see her now. See to the preparations."

Martha Tucker looked up from her dark contemplations when Geoffrey Benton-Howell entered the small, bare pantry in which she had been confined. She had been separated from her children the moment they arrived at the ranch. That troubled her a good deal more than the constant insistence that she sign the ranch over to the Englishman. Jimmy would be all right, she felt certain, but little Rose and Tommy could be easily frightened. When her eyes fixed on her visitor's face, she noted at once that something seemed to have ruffled his usual icy composure.

"Mrs. Tucker, I'm afraid I really must insist on you signing the quit claim deed form I provided. Time is—ah—running short."

"For you or for me?"

"For both of us, I regret to say."

Again, Martha noted a flash of distress, and seized upon it at once. "What is it, Mr. Benton-Howell? Is Smoke Jensen closing in on you?"

Damn the woman, Benton-Howell thought furiously. Had she heard anything, even locked away here? He fought to retain his calm demeanor. "Smoke Jensen has nothing to do with the business between us. What I want is your ranch."

"Smoke Jensen has *everything* to do with it," Martha surprised herself by saying. "I see it now. You tried to frame Mr. Jensen for the murder of my husband."

"Damnit, madam, I'll not have that sort of talk from you. I had nothing whatever to do with that sorry incident." He omitted mentioning Miguel Selleres and Quint Stalker. "The matter is plain and clear. I—want—that—ranch."

"How much are you offering for it?"

Benton-Howell pinned her with icy eyes. "Your life, and the lives of your children."

"I have had better offers than that," Martha snapped.

"Which you chose to spurn. My patience is growing short. Perhaps I should have one of the youngsters brought here. I assure you my men have ways that are most persuasive when dealing with a child."

Martha paled, then red fury shot through her cheeks. "You'd not dare harm one of them."

"Ah, but I would, indeed. If my wishes are not acceded to. The form is on the counter there, and pen and ink. I recommend you sign now."

"Why do you want our ranch so badly?"

"That's none of your affair. Sign that paper, madam."

"Or else?"

Benton-Howell thought a moment. "That younger boy of yours, ah, Tommy I believe. Is he a good scholar?"

"He does very well in school."

A smirk twisted Benton-Howell's aristocratic visage into a mask of ugliness. "He wouldn't do so well missing a couple of fingers, would he?"

Outrage and horror choked Martha Tucker. She made no sound as she leaped to her feet. Her fingernails flashed like the talons of an eagle, as she raked them down the face of her tormentor. Benton-Howell cried out in an almost feminine shriek, and he pushed her roughly away. He stormed to the door and hurled his last threat over one shoulder.

"Sign it or suffer the consequences."

By late afternoon, half a dozen hard-faced men had ridden in and tied horses at the Socorro livery. Smoke Jensen observed to Jeff York that there must be an inexhaustible supply of second-rate gunhawks in New Mexico. They decided to delay their departure from town. One of the hands who had volunteered to help was sent back to the Tucker spread to make contact with the trackers, and bring their discoveries to Smoke. Now, with twenty gunmen locked in jail, more than half of them wounded, the town began to fill up with more of the same.

"By this time tomorrow, it'll be every bit as bad as it was when we rode in," Jeff stated in disgust, as he sipped at a beer in the Hang Dog.

"Too bad we couldn't keep the Apaches in town," Smoke observed.

"The good people of Socorro would have died of heart failure left and right. Some of my own men were concerned about how Black Knife's bucks would behave when they got the killin' hunger on them."

"They're damn good fighters," Smoke said tightly.

"They're that. They're also savages. No different from any other tribe. They got their ways; we've got ours. There isn't often that the two meet and work well together, like we did here yesterday."

Smoke lifted the corners of his mouth in a hint of a smile. "It worked well enough, I'd say. Of course, we had common cause. Some of those men you chased down were responsible for killing those Apache kids. I'll give you that if we go into their country next week, there's no guarantee they won't lift our hair. Like Preacher used to say, 'Injuns is changeable.' "

Boots clumped importantly on the porch outside. Sheriff Jake Reno bustled through the doorway and came directly to Jeff York. "I see you are still in town, Ranger. Maybe that's a good thing. There's more of that border trash drifting in every hour. I'm danged if I know what got them stirred up."

Jeff York put on a big grin and hooked a thumb in Smoke Jensen's direction. "Maybe it's that big reward you put out on my friend here."

Sheriff Reno turned to see whom the Arizona lawman meant. He came face-to-face with Smoke Jensen. His jaw sagged, and the color drained from his cheeks. He staggered back a few small steps. At first, no sound came. Then, a wheeze and squeak slid past rigid lips. A moment later, he found full voice, and bellowed, albeit with a quake.

"Goddamnit! It's Smoke Jensen!"

"In person, Sheriff. How's tricks?" Smoke asked with a mischievous twinkle in his eyes.

Sheriff Reno choked over the words that rushed to spew from his lips. He reached for his Smith American and handcuffs at the same time. "S—sta—stand ri-right there, Jensen. You're under arrest. Give up, or by God, I'm gonna gun you down right here."

Smoke Jensen backhanded Jake Reno so swiftly the sheriff never saw Smoke's big hand. The impact sounded like a shot. "You're not arresting anyone, Sheriff," Smoke told him in a flat, deadly tone.

No small man, Jake Reno balled huge, ham fists and swung at the taunting man before him. Smoke easily slipped the first blow and caught the second on the point of one shoulder. He brought his hands up and worked on the sheriff's soft middle. The fat yielded easily and, to his surprise, Smoke found a hard slab of muscle beneath. Reno grunted and punched Smoke in the face.

Smoke's head snapped back and heat flared in his eyes,

as he drove a hard left to the side of Reno's jaw. Jake Reno backpedaled rapidly until he struck the bar. Smoke followed with hard rights and lefts to the sheriff's ribs. He felt bone give under his pounding, and shifted to Reno's gut. Stale whiskey breath gusted from behind yellowed teeth.

A hard right from Smoke stopped that when it cracked three of Reno's teeth and mashed his lips. Blood flew through the room when Sheriff Reno shook his head violently in an effort to clear his fogged mind. He managed to get his guard up in time to parry two more solid swings, then Smoke broke through and did more damage to Reno's mouth.

Jake Reno sagged slowly, desperately seeking his second wind. It came gradually as his vision dimmed. With a blink of his eyes, he saw everything clearly again. He lunged awkwardly for Smoke Jensen and planted a left on the gunfighter's cheek. Smoke took it without a flinch. Smoke's own knuckles stung—he had not had time to put on his gloves before handing out this lesson in restraint. He ignored it and planted another fist in Reno's face.

Reno countered with a vicious kick aimed at Smoke's crotch. With a slight bob, Smoke slapped the booted foot away and then yanked upward on it. A startled *whoop* came from Jake Reno as he fell flat on his butt. Smoke closed in and stood over the seated man, to pound blow after blow onto the top of Reno's head. Reno began to gag and spit up blood. He must have bitten his tongue, Smoke considered.

With what would prove to be his final defiance, Jake Reno reached out with both arms and encircled Smoke

Jensen's legs. He hauled with rapidly dwindling strength. When he put a little shoulder in it, he dislodged Smoke's boots from the plank floor and toppled the mountain man.

Smoke recovered quickly though, and popped Reno on one ear with a stinging open palm. It had the effect of a gun going off beside the sheriff's head. Through the ringing, with eyes tearing, Jake Reno pawed uselessly at Smoke Jensen's torso while Smoke drove hard, punishing blows into already weakened ribs. Without warning, Jake Reno uttered a small, shrill cry, arched his back, and fell over backward. His head thudded in the sawdust.

Panting, blood dripping from the cut under his left eye, Smoke Jensen came slowly to his feet. He reached gratefully for the schooner of beer Jeff York offered him. He rinsed his mouth and spat pinkish foam into a brass gobboon.

"We've got enough evidence on the good sheriff to lock him up, don't we, Jeff?"

"I'd say so. It'll be up to the prosecutor if he's tried for anything."

"Then get this trash out of here. Put him in his own jail, and make sure he stays there."

"We found sign about three miles from the ranch," one of the trackers Smoke Jensen had sent out reported late the next day. "The Tuckers were taken to the B-Bar-H, sure enough. The closer they got, the less careful they were about covering their trail. An' something else, Mr. Jensen. That place is being turned into a fort. Armed riders everywhere, fence lines are being raised higher, the windows of the main house are boarded up."

Smoke considered this report while he sipped coffee. "Kevin, how many men do you figure are siding with Benton-Howell and Selleres?"

Kevin Noonan evaluated the quality of the gunmen they had seen. "I'd say twenty-five to thirty of them are average to good. They stay off the ridge lines, keep to the trees where they can, most don't smoke at night. There's another twenty or so who just don't measure up; trash with a gun strapped on. And there's more driftin' in all the time, five to ten a day."

Those numbers didn't appeal to Smoke Jensen. Even a poor shot could hit someone sometime. He simply didn't have enough men for a head-on fight. "It sounds like they're getting ready to stand off an army."

"Could be that this Englishman is trying to buy time," Walt Reardon suggested.

"For what purpose?" Jeff York asked.

Smoke Jensen picked it up from there. "He did have all those politicians out there for a big party. While you were there, did you gather that they were being paid for favors already done?"

"More like Benton-Howell was courting them," Jeff recalled. "It could be that they haven't come through so far."

"Yes. So he has to stall us, until whatever he is doing becomes legal," Smoke completed the thought. "Which means we should do a little pushing right soon. We have to force the issue *before* he can get whatever he's after out of the politicians."

"How soon?" Walt Reardon asked.

Smoke thought on it. "In a day or two. First we have to make Socorro unpopular with the sort Benton-Howell is attracting to town."

Walt Reardon lightly touched the grips of his six-gun. "We'd best do that before the place fills up again."

"Right about now should be a good time to start," Smoke announced, rising to his boots.

Orin Banning turned away from the lace curtains that covered the window of the parlor in Fanny Mae's Residence for Refined Young Women. "I never saw a town with so many badge-toters in it," he grumbled.

Beyond him, in the street, Arizona Rangers busily nailed up small, neat posters. One of the six men who had ridden with Banning to Socorro to answer the call put out by Benton-Howell made his way toward the brothel, eyes fixed on the industrious lawmen. After one had fastened a notice to a lamppost, he ripped it down and made his way quickly to the front door.

"Hey, Orin, lookie at this. We're being posted out of town."

"You mean *us?*" the would-be gang leader demanded.

"Well, yeah. Us an' everybody else. It says here that, 'Everyone not a resident of Socorro, New Mexico Territory or its environs'—whatever that means—'is hereby ordered to be out of town by noon Tuesday.' That's tomorrow."

"Who is going to be doin' the throwin'?"

"Them Rangers, I reckon. Oh, an' I heard a funny thing down at the Hang Dog. A feller said Smoke Jensen was in town."

Banning frowned. "Jensen would never mix into something like this. Thinks he's too damned good to work for another man."

"Maybe so, maybe not," the gunslick opined. "Anyway, what'er we gonna do?"

"For starters, we're not going to leave," Banning told him firmly.

By late afternoon, some of the least confident among the gunmen began to drift out of town. A few more joined them the next morning. Many hung around though, to see how this hand would be played. Some soon learned, when the Rangers—and some local residents who had been deputized—began to make sweeps of the streets.

"You ride for one of the ranches around here?" Tallpockets Granger asked a pair of wannabe gunhawks lounging outside the barbershop.

"Nope."

"Then fork them scruffy mounts of yours and blow on out of here."

"What if we don't want to?"

Tallpockets's eyes turned to ice. "Then you'll be in jail faster than you can whistle the first two bars of 'Dixie.' "

From down the block, a voice of authority made a hard demand. "Move along. You don't have business in this town anymore. I'd make it fast, if I was you."

Three Arizona Rangers filled an intersection off the main street and began to walk along the dirt track. Every time they looked at a man, the subject of their scrutiny shied his eyes away and silently mounted up to ride out.

Slowly, the crowd of low-grade gunfighters began to thin noticeably. Most of them knew who was hiring and how much would be paid, Smoke Jensen believed, and many even knew how to find the B-Bar-H. No doubt they'd be heading that way.

He had to admit to Jeff and Walt that there was little they could do about it. They had spoken on the matter only a minute before one of Granger's men approached. "There's some hard cases over at Fanny Mae's parlor house say they're comin' out shootin'. One of them with a big mouth told us that they'd take on all comers at that windmill in the center of town."

Jeff and Walt cut their eyes to Smoke. The legendary gunfighter quirked his lips in a hint of a smile, and hitched up his cartridge belt. "Then I guess we'd better get down to the *Plaza de Armas*. This might get interesting after all."

Twenty-one

Seven self-styled *pistoleros* stood spread out in the central plaza of Socorro. A wooden windmill squeaked and groaned above them, the blades turning listlessly. The pump below musically sloshed water into a cuplike, leather harness over its spout. From there it ran through a pipe to a large, square, wooden tank that provided water for any horses so inclined, the local stray dogs, cats, and birds. Water lily pads dotted the surface. From its pedestal opposite, a statue of an armored Spaniard, bearing a long, lancelike cross, wrapped in the *Chi-Rho* flag of the Church of Rome, looked down on it all. When Smoke Jensen, Jeff York, and Walt Reardon rounded the corner of the adobe block building that housed the Mercado Central, the one in the middle took two long strides ahead of his henchmen.

"Hold it right there," he demanded. "I hear you badge-pushers done run some friends of mine out of town. I'm here to tell you that you ain't runnin' me out."

"Carry you out, more likely," Smoke replied in a tired voice.

"You ain't man enough. Ain't got the guts. Uh—who might you be?"

"Capt. Jeff York, Arizona Rangers," Jeff introduced himself.

That didn't seem to faze Banning, but he paled slightly when Walt said, "Walt Reardon. No doubt you've heard of me."

"Y-yeah. Can't believe you've turned lawdog. How about you," he directed at Smoke.

"Smoke Jensen."

Right then Orin Banning did a right peculiar thing, considering he faced three of the best gunfighters on the frontier. He gave his sidemen the signal and went for his gun. Most of them didn't clear leather before Smoke, Jeff, and Walt fired their first rounds.

One of the outlaws went down gagging, a hand clutching his belly. Another spun sideways, then turned back to the action with a vengeance. He put a bullet through Walt's left arm a moment before he died of .44 caliber poisoning from the pistol in the hand of Smoke Jensen.

Bullets zipped through the small garden of the *Plaza de Armas* as Smoke sought another target. He soon found one. A hard case from the short-lived Banning gang crouched behind the edge of the pedestal of the unknown Spanish don. He rested the barrel of a Winchester on the smoothed surface of granite. Smoke put stone chips in the man's eyes with a quick round. The shooter fell back screaming. A hearty boom came from the barrel of the short-barreled L.C. Smith double ten that Walt Reardon had swung up from behind his back, after he emptied his six-gun.

The shot column of 00 Buck lifted a short, squat gunslick off his boots and planted him in the water tank. He went under without so much as a second splash. Walt cut his eyes to Smoke, then Jeff, to make sure of their where-abouts, then swung the shotgun toward a new target. The wound in his arm bled profusely. Smoke Jensen headed his way, when he saw Walt Reardon's knees start to buckle.

"Hang on, old friend," Smoke encouraged. "We've got to stop the bleeding."

"In the middle of a shoot-out?" Walt asked wonder-ingly.

"Damn betcha," said Smoke as he forced a grin.

Bullets cracked overhead and to both sides, as Smoke quickly bound Walt's arm. He helped Walt to the edge of the artificial pond created by the water tank, and eased the younger man to the ground.

"You can cover us from here." To Jeff, "Time to clean out the rest of this vermin."

"I'm with you," Jeff agreed.

They faced only three living enemies. Orin Banning would have been fortunate to have died first. That way he wouldn't have to see the destruction of his gang. Smoke gave that passing thought as he darted between the neatly trimmed clumps of hedge that defined walk-ways through the plaza. He saw a flicker of movement to his left and spun on one heel.

Gunfire had attracted more of the ne'er-do-wells, like vultures to carrion. The newcomer had only a brief in-stant to see the badge on the chest of Smoke Jensen before the famous gunfighter busted a cap and sent the gunhawk off to join Orin Banning's men in Hell.

"Awh, damn," Smoke grumbled, as two more took the dying one's place.

* * *

Wildcat Wally Holt could not remember a time when he didn't have a gun in the waistband of his trousers or on his hip. He'd killed his first man at the age of eleven; shot him in the back. He had killed a dozen more since. At nineteen, Wildcat Wally saw himself as one of the best gunfighters in New Mexico Territory. Why, he had even been so bold as to compare himself with Billy Bonny. In less than thirty seconds, he was about to learn that he had nowhere near the speed, accuracy, or determination of Billy the Kid, let alone the man he suddenly found himself facing.

"You gonna use that thing, or sit on it?" Smoke Jensen asked of him as the youthful tough skidded into the center of the gunfight on the plaza.

"Yeeeaaaaah!" Wildcat Wally roared as he drew his Colt.

Or at least he tried to draw it. Suddenly his right arm would not obey him. Immense pain radiated from his shoulder through his chest and neck. Wildcat Wally jolted backward a few wobbly steps, and again tried to raise his six-gun. Nothing happened. Swiftly he made a grab for the Peacemaker on his left hip. He had it clear of leather when some unseen force punched him solidly in the center of his body, right below his ribs. A splash of crimson droplets rose before his eyes, as they started dimming.

Wildcat Wally next discovered that he could not breathe. He willed himself to draw deeply, yet his chest never moved. Slowly he dropped to his knees, an unbelieving expression on his face.

He worked his mouth. "Wh—who are you, Marshal?"

"Smoke Jensen."

"Go—good. At least it took the best to do me in." So saying, Wildcat Wally Holt lost all his wildness and slipped into the long slumber of death.

"Smoke, behind you!" Walt Reardon shouted from the water tank.

A Winchester gave its familiar .44-40 bark and Smoke Jensen felt a tug and fiery burning sensation along the right side of his ribs. He had dodged and started to turn at Walt's shout, which had saved his life. Now he faced the back-shooter and watched fear drain the smirk of triumph off the coward's face. Blood ran freely down Smoke's right side as he raised his gun and put a .44 period right between the would-be killer's running lights. The back of his head left with the gunman's hat, and he did a high kick backward into oblivion.

"Thanks, Walt."

"Any time, Smoke."

Three more hard cases, lured by the sound of action, dashed onto the plaza, weapons at the ready. Walt cut the legs out from under one of them with a load of buckshot. The other two turned in his direction to see the double zeroes of the L.C. Smith pointed their way. They also saw Smoke Jensen off to the right. The wounded man managed to fish his six-gun out from under him, and died instantly from a gunshot wound delivered by Jeff York, whom they had not seen off to their left.

Made desperate by the sudden confrontation, the remaining pair swung weapons toward Smoke and Walt. The scattergun ripped one's chest apart. Smoke pumped a round into the last man, who draped himself over the back of a wooden bench. A dozen others, wishing to

have no part of these deadly gunfighters, gave up a bad
cause.

It was then that Orin Banning reared up from behind
a low hedge and, screaming defiance, emptied his six-
gun in wild, stray rounds that hit no one. He jammed the
smoking weapon in his waistband and hauled another
six-gun from his left-hand holster.

"Smoke Jensen, you baaastard!" he yelled as he opened
fire.

Smoke dodged the first bullet, then returned fire. Banning grunted and staggered to one side. He got off another round, which plowed the ground between Smoke's
legs. Then Smoke's second slug caught Banning full in
the chest. That dropped him at last, amid the useless
dregs of human garbage that had formed his gang. All
at once the shooting stopped.

"Lay down your weapons and put hands in the air,"
Smoke Jensen demanded.

"What are you goin' to do to us?" one bleated.

"You're going to jail. When we have time to sort you
all out, we'll send you home," Jeff York added.

A straggly parade of glum, disgruntled would-be gunhawks wound along the way to the jail. Inside, Ferdie
Biggs had been talking with Sheriff Reno. When the prisoners trooped in, led by Jeff York, Ferdie cut his eyes to
the disgraced sheriff. He received a slight nod in response.

"Lock 'em up yourself," he grumbled to Jeff York.

Jeff took the keys from Ferdie as the latter pushed past
him. A moment later, Ferdie Biggs reached the office
section. Smoke Jensen bent over a seated Walt Reardon.
He changed the makeshift bandage and again insisted

that Walt see a doctor. With Smoke's back turned, Ferdie had all the encouragement he needed. His six-gun had already cleared leather with a soft, wicked whisper.

Before Ferdie Biggs could ear back the hammer, Smoke Jensen turned in an eye blink, his right fist filled with a big .45 Colt. Transfixed by surprise, Ferdie stupidly tried to continue. Smoke shot him twice before Ferdie could squeeze his trigger.

Ferdie's legs reflexed violently and catapulted him over the former sheriff's desk. He sprawled on the floor behind, twitched and shuddered, then sighed out his life.

"Damn, how'd you know?" Walt Reardon gulped out.

"I saw your eyes narrow," Smoke answered.

"I was going to call a warning to you."

"Ferdie didn't give you enough time, Walt. But that squint did enough to tip me off."

"What now?"

"We drag that garbage out of here, and get on with it," Smoke answered with a glance at the corpse.

With their assorted wounds properly tended to, Smoke Jensen, Jeff York, and half of the Rangers with Tallpockets rode directly toward the B-Bar-H. Walt Reardon stayed behind to hold the jail. Even as they rode past the town limits, more fast-gun types drifted into Socorro.

"We're mighty short on numbers," Jeff observed tight-lipped.

"I thought about that before we left." Smoke flashed a white-toothed grin. "So I brought along enough dynamite to lower the odds a little."

Jeff let out a low whistle. "Reckon this is the last go-round."

"It had better be."

They rode on in silence for a while. By late afternoon they reached the boundary of Benton-Howell's ranch. Smoke noticed it first. The split-rail fences had been filled in with rocks and dirt, to form parapets; behind them stood some twenty rifle-toting gunhawks, lured by the high money paid and a chance to test themselves against Smoke Jensen. Smoke and his men reined in just out of range.

"We aren't going through there, even with dynamite," Jeff opined.

"Don't go off too sudden, Jeff. What we need to do is look around a little more. We'll ride around the whole spread, and see how much is done up like this."

They made it only halfway around the ten sections controlled by Benton-Howell by nightfall. So far it appeared that only a half-section, some three-hundred-twenty acres, had been sealed off. Not all the approaches were covered by so many men. Smoke had led them out of sight of those guarding the road and gate, when they had been able to cross over onto the ranch property. Well-accustomed to the rigors of man hunting, the rangers made a cold camp.

Smoke sat, chewing on a strip of jerky, and took council from the stars. After a while, he rose to his boots and walked over to where Jeff York had already bedded down for the night. He squatted beside his friend and spoke softly.

"I've made up my mind. Come first light, we'll ride back to the Tucker place and send for the rest of Tallpockets's men. Then I'm going to fix up something that will get us through all those defenses."

"What do you have in mind, Smoke?"

"The dynamite got me to thinking on it. That and the wide gaps along this side that aren't being watched. You'll see what I'm doing when we get to working on it."

Smoke Jensen had added to the mystery by instructing the young Ranger headed for Socorro, "Bring the wainwright from town out here, when you come back."

Now, two days later, with night on the sawtooth ridges to the east, the curious among the Arizona Rangers stood around, watching while the wagon builder rigged an unusual attachment to a buckboard which Smoke Jensen had purchased from Martha Tucker. One of the older—which meant a man in his late twenties—Rangers scratched at a growing bald spot in his sandy hair, and worked his lips up for a good spit.

"Now, what the heck kind of thing do you call that?"

Laughing at something said inside, Smoke Jensen stepped out of the house and walked directly to the curious lawman. "That's a quick release lynch pin, to let the team get away from the wagon in time."

"Time for what?" the sandy-haired peace officer fired back.

"Come along with me and you'll see," Smoke promised.

At the rear of the buckboard, eleven wooden cases of dynamite, from Lawrence Tucker's private powder magazine, were being carefully loaded into the wagon. Baskets and barrels of scrap metal from the blacksmithy and sheds of the ranch were being emptied around and over the explosives, except for the one in the middle. It had its top off, and several sticks of sixty percent dynamite were missing.

"You buildin' a bombshell?" the seasoned Ranger asked.

"I thought you'd figure it out right quick," Smoke praised him. "When we get done, this will be like the largest exploding cannon shell in the world."

"How come that one case is open?"

"We get to that one last. After the wagon is in position for what I want it to do. That's the primer that's going to set off all the rest."

"Gol-ly, Mr. Jensen, I ain't never seen anythin' quite like this."

"Those on the receiving end will wish they had never seen this one."

"I want everyone to get a good night's rest," Jeff announced as he joined Smoke at the wagon. "We leave for the B-Bar-H at first light." To Smoke, he invited, "Time for another cup of coffee?"

Smoke Jensen cut his eyes skyward. "If I do, my eyes will turn brown. I'm going to grab a few winks."

"Sleep well," Jeff offered.

"You know it's funny, but I never do the night before a big fight," Smoke responded on his way to the bunk-house.

Twenty-two

Smoke Jensen saw at once that the time they had taken to prepare for the attack on the B-Bar-H had a double edge. It had given Benton-Howell the opportunity to strengthen his defenses. Instead of penetrating the outer ring of hastily made revetments on the north, they had to go around to the east, because of reinforcements who now patrolled where none had been before. It took some doing, and cost several hours to move slowly enough not to reveal the presence of their force of some twenty-five men and the wagon. Smoke oversaw the operation with patience and good humor.

"Look at it this way," he advised a grumbling ranch hand from the Tucker spread. "The longer goes by without an attack on the B-Bar-H, the more restless and bored those second- and third-rate gunhands are going to get. When we do hit, it will shock them right out of their boots."

"When do we hit them, then?"

"Tonight, well after dark, when all of them are relaxed and off their edge. The big thing is to get a hole cut in the outer defenses, wide enough to drive the wagon through without being detected."

"We have enough shovels along," Jeff York added, as

he rode up beside the buckboard being driven by Smoke Jensen. "Should go fast."

"That is if they aren't as thick around there as on the north," a gloomy Ranger commented.

"Ralph, you always look on the dark side," Jeff snapped.

"He has a point," Smoke Jensen injected. "Even if Benton-Howell doesn't have enough reinforcements now to cover the whole perimeter, we'll have to get rid of those on the east without making a sound. Knives and 'hawks if you've got them," he concluded through the scant opening between grimly straight lips.

Darkness had come an hour before and Pearly Cousins had given strict instructions to the gunmen who had accompanied him not to light up a smoke during their time on watch. It was hard enough seeing before the moon rose, let alone to be blinded by the flare of a lucifer. He yawned and stirred in his saddle. Pearly had been up late the night before, and had only five hours sleep in the past two days. We're stretched too thin, Pearly thought to himself. Best be checking on the lookouts along the east side of the wall. Some of them aren't wrapped all too tight.

Pearly didn't find the rider at the northeast corner. "Must be patrolin'," he muttered aloud. He turned south.

Close to where he expected to find two of the eight men guarding this side of the defenses jawing instead of doing their work, he came upon a riderless horse. That was something Pearly hadn't expected. It ignited the first suspicions.

"Lupe, you takin' a leak, or what?" Pearly asked in a muted voice.

When he received no answer, Pearly edged his horse forward and caught up the reins of the abandoned mount. Then he started inward to seek the negligent sentry. He did not go far before he dimly saw a huddled form on the ground. The black silhouette of a big Mexican sombrero two feet from the body identified it as Lupe. His alarms jangling now, Pearly dismounted and crouched beside the unmoving man.

Pearly rolled Lupe onto his back. Pearly saw that Lupe's throat had been slit from ear to ear. Stealthy motion caught Pearly's eyes, as a huge human figure rose from the brush directly in front of him. He heard a soft *swish* a moment before the tomahawk in the hand of Smoke Jensen split Pearly's skull to his jawbone.

Smoke wrenched his 'hawk free and cleaned it on the dead outlaw's shirt front. He tucked it back behind his belt, and set off for the spot he judged to be directly in line with the ranch house. When he reached the place, he found the other night stalkers there ahead of him.

"Had an extra one to take care of," he explained. "We had better get started."

Taking turns at the dirt barrier, the lawmen spent only half an hour opening a space wide enough to admit the buckboard. Smoke drove, while Jeff led the mountain man's roan stallion. The Arizona Rangers and ranch hands formed a crescent-shaped line to right and left.

A mile inside the outer defenses, Smoke called a halt. "Time to set the primer charge," he announced tightly.

With that accomplished, the posse started up again. Smoke had allowed enough fuse for what he thought approximated twenty minutes. He would light it a moment before they topped the rise to the east of the house. Then he would set the team in a gallop, and make ready for the rest of the plan. If it didn't work the way he expected, if the fuse burned too quickly, then he would never know it.

"Good luck," Jeff York said tightly thirty minutes later, as the lawmen dropped back to let the wagon take the lead.

Smoke Jensen lit the fuse, and slapped the reins lightly on the rumps of the wheelers. The team dug in, the sixteen hooves of the draft animals pounded the ground with increasing speed. They crested the steep swale, and the velocity increased. Smoke snapped the reins again. He stood upright now, a small rope wrapped around his gloved left hand. The rumbling of the buckboard's wheels drowned out the sound of the mounts of the lawmen with him.

Closer loomed the mounded dirt that formed the inner fortifications. Smoke Jensen drove straight at the parapet. Flame lanced at the wagon from half a dozen places. Still Smoke remained upright, swaying with the erratic motion of the heavily laden buckboard. The vehicle careened onward. Closer, ever closer . . . the blackness of the hastily erected defenses filled Smoke's field of vision. He pulled slightly on the cord in his left hand, felt the lynch pin loosen. Any time now . . . any . . .

NOW!

Smoke dropped the reins and yanked the lynch pin.It came free, and the horses, undirected now, curved from the mass before them, the tongue carried between their churning bodies. Smoke jumped free and rolled in the tall grass. Suddenly Jeff York swerved in close at the side of Smoke Jensen. He trailed the reins of Smoke's roan. Without breaking stride, Jeff flashed past. Smoke readied himself and leaped for the saddle horn. He caught it and swung atop his rutching stallion.

Immediately they all curved away and outward from the barrier. Five seconds later, the wagon struck the solid wall of dirt with a thunderous crash. A heartbeat later it exploded with a roar that came from the end of the world.

Waiting for an attack that might or might not come had started to get on his nerves. Geoffrey Benton-Howell paced the thick oriental rug in his study, hands clasped behind his back. His eyes cut frequently to the crystal decanter of brandy on the sideboard that formed part of a wall of bookshelves. No, that wouldn't do, he thought forcefully.

This was no night to get lost in the heady fumes of the grape. Not any night was fit for tippling until that offensive son of a bitch, Smoke Jensen, had been hunted down and eliminated. Nearly a week had passed since Jensen and the Rangers had cleared out Socorro. It did little to improve his outlook to know that the town had filled up once again with eager fast guns. Most of the Rangers had disappeared, and the remainder had forted up in the jail. He needed to get those new men involved in a search for Jensen. Benton-Howell sighed heavily, almost a gasp, and crossed to the door.

He leaned through the opening and called down the hall to the large sitting room. "Miguel, I need you in here for a moment."

When Miguel Selleres entered the paneled study, Benton-Howell had arranged his thoughts in order. Selleres likewise declined any liquor. He seated himself in a large, horsehair-stuffed leather chair and rested elbows on the arms. He steepled his long fingers and spoke over them.

"So, you have grown tired of waiting, *amigo?*"

"Just so. I want you to take two of the better gunmen and ride into Socorro. Organize that rabble, and set them off hunting for Smoke Jensen."

"I thought we had agreed to make him come to us here."

"We did. Only I don't think it is working."

Suddenly, as though to put the lie to Benton-Howell's pronouncement, a ragged volley of gunfire broke out at the dirt barricade that surrounded the house and barn. There followed a moment of silence, then a violent crash of splintering wood. Then the darkness washed away in a wall of sheer whiteness. The sound of the explosion, like a thunderclap directly overhead, came a second later. The shockwave blew every window on that side of the building inward.

It knocked books from the shelves and set the brandy decanter to dancing. Stunned to immobility, the two plotters stared at each other. Fighting for words, Benton-Howell got control of his voice first.

"They're attacking! Take charge of the men. There's no time to head for town. We have to stop them."

"Someone else can go, Stalker perhaps, and bring the others back. They could hit the Rangers in the rear."

"It's half a day in and the same back," Benton-Howell reminded. "By then we could all be dead."

"Or worse, on the way to jail," Miguel Selleres riposted.

Shuddering, Benton-Howell dismissed such weakening visions and began to organize the defenses. "Get torches lit; the men can't see which way to shoot. Are the sandbags in place around the outer walls?"

"Yes, since yesterday. Both floors."

"Have men at every window. Bolt the doors."

Sparks from the fuses in single sticks of dynamite began to make twinkling trails through the black of night. The blasts began to rout men caught in the open yard. Some bolted for the covered passageway that led to the well nearest the house. They made it without incident, only to be forced to cringe on the ground when holes began to appear in the wooden walls, as hot lead cracked through at chest level.

Sharp blasts illuminated the yard, as the dynamite began to explode. Their flashes strobed the action of the disoriented outlaws in the ranch yard. Two went down, shot through the chest, and a screech of agony came from another who had caught a short round in the groin. With a muffled curse, Miguel Selleres rushed from the room to bring order out of the chaos.

Fully a third of the defenders had been knocked off their feet by the tremendous explosion, Smoke Jensen noted as he and Jeff rode through the breach created in the parapet. Dust and the acrid odor of dynamite smoke still hung in the air. Jeff pointed to the rubble of scattered earth.

"If they'd used gabions, that wouldn't have worked," the Arizona Ranger said.

"What are those?"

"Sort of tubelike baskets, made of reeds or thin tree branches; they're used in building fortifications." Jeff looked sort of embarrassed. "I learned that from General Crook, when I scouted for the army."

Smoke grunted. "Good thing the one who built this didn't know it."

Bullets cracked past Smoke and Jeff, and they saw that some of those not effected by the blast had recovered enough to offer resistance. One of the Tucker hands yelped, and clapped a hand to a profusely bleeding wound in his right arm. The shooter didn't have time to celebrate his victory. Smoke Jensen put a .44 round in his ear, and sent him, brainless, onto the outlaw level of Hell.

Suddenly a pack of dogs charged into the yard from a run behind the house. One launched itself and sank fangs into the leg of an Arizona Ranger. The lawman screamed as the teeth savaged him. He swung with the barrel of his revolver. It made a hollow sound when it struck the flat, triangular head of the bristling mastiff.

That had no effect on his grip though. He hung on, his body weight sagging downward, ripping his fangs through tender flesh. Tallpockets Granger whirled in his saddle and shot the vicious monster through the head. It fell away with a whimper and twitched violently on the ground. Another of the beasts, crazed by the explosive blasts, leaped on the back of one of the hired guns. His shrieks could be heard until the huge dog reached his throat. h'

"Keep clear of them," Smoke called out. "They'll do us more good than harm."

Smoke pulled a fused stick of dynamite from his saddlebag and lit it from a cigar clinched in his teeth. He hurled it toward the house. It hit the window frame and bounced off. A moment later it went off with a blinding flash and roar.

More quickly followed from the Arizona Rangers. Two more of the savage dogs died in attempts to attack strangers among the outlaw defenders. Smoke rounded the house and found himself facing two hard cases with sixguns cocked and ready. His right hand dropped to the curved butt-grips of his .44 Colt. One of the gunslingers fired before Smoke finished his draw.

His bullet cut a hot trail along Smoke's left side, below the rib cage. Then Smoke had his Peacemaker clear and in action. It bucked sharply, and he emptied the saddle of the second outlaw. Hammer back and another sharp recoil as the .44 belched. It spat hot lead that ended the ambitions of a would-be giant-killer. Smoke chucked another stick of explosives through a window and spun away.

The blast, muffled somewhat, blew out two walls of the kitchen. Plaster dust and powder smoke made a heavy fog that was all too easy for the hard-pressed gunhawks to hide in. Smoke knew that the noise they had made would soon attract the larger portion of the gunslick army from their outer defenses. He had taken that into consideration in his plans. Now, he decided, would be the time to pull out. He worked the thin leather glove off his right hand and put thumb and forefinger between his lips.

He whistled shrilly and headed at once for the gap

blown in the defenses. The Arizona Rangers and Tucker ranch hands streamed behind him. Only a few random shots followed them. That and the shrill, patently hysterical curses of Geoffrey Benton-Howell.

In the cold, hard light of dawn, Geoffrey Benton-Howell and Miguel Selleres surveyed the damage. Every window in the house had been blown out again. Two walls of the kitchen had been scattered over the ranch yard, and the second-floor extension sagged precariously over what remained. Food had to be prepared in the bunkhouse and the outdoor rock-lined fire pits. Those of the hired guns who remained, shivered in the chill, early morning air as they waited in line for coffee, beans, and fatback.

Half an hour later, as the partners accepted plates of food from the grizzled range cook, a patrol sent out at first light returned.

"Then Rangers blew holes in the barricades in half a dozen places on their way out," Charlie Bascomb, who had led them, reported. "Any time they want, they can pour through on us like water through a sieve."

"Damn him to eternal hell!" Benton-Howell blurted. "It's the doing of Smoke Jensen, you can be certain of that."

"*¡Oye, amigo! No te dejes poner los verdes.* He is only a man," Miguel Selleres jokingly told his partner.

"I am *not* letting him pull the wool over my eyes," Benton-Howell snapped angrily. "You know as well as I what that man has done to us. It's not natural, not . . . human! We started this project off with him waiting a lynch mob in the Socorro jail. Now he has nearly destroyed my home."

"What do you propose?" Selleres prompted.

Benton-Howell considered that a while. "It's obvious that the ranch is not secure enough. There are ample gunmen waiting in Socorro to assist us. If we move the Tuckers into town, Smoke Jensen will hear of it. We can draw him out and make him fight on ground of our choosing."

Selleres played the devil's advocate. "What if he's waiting for us on the way?"

Benton-Howell shaped his plan aloud. "We'll take everyone from here, form a screen of protection around us and our hostages. Once we reach town, we'll be safe enough. You'll see."

Walt Reardon met the raiding party when Smoke Jensen brought the men back to the Tucker ranch. His grim expression alerted Smoke to possible new problems. He and Jeff met with the ex-gunfighter in the kitchen over coffee and sweet rolls.

Walt chomped on a yeasty cinnamon roll, and washed it down with a long swallow of Arbuckle's Arabica before revealing what brought him to the ranch. "Something big is building up in town." Walt cut his eyes to Jeff. "The Rangers you left me have been overpowered one by one, and completely disappeared. Socorro's runnin' chock-a-block with ne'er-do-wells and gunslingers. Somethin' big's cookin', I can feel it in my bones."

"Any ideas?" Smoke prompted. "We did a fair job of rattling Benton-Howell and his gunhands on the ranch."

He looked at the table, chagrined by the admission he had to make. "We were too outnumbered to make a push to get the Tuckers out."

Walt shook his head. "I got this feelin' somethin' big is comin' on. If nothin' else, we need to find those missing Rangers."

Smoke Jensen came to his boots, thumbs hooked in the front of his cartridge belt. "I agree. Cuchillo Negro's warriors are needed to guard the ranch, so I suggest we take the Rangers we have on hand, any hands who volunteer, and head for Socorro."

Twenty-three

Clear, sharp eyes, undimmed by long afternoons and nights of drinking and carousing in the saloons of Socorro, first spotted the large plume of dust that rose from the horses of the Rangers and ranch hands. It took little time to realize that trouble rode toward town. Even so, the alert gunhawk placed on lookout on the north edge of Socorro waited until he could count heads, make certain who and how much trouble was headed his way. Then he sent one of the hungover wannabes to report his findings.

"Go to the Exchange Hotel and tell Mr. Benton-Howell that twenty-three men are headed this way. Tell him Smoke Jensen and that Ranger are in the lead."

The two-bit gunslick ambled away, while he held his head with one hand and licked dry lips, wishing for a little hair of the dog—no, wolf—that had bit him the night before. He found the lordly Englishman in the saloon of the Exchange, which gave him an excuse to get a drink.

First he had to report, which he did, cringing a little from the expression of wrath that grew on Benton-Howell's' face. When he delivered the message, he turned toward the bar. "No drinking. Not today," Benton-Howell declared imperiously. "Every man must be sober for what is sure to come." He turned to Quint Stalker, who sat at a table drinking coffee, which he had surreptitiously laced with rum in defiance of the orders of the big boss.

"Quinten, I want you to deliver a message to Smoke Jensen. Under a flag of truce, naturally."

"Sure, Boss. What do you want to say?"

Benton-Howell told him and sent the gang leader on his way. On the slow ride to the edge of town, Quint Stalker tied a strip of white petticoat to the barrel of his Winchester. He had torn it from the undergarment of a soiled dove he had encountered on the street. He reached the city limits only a minute before Smoke and the posse thundered up to the wooden bridge that crossed the dry creek. Quint hoisted his white flag, and showed himself in the middle of the road.

"I got a message for Smoke Jensen," he called out.

Smoke edged forward on his roan stallion. "Spit it out."

"Mr. Benton-Howell done told me to tell you that he's turned Miz Tucker an' her brats over to Miguel Selleres. *Señor* Selleres has orders to kill them slowly, starting with the youngest kid, if you don't give yourself up within one hour."

Anger flared in Smoke's chest. He dare not risk the lives of the Tuckers further, yet he had no intention of providing target practice for a bunch of second-rate *pistoleros*. He had to buy some time.

"Do you know what happened in the Middle Ages when a messenger brought bad news?" he asked Stalker.

"No, what?"

"They killed him."

Stalker blanched. "Now, look, I'm under a flag of truce. You got no call to kill me. It ain't fair," he ended with a nervous titter.

"Very little is in this life," Smoke returned.

Stalker knew enough about the gunfighter business to know Jensen wanted something, a deal, a way out. "You got that right. What are you after, Jensen?"

A bleak smile answered him for a long moment, and Quint Stalker felt a chill as the icy gray eyes of Smoke Jensen bored into him. "Time. I didn't expect to find the Tuckers here. need to rethink things."

Sensing he had regained the upper hand, Stalker snapped, "You've got an hour, that's what The Man said."

"I need more than that. Make it two hours. Tell Benton-Howell that if I see the Tucker family, alive and well, after that, I'll come in alone."

"No tricks?"

"Your boss has all the aces, Stalker," Smoke Jensen replied in a disarming tone.

"I'll see what I can do." Smirking, Stalker turned on one boot heel. Then he threw over his shoulder, "If you hear a gunshot an hour from now, you'll know Mr. Benton-Howell has rejected your terms."

"Damn! What do we do now?" Jeff York exploded.

"It's a rigged deck, the way I see it," Smoke told him bluntly. "It's too obvious to mention what will happen, if I go in there alone. If I don't go in, the Tuckers will die. Benton-Howell is a desperate man."

"I can believe that," Jeff allowed. "He has to see that

his scheme is falling apart. Even if he gets you, there's no way he can bring it off."

"My thoughts, too, Jeff. So, here's what we'll do," Smoke offered. Without hesitation he laid out his plans.

Ten minutes went by before Tallpockets Granger walked his mount down the main street of Socorro, a white shirt tied to the muzzle of his rifle. He stopped outside the Exchange Hotel and called out for Quint Stalker. When Quint appeared, Tallpockets waved the white flag over his head to make it clear that he was under truce. Then he leaned forward and spoke eye to eye with Stalker.

"Smoke Jensen wants to talk to you again. He says he wants to spell out the manner of his surrender."

"I'll be right with you." Stalker returned to the hotel, to walk back out in less than half a minute. "The Boss says that's all right with him."

They rode together to the edge of town. There, Stalker threw a look of contempt at Smoke Jensen and spoke in a crisp tone of command. "Mr. Benton-Howell said you were in no position to set terms. But he agreed to listen this time. What is it you have in mind?"

"I've decided to turn myself in. Provided that the Tuckers are unharmed. And I want to see them riding away from town, alone, or no deal. They go free before I reach the center of town. And no back-shooting, or the rest of my friends here will take Socorro apart, regardless of what happens to me or the Tuckers. Benton-Howell and Selleres will hang, and there won't be a one of those two-bit *pistoleros* left alive."

Anger rose to choke Stalker, so that he spluttered when he snapped, "That's bluster, Jensen, and you know it. You must be gettin' old. Old and yellow, deep down in your core, or you'd not be runnin' yer mouth instead of your gun."

Fire replaced the ice in the eyes of Smoke Jensen. "You want to try me now?"

Quint Stalker hesitated a moment, and Smoke Jensen thought, *gotcha!* "Another time. I'll take what you said to the Boss, and we'll see." He turned his mount and rode away.

Fifteen minutes later, he returned. "Mr. Benton-Howell agrees," Quint Stalker shouted across the dry creek. "I'm to accompany you to the jail to see there are no tricks . . . from either side."

"How noble of you," Smoke responded sarcastically.

Stalker looked hurt. "I insisted on it. I admire you for this, Jensen, and I wanted to make sure there was no hanky-panky on either side."

Quint Stalker's words raised Jensen's assessment of the outlaw leader. He shrugged and cut his eyes to Jeff, "You know what to do." To Stalker, "Let's get on with it." Smoke eased his roan onto the bridge.

From that first step, Smoke felt his gut tighten with sour tension. At each step the horses took, a spot between his shoulder blades grew warmer and tingled with anticipation of a bullet to rend and tear his flesh and end his life. Not one to fear death, the mountain man still had a healthy regard for living. By the end of the first block, with not a hard case in sight, Smoke began to gauge each building as the possible spot from which the assassin's bullet would come.

Beside him, Quint Stalker appeared to be equally apprehensive. His eyes cut from side to side, suspicion deeply planted on his face. Sweat popped out on his brow, and he licked his lips continuously. Smoke suspicioned that Stalker's palms oozed moisture inside the black leather gloves.

"Don't you trust your masters?" Smoke taunted, partly to break his own chain of anxiety.

"Of course—come to think of it, not a hell of a lot. It's me that's the target out here, not them."

"Good thinking, Stalker."

Another block further along, Stalker nodded toward the balcony of the Exchange Hotel. "Over there."

Smoke cut his eyes to three tiny figures standing there. Jimmy, Rose, and Tommy Tucker huddled close together, the older boy's arms protectively around the shoulders of his siblings. They had all been crying, and began again at the sight of Smoke Jensen riding in a prisoner.

"Don't let 'em do it to you, Smoke," Jimmy's high, thin voice cut through the dust haze to Smoke's ears.

Smoke gave the boy a short, friendly wave. Lace curtains at a second-floor front window fluttered and drew apart. A Mexican *pistolero* stood beside Martha Tucker, a wicked grin whitening his face under a thick, drooping moustache. Smoke reined in. He jabbed a finger at the hostages and spoke harshly.

"Bring them down here. Now."

Quint Stalker sighed heavily and shrugged. "This is the part makes me uneasy. They don't get loose, until you're locked in jail. The Boss ordered it that way."

Smoke Jensen started a curse, broke if off, knowing it to be futile. If the shooting started now, the Tuckers would die for certain. "Never could abide two-faced bastards like your Benton-Howell," he growled bitterly.

"Truth to tell, I ain't too fond of him, myself," Stalker muttered.

Smoke eyed him thoughtfully. "Ever think of changing sides?" From the light that glowed in Stalker's eyes, Smoke knew that he had planted a seed in fertile soil. "Let's get on with it."

At the jail, without a shot fired, Stalker dismounted, tied off his horse, then drew his six-gun. He covered Smoke while Jensen climbed from the saddle and let himself be led into the office. With Ferdie Biggs no longer among the living, a new jailer had been selected. His smirking grin revealed a missing front tooth and the yellow stain of an inveterate tobacco chewer. Quint Stalker removed Smoke's cartridge belt and twin .44s and tossed them on the desk. Then the jailer revealed his nature to be much like his predecessor.

He took two quick steps forward and solidly punched Smoke Jensen in the ribs. Pain shot through Smoke from the bullet scrapes on both sides, as he rocked with the blows. He caught another pair in the gut, and fought the urge to double over from the effect. Carefully he sucked in fresh air.

"Are you any relation to Ferdie Biggs?" Smoke asked in as calm a voice as he could manage.

"Naw, I ain't no kin of his."

"Funny, there's such a resemblance," Smoke taunted.

Smoke's taunt had the desired effect. With a roar the lout lunged forward again without any caution. Smoke's hard, looping left caught him on the point of his protruding jaw; the gunfighter put all his body behind it. He had the satisfaction of hearing a loud snap and feel the loose wobble of bone before the jailer dropped like a stone.

"Gawdamn!" Stalker blurted.

"He needed that."

Awe filled the eyes of Quint Stalker, as he nodded his head in agreement. "I still gotta lock you up. You know the way."

Down the corridor of the cellblock, Smoke found three of the missing Rangers, locked together in one large cell. No doubt the holding tank for drunks. They all had depression written on their faces.

"In you go," Quint Stalker said with a wink.

He opened the cage, and Smoke joined his three allies. Without further comment, Stalker left the cellblock and the jail and returned to the Exchange Hotel.

Deft, brown fingers worked at the fastenings of the wire basket that enclosed the cork. With it pried open and removed, two thumbs pried the cork until it popped loudly and flew to the ceiling of the men's bar in the Exchange Hotel. A shower of bubbles followed. Laughing, Miguel Selleres turned to the four other men in the room.

"We have much to celebrate, *Señores*. Our good friend, Sheriff Reno, is out of jail and . . . Smoke Jensen is inside!"

"Not to mention we still have the hostages, old boy," Geoffrey Benton-Howell chortled as he presented his glass to be filled.

"More important, the Tuckers will not be released until

the ranch is signed over to the three of us," Dalton Wade crowed.

"They'll not be released even then," Benton-Howell stated quietly, instantly drawing the attention of Sheriff Reno, Dalton Wade, and Miguel Selleres.

"Whatever do you mean by that, Sir Geoffrey?" Dalton Wade asked, concern creasing his brow.

"There's no percentage in leaving behind any living witnesses. Surely you see the wisdom of that, Dalton."

"My word. I'd never given that problem any consideration. Isn't it a bit savage to take the lives of women and children?"

Benton-Howell peered at his partner over the rim of his champagne glass. "We live in brutal times, my friend. We cannot afford to have anyone—outside of ourselves— left to bear tales of how we obtained all this property and the wealth of that gold field in the White Mountains. Oh, yes, I have been assured the transfer will take place as promised. You can see the importance now, can you not? Not even these troublesome Arizona Rangers must escape our little cleanup."

"Yes," Selleres agreed. "Which brings us to what means to use to dispose of Smoke Jensen."

All four men remained silent with their thoughts a moment. Then a beatific smile spread on the face of Benton-Howell.

"I think the most demeaning, humiliating, degrading form of death should be applied to Smoke Jensen. Unfortunately, there is not a single guillotine to be had in this forsaken country. So, I suggest we hang him. How ignoble."

Soft applause came from Dalton Wade and Miguel

Selleres. Sheriff Reno nodded approval. As did Quint
Stalker, who had to fight to keep his face rigidly devoid
of any expression. The plotters were convinced of the
complete defeat of Smoke Jensen, only the outlaw leader
felt no surprise when a cacophony of sound blasted into
the elegant barroom, followed by the crumbling of stone
and brickwork from the direction of the jail.

Following Smoke Jensen's instructions, the Rangers
watched until he disappeared into the jail, then drifted
off in groups of threes and fours. They made their way
out of sight of town at the slow pace of men who had
reluctantly admitted their cause to be lost, yet unwilling
to leave in a body. The ruse worked, Jeff York realized
half an hour later when no pursuit had begun against
them.

At that point, Geoffrey Benton-Howell had as yet to
pronounce their death sentences along with the rest. After
the Rangers departed, Quint Stalker had withdrawn the
lookouts, leaving only some of the hungover dregs to
keep watch, so that his men could join in the celebration.
Before he had returned to the hotel, he noted a number
of those who had come bounty hunting, drift off toward
more promising fields. He would soon regret that.

Jeff York and six men had no difficulty in slipping
unobserved into Socorro. They went directly to the jail,
located the cell holding Smoke Jensen and the missing
Rangers. They cut short any reunion for the business at
hand.

"Get mattresses," Jeff instructed curtly. "Sit down
clear of this wall, cover yourselves, and hold your ears."

"Awh, crap, Jeff, you ain't gonna blow us outta here, are you?" one lanky, horse-faced Ranger complained.

"Come up with a better way, and I won't have to," Jeff quipped.

While he spoke, Jeff rigged a bundle of dynamite sticks to the wall, close to the small window, which he figured for the weakest point. With everything in readiness, he lit the fuse and cleared out with his Rangers. The blast reverberated all over town, bounced off the steep walls of the gorge in which the village had been built, punished ears for a quarter mile, and set dogs to howling hysterically.

It didn't do too much for the men in the cell, for that matter. The brick wall within the native fieldstone one pummeled them with chunks that would leave bruises the next day. Even with fingers in ears and mouths open, the pressure was enormous. Two Rangers lost consciousness, and Smoke Jensen discovered he had a bloody nose. A tad bit more dynamite, and they'd all be playing harps for St. Peter, he thought dazedly as the caustic fumes and mortar dust swirled around him. Only indistinctly did he hear the pound of hooves, as Jeff and his volunteers rushed back to extricate them from the jail.

Upright beside Jeff York, Smoke Jensen gestured to the ruined building they had just exited. "We have to get our weapons."

"Already taken care of."

Smoke frowned as the import of that struck him. "Then why in Billy blue hell did you try to turn us into red mush?"

"Thought it might scare hell out of some of these tender feet gunhawks."

"You did a fair job of that on us." Jeff gave a shrug, so Smoke continued, "Give me my rig, and let's go get these bastards who hide behind women and children."

Twenty-four

Geoffrey Benton-Howell had no doubt as to the source of the explosion. He immediately sent Quint Stalker to organize the horde of gunslingers who milled about the streets of Socorro, most of them confused as to what was going on. Miguel Selleres went upstairs at once, to make sure the Tuckers remained secure in the Exchange Hotel. He spoke urgently to the guards outside the door to the room that held the children.

"No one gets in there, none of our own or any lawmen."

"Sí, Señor Selleres," one Sonoran *pistolero* responded respectfully. "Not a soul will get past us."

"See to it." Selleres went on down the hall to where Mrs. Tucker had been kept. "Unlock it," he demanded. Inside, he crossed to a small table where Martha Tucker sat taking her evening meal. He shaped his features to show pleading. *"Señora,* there is going to be a great deal of bloodshed. You can prevent it. Simply sign the ranch over to us . . ." Selleres ended with hands outstretched, palms up in silent appeal.

"I do not believe in fairy-tales, *Señor* Selleres. The moment I sign those papers, myself and my children are dead. On the other hand, I can trust that for now, no stray bullet will strike any of us."

Selleres hardened his face. "Can you trust that we will not kill you outright, rather than let you fall into the hands of Smoke Jensen?"

A chill-ran along Martha's spine. She girded herself for the answer she knew she had to make. "If you are that thoroughly reprehensible, then I can only place my trust in the Lord . . . and Smoke Jensen."

A burst of gunfire from down the street interrupted the hot retort that started from the lips of Miguel Selleres. He turned on one boot heel and started for the door.

Two gun-toting henchmen appeared high up in the windows of the feed mill. The tinkle of broken glass alerted those below. Smoke Jensen went to one knee and snugged the Winchester .44 carbine to his shoulder in one smooth motion. Jeff York raised his Colt, and put a .45 round through the corrugated metal skin of the grain elevator.

It expanded as it went its way, and slammed into flesh an inch above the buckle on the cartridge belt of one hard case. He jolted forward in reaction to his wound, and lurched through the window sash. His startled companion had only a moment to hear the agonized scream, as Smoke Jensen put out his lights for all time with a hot lead snuffer. The sniper's body jerked backward and out of view.

"That was close," Jeff observed.

"They never got off a shot," Smoke reminded him.

Halfway down the next block, four men ranged across

the street. They had a variety of mismatched weapons, which spoke for their lack of expertise. What they lacked in knowledge they made up for in courage—or foolishness. All four entered the dance with blazing six-guns.

Smoke Jensen downed one easily, and heard the nearby crack of a bullet that sailed past his head. He lined his sights on another as two more weapons opened up through windows on the second floor above the general mercantile. He made a quick shot at his target, missed, and swung the muzzle of the Winchester upward. Three rounds levered through the Winchester silenced one of the hidden assassins. From behind Smoke the six-gun of Tallpockets roared and spat flame.

"They ain't gonna do any back-shootin'," the lanky Arizona Ranger remarked casually.

"We have to get to the Exchange Hotel fast," Smoke urged. "Every minute puts the Tuckers in more danger."

"Was I doin' it," Tallpockets drawled, "I'd get me away from here an' come at 'em from behind. Let me an' the boys take care of Main Street."

Smoke smiled broadly. "I appreciate the offer, Tallpockets. And I'll take you up on it. Jeff, Walt, and I will take this alley and come at the hotel from the back door."

"Three of you gonna be enough?" Tallpockets asked, then he looked over the trio indicated, grunted, and answered his own question. "I reckon so."

The street fighting grew fiercer as the outlaw scum and bounty-hungry drifters realized a major push was on against them. The way they saw it, they had to stand their ground; they simply had no way to go and no money to take them there. While they hotted up the battle,

Smoke, Jeff, and Walt darted down an alleyway and turned into the one that paralleled the main street. Three blocks to the hotel, and no way of knowing how many of Benton-Howell's gunhands they would encounter.

They made it only a block, and ran into half a dozen desperate men forted up in the rear of the saddler's shop. Lead flew thick and fast. Smoke Jensen felt a searing pain just below the point of his right shoulder, and cut his eyes to a ragged tear in the cloth of his shirt. Another fraction of an inch, and he'd be dripping blood again. Suddenly one of the defenders showed enough head for a clear shot.

Smoke took it with his old .44. The hat of the hard case flew off as his head snapped back. His eyes glazed as he sagged to the floor. A pair of boot heels could be heard pounding on the floorboards, headed for the front. That slackened the fire enough for Jeff York to dart along the alley, past the shop. From that angle, he poured fire into the back of the saddlery. Smoke and Walt did the same.

A couple of yowls of pain came from the interior. Then the firing lessened. A table, hastily put in place to barricade the back door, slid noisily across the floor. Nervous sounding, a voice called to them.

"That does it. We give up! We're coming out."

Smoke Jensen knew the darkness served as an ally to the dangerous men inside. He set himself and responded, "Come out one at a time. Hands in sight."

"Sure—sure. Don't shoot us, huh?"

A moment later the door opened, and a man's silhouette appeared in the frame. He advanced, hands at shoulder height, palms forward. So far, so good. Another man followed a moment later. When the body of the first to surrender blocked the view, the second man reached forward and yanked a hidden six-gun from the small of his partner's back. He threw a shot in the general direction of Smoke Jensen.

And died for his treachery. Smoke drilled him through the left eye. Bleating his nonexistent innocence, the first man went to his knees. The three lawmen ignored him for the moment, and concentrated on the others. A trio of rounds sped through the doorway, and the others came out so docile that one would think they were in church.

"That's more like it," Jeff York growled.

They quickly trussed up their prisoners and left them for the other Rangers to tend to. Of one accord, Smoke and his companions started off toward the hotel. Smoke found the back door first. He tried it, found it latched, and pondered their problem.

"This isn't going to be as easy as we thought," he advised the others. "If we make any noise going in there, they just might kill Martha and the children."

Whether by chance or design, the beleaguered gunfighters in the streets of Socorro drew back on the Exchange Hotel and the few buildings immediately around it. There they rallied and put up a determined resistance. Without a foolish risk of life, the Arizona Rangers could not expose themselves to make a frontal assault. Gradually it became obvious to everyone that the battle had degenerated into a standoff.

By one-thirty in the morning, only a few of the more aggressive individuals took potshots at their counterparts.

Another problem presented itself, brought to the attention of Smoke Jensen by Walt Reardon.

"We've got more prisoners than places to put them. Blowin' out that wall weren't such a good idea. That drunk tank could hold an easy twenty, twenty-five."

Smoke thought a moment. "Go to the Tinto Range Supply. There should be some barbed wire there. Use all you need to crisscross that opening like a spiderweb. Then put some men to guarding it. Some of the Tucker hands should be fine for that. They aren't getting paid to be shot at. Jeff and I will hold the fort here."

"Mighty interestin' idea. Just might work." Walt scooted out of there.

Within half an hour, prisoners had begun to be shifted from the grain bins of the livery into the holding cell of the jail. The first ones inside stared in stunned disbelief at what appeared to be a gaping hole in the wall.

"C'mon, boys, let's make a break for it," Wink Winkler muttered to those nearest to him. He made a dash for the opening, only to be caught in midair on the all but invisible strands of barbed wire. He howled in agony and thrashed a while, until he realized he only made it worse.

"Never did like that damned stuff," one hard-faced gunman remarked.

"Been more than one war fought over it," another agreed.

"Git me down offa here," Winkler wailed.

"Sure, but it'll smart some."

"You get close to that wire, and I'll blow your head off," came a voice from outside.

"Do something, get me off of here!" Wink Winkler wailed on the verge of hysteria.

"Reckon I could shoot you, to put you out of your misery," the Tucker wrangler suggested.

Morning brought no change in the stalemate. It also did not provide any easy access into the hotel. Smoke Jensen left Jeff York and three Arizona Rangers to watch the back exit to the Exchange Hotel, while he scouted for ideas. He found a possible solution within a block of the two-story structure.

He also received some bad news. Simms, one of the Rangers, came upon Smoke while he was trying to drag a tall ladder out of a litter of barrels and boxes outside the back of a store. The bantam rooster of a lawman announced that he sought Jeff York.

"Jeff's at the Exchange Hotel back door."

"We've got more troubles," Simms replied. "Durin' the night, more of this border scum drifted into town. Seems as how they got us caught between the ones we've corralled, and themselves."

Smoke Jensen gave it only a moment's thought. Using the ladder to scale to the second floor windows at the back of the hotel would have to wait. "When you're surrounded, there's only one thing to do."

"Surrender?" Simms asked doubtfully.

"Where've you been all your life? What we're going to do is attack in both directions at once." Smoke set off immediately to inform Jeff.

Eyes glazed with blood lust, the newcomers to Socorro sensed an easy kill. They moved in on the thin line of

Rangers with weapons in hand. Their shock was complete then, when half of the lawmen turned on them and opened fire, while the remainder yelled chillingly and charged buildings to either side of a large hotel. The rapid-fire crackle of rifles and six-guns drowned out the exclamations of consternation.

Three of the hard cases went down in a hail of bullets. Two ran toward the partial shelter of an alleyway, only to be met with the flat report of a shotgun. A scythe of buck shot kicked them off their boots. Writhing in the dirt, their multiple wounds gradually went numb.

Few among their fellow gunfighters took notice, as the downed gunhawks lost their struggle to hold onto life. After a moment of stunned inactivity, the remaining fast guns released a ragged volley of their own. By then the astonished defenders inside the buildings nearest the Exchange Hotel found themselves overwhelmed by the surprise assault. Smoke Jensen led the way into the dry goods store.

Smoke's .44 barked with authority, as he jumped through a shattered window and pushed aside a mannequin in the display case. It bounced off a rack of dresses, and a member of Quint Stalker's gang used its distracting motion to cover his move to get Smoke Jensen.

Rising up, he swung the muzzle of his Colt into line with Smoke, only to find himself staring down a long, black tunnel to the afterworld. Smoke Jensen fired first. Hot lead released a thunderous pain in the chest of the outlaw, who slammed backward to upend over an island of discounted women's shoes. High-top button creations in uniform black flew in three directions.

When the powder smoke cleared, Smoke Jensen saw

his man lying still in death. "Put some men in place to hold this window," Smoke told the nearest Ranger.

Numbers began to tell. Doing the unexpected had gained the Rangers the dubious shelter of two wooden frame buildings, only to be pinned down by concentrated fire from outside. Several of the lawmen gave fleeting thought to how Benton-Howell's defenders in the hotel must have felt. Smoke Jensen took a quick mental inventory.

It didn't look good. Not counting those who broke through the ring of guns in the hands of the newly arrived hard cases, he could account for only some seven men not wounded or dead among the Rangers. They still faced some thirty or more guns. He had to find a way into the hotel. In memory, the ladder beckoned.

"Can you hold them here?" Smoke asked of Tallpockets.

He received a curt nod. "Don't know how long, but we'll do our best. Jeff an' the other boys should be hittin' 'em from behind soon. What'er you gonna do?"

"Get in that hotel." Not waiting for a response from the Arizona Ranger, Smoke headed for the rear of the shop.

A small loading dock behind the dry goods store could be accessed by three heavy plank steps. Smoke Jensen didn't waste time on them. A small shock ran up his legs when his boots hit the ground. He turned right and soon located the ladder. Fighting a sense of being too late, he lugged the heavy wooden object back to the hotel. Smoke leaned it against the clapboard siding of the hotel under a window. Colt in one hand, he started upward.

When he reached a position below the sash, Smoke

Jensen crouched and removed his hat. He held it in his left hand, while he raised his head and six-gun to peer inside. The room was empty. Smoke suddenly realized that he had been holding his breath. Stale air gusted out of his lungs, and he drew in a fresh draught. He tried the window, but it had been secured by a slide latch.

No time for finesse. Smoke cracked the lower center pane of glass, and reached through to slide the bar out of place. Then he raised up the lower half of the sash. He climbed into the room without incident. He crossed the room in four long strides, and paused at the door.

Smoke strained his keen hearing to gauge the unknown surroundings outside. At first he heard nothing, yet caution urged him to open the door only a crack. His first glance of the hallway showed him some ten gunmen lounging around, worried looks on their faces. Then all hell broke out on the street in front of the hotel.

Twenty-five

Jeff York levered rounds through the Winchester in a blur of speed, as he advanced on the hard cases milling in the street. One of the steadier of the band of thugs placed a round close enough to put Jeff down behind a full watering trough. He hunched forward on his elbows and took aim at one gunhawk's left kneecap. The Winchester bucked, and the man screamed as he went down.

But not out of the fight. His six-gun cracked and brought a shower of splinters from the trough. Stinging pinpricks on his face, told Jeff that the man could definitely shoot. His next round ended the contest with the border ruffian doubled over his perforated intestines. Jeff sought another target.

He had all too many, Jeff reflected on the situation. Enough that they were no longer intimidated by gunfire from the Rangers. They gathered their ranks and actually began to advance. A shirtless ruffian bounded out of the barbershop two doors down from Jeff, and raised a Smith and Wesson American to blast the life from the Arizona Ranger.

Jeff saw him first and put the last round from his Winchester through the small white button, third down on the front of the thug's red, longhandle underwear top. His mouth formed a black oval in his shaving cream-lathered face, and he did a pratfall on the boardwalk. His weapon discharged upward and shattered one square pane of glass in a streetlight. Dead already, he didn't feel the shards that pierced his scalp and chest. Three more popped up seemingly out of nowhere.

Screams of rage reached Jeff's ears a moment before he heard the distinctive yowl of a coyote. The voices of several desert birds joined, then came the thunder of hooves. Jeff York looked behind him to see seven riders, hugging low on the necks of their horses, rumbling toward the center of the fight.

Bands of red and yellow cloth fluttered from the forestocks of three rifles, and he saw the sharp curve of a bow a moment before an arrow flashed overhead and buried its point in the stomach of a would-be gunfighter not five feet from where Jeff lay.

Cuchillo Negro and six of his warriors had come through at a crucial time. They pounded down on the suddenly disorganized outlaws, and brought swift death with them. Several of the wiser among the hirelings of Benton-Howell took off running toward the nearest empty saddle. They took flight in utter panic, leaving all possessions behind. Others chose to fight it out.

They got a poor bargain for it. Hot lead laced the street from both Ranger positions. Black Knife operated his trapdoor Spencer with cool, smooth expertise. Round after round of lethal .56 caliber slugs smacked into flesh. One gunhawk went down with two Apaches swarming over him, knives flashing silver, then crimson in the sunlight.

In that mad, swirling instant, what had been certain

defeat for the Arizona Rangers turned into a promise of victory.

Boot heels thumped along the carpeted upstairs hall in reaction to the rattle of gunfire. Smoke Jensen watched the retreating backs of the hard cases, as they responded to the increased fighting outside. When all but two started down the wide staircase, Smoke Jensen stepped out of the room he had entered moments before and took stock.

A pair of men stood at the door to each of two rooms. Guarding the bosses? Smoke pondered a moment. At the far end, one gunhand was mostly out the door of the balcony that fronted the establishment. Another waited his turn. That meant five guns against Smoke. Six in the worst case. An arrow thudded into the wooden panel of the balcony door with enough force to wrest it from the hand of the youthful outlaw. A moment later he went to his knees, hands clutched to the shaft of the projectile that protruded from his chest.

Only five guns now. Considering who Smoke Jensen suspected had been confined behind those guarded portals, he could not simply leave well enough alone. When he opened up on the gunmen below, they would no doubt kill the hostages at once. He walked up to the Anglo pair guarding the center door.

"Benton-Howell said for me to relieve you two. He needs more guns in the fight downstairs."

Suspicion shined in the eyes of the nearer outlaw. "How'd he tell you that with you up here?"

"Don't you know anything about this place? There's a

brass speaking from the desk connected to every room." Smoke had noticed the device beside the door as he had exited, and took the chance that everyone was aware of them. "He just blew into it, and it whistled in my room. I answered and got told what to do."

"Yeah. I guess I did see them things. Looked like a pipe organ behind the counter."

"That's the one. Now go on, before those damned Rangers get inside the building."

They turned away with a dubious look, then joined the third white man at the top of the stairs. "I ain't gonna go out there. Damn Injuns have ridden in," he told them. "I'll go with you boys."

Once the three were out of sight, Smoke turned his attention to the two sombrero-wearing *bandidos* at the other door. He walked up to them, displaying a casual manner. A smile and his poor and rusty Spanish should help put them off guard, Smoke reckoned.

"Oye, my Spanish she is not so good," Smoke greeted in mixed language. "Your *jefe,* he says for me to tell you that they need more guns—*mas pistolas*—downstairs. You are to go at once."

"Don Miguel ordered us to stay here, not to leave unless he told us," the burlier of the pair protested in rapid-fire Spanish.

"¿Como? You speak too fast for me."

"Not too fast for me," a heavy voice rumbled from the head of the stairs.

A sharp crack of a .44 round from his Merwin and Hulbert punctuated Quint Stalker's statement. The bullet burned along the meaty portion of the small of Smoke Jensen's back. Smoke sprang across the hallway, out of reach of the two Mexican bandits, and spun to face Stalker.

"I see you got out of jail."

, "Damn right, Jensen. You an' me got a score to settle."

"Words are cheap. Let's get to it," Smoke grated, hand on the grip of his pistol.

"I don't think so. Ramon, Xavier, grab him."

For all the girth of Xavier, he moved like a startled cat. As his ham hands closed on the arm of Smoke Jensen, he left his ample belly open to ready attack. Smoke did not overlook it. He drove two hard, fast rights into the swell of gut before him. Xavier grunted and yanked Smoke toward him. By then, Ramon had Smoke's other arm. Smirking, Quint Stalker advanced along the hall. The Merwin and Hulbert drooped indolently in his gunhand, but even with his victim held captive, he took no chances with Smoke Jensen.

When he reached an arm's length from Smoke, Stalker cocked a solid left and drove knuckles into Jensen's face. "Hold him up," Stalker commanded. Another punch to the cheek, and Smoke Jensen went slack in their grasp.

Quint Stalker leered at the apparently dazed Smoke Jensen. "I'm gonna make this last, Jensen. Go real slow, give you a lot of pain . . . before I kill you."

Smoke gasped as he imperceptibly tightened his muscles, positioned now with his weight supported by the Mexican outlaws. His ears caught a distinct sound from outside. "You . . . may not . . . have time, Stalker. Those Apaches still want to get their hands on you."

The word Apaches galvanized Quint Stalker. He turned his attention away from his intended victim to listen to the war whoops that drifted through the open doorway.

Then he saw the dying hard case with the arrow in his chest. Time to move, Smoke Jensen judged. Swiftly shifting his weight, Smoke drove the pointed toe of his boot into Stalker's groin.

A banshee shriek ripped from the throat of Quint Stalker. Following it came a wet, sucking sound, as the hurting outlaw leader fought to pull air into his body and stop the misery. He doubled over until his chin touched his knees. Before the Mexican bandits could react, Smoke kicked Stalker in the face. Then, his feet planted firmly on the carpet runner in the hall, Smoke Jensen flexed powerful muscles in his shoulders and slammed Ramon and Xavier together face to face.

Their foreheads met with a *klonk!,* and Ramon went slack-legged to the floor. Quint Stalker lay twitching on the carpet strip. Smoke Jensen had no desire to trade punches with Quint Stalker, let alone the massive Xavier. He had his .44 halfway out of the holster when Xavier spotted the motion and, still dazed by the ramming, groped for his Mendoza .45 copy. He freed it and fired too soon. The slug zipped between the legs of Smoke Jensen and ploughed into a floorboard. Vibration from the hammer blow partly revived Quint Stalker.

He squinted and blinked his eyes to fuzzily see that Smoke Jensen had his Colt leveled. Smoke fired while Xavier tried desperately to cock his six-gun again. The, slug slammed into Xavier's hip; he staggered and finished cocking. Eyes tearing in pain, he sought to sight in on the insubstantial target of Smoke Jensen.

Eyes fixed on Xavier, Smoke brought his pistol to bear and tripped the trigger. Ramon's hand closed on Smoke's ankle, and he yanked as the hammer fell. The .44 bullet went wide of its intended mark. With his attention now divided between the Mexican bandits, Smoke did not notice Stalker's stealthy, crablike crawl away from the conflict.

His strength rapidly waning, Xavier sent a round over Smoke's left shoulder. Smoke Jensen had had enough of this. His next round shattered Ramon's shoulder, and the grip on his leg released at once. He turned back to Xavier, as the pudgy Sonoran went white-faced and sagged back against the opposite wall. Internal bleeding had sapped him of all his strength. He slithered to a sitting position and sighed regretfully before he passed out.

That's when Quint Stalker regained reason enough to take a shot.

Quint Stalker's bullet cracked past Smoke Jensen's head close enough for the gunfighter to feel its hot breath. One thing he knew for certain, he did not want Stalker to reach the ground floor and bring the news of Smoke's presence in the hotel. Far too many guns waited him down there, and what little element of surprise remained was all Smoke had going for his plan to free the Tuckers. Quint Stalker had already negotiated the top three treads, his weight borne by the banister, over which the outlaw leader had draped himself heavily.

A quick memory check told Smoke that he had emptied his right-hand gun. He holstered it and went for his second .44. The time lapse got Stalker to the upper landing, where he paused, gasped, and looked upward. He was out of sight of Smoke Jensen and glad of it. Determined not to let Stalker get away, Smoke advanced down the hallway toward the head of the stairs.

When he reached his goal, the wooden ball on top of the newel post exploded in a shower of splinters. Several stung and bit into Smoke's cheeks. Ignoring them, he threw a quick shot down the stairwell. Hot lead brought forth a yelp of alarm, when it tugged at the shoulder piece of Stalker's vest. At once, Smoke bounded down four steps.

Stalker fired again and, with his strength returning, retreated downward before he could check the results. There were none, except for a hole in the plaster high over Smoke Jensen's right shoulder. Smoke came after him at once. At the central landing, feet planted squarely on the level, Quint Stalker's bullet caused Smoke Jensen to dive to one side to avoid a mortal wound.

Crying out at this near-triumph, Stalker started off down the final flight of stairs. Smoke Jensen reached the platform seconds behind Quint Stalker. He steadied his arm and took aim. Stalker looked back, spun on a boot heel, and tried again to blast Smoke out of existence. Smoke Jensen fired first.

Smoke's slug took Quint in the chest, to the right of his sternum. The outlaw boss rose on tiptoe and a thin whine came through his lips. He tried to raise his gun barrel . . . and failed. Smoke shot hid in the center of the chest.

Stalker teetered backward and cartwheeled down four treads. His body went slack, and he rolled the rest of the way to the bottom of the staircase. Smoke Jensen was already heading upward. He took the steps two at a time. Excited voices followed him.

"Have the savages gotten in?" Benton-Howell's English accent floated upward.

"Someone has," another voice answered, as he spotted the body of Quint Stalker.

"Then go after them," Benton-Howell commanded.

Half a dozen hard cases started for the stairway. At the same moment, chunks of plaster showered into the room from the wall dividing the hotel from the dry goods store. Another crash drove the heavy metal base of a display rack through the lath. The barrels of rifles and shotguns followed.

A few of the hired guns made instant response, only to be cut down in a hail of lead. Not bound by years of loyalty, the majority saw the inevitable end for their kind, and deserted the cause. They rushed out into the street to surrender, hope filling them that the Indians had ridden on to other depredations.

There the Arizona Rangers began to disarm and handcuff the demoralized mob of shootists. Jeff York detached himself from his men and made for the hotel. Upstairs, Smoke Jensen caught a glimpse of a flat-crowned Cordovan sombrero disappear down the back stairway. Suspecting defeat, he hurried to the first of the two rooms that had been guarded.

He threw open the door . . . and found the stark cubicle empty.

"Selleres has them," Smoke Jensen shouted to Jeff York, when the Arizona Ranger's head topped the stairs. "He went down the back."

Jeff didn't waste time asking if Smoke was sure.

Smoke Jensen rarely made such a statement if he didn't know for certain. Instead, he strode rapidly to where Smoke stood at the top of the back staircase. As he did, Jeff passed two open doors, the rooms behind them gaping emptily.

"We're going after them?" Jeff asked.

"Just you and me. I don't want to frighten Selleres into killing any of them."

They started down, only to find the way blocked by three of Quint Stalker's loyalest men; Vern Draper, Marv Fletcher, and Charlie Bascomb. Bascomb fired first. His bullet cut the air between Smoke and Jeff. Smoke got a slug into the leg of the young gunslinger, and sent him tumbling back down the stairs. That bought Smoke and Jeff half the flight, before a muzzle appeared around the corner of the hallway and sent a bullet winging upward.

Hunkered down, Smoke and Jeff duck-walked uncomfortably down the next five treads. A six-gun blazed in their direction, and Smoke put a round through the wall. A soft grunt answered him. No more shots came, and they made it to the bottom. A quick look showed Charlie Bascomb sprawled on the floorboards of the rear hallway in a pool of blood. He wouldn't be holding them up any more.

"Out back," Smoke prompted.

He made his way cautiously to the open back door. The moment Smoke Jensen's head appeared around the jamb, Vern Draper and Marv Fletcher opened up. Smoke jerked back in time. The slugs whistled down the corridor. Smoke saw that Jeff had wisely flattened himself against the far wall, out of the line of fire.

"We'll lose too much time going around the long way,"

Smoke figured aloud. "Nothing for it but to rush them." At that moment he would have given anything for Walt Reardon's 10 gauge L.C. Smith.

Both he and Jeff took time to reload. Then, with a six-gun in each hand—something Preacher had told Smoke never, ever to do—he crouched low and went through the doorway, his, matched pistols leading him. They blasted alternately in a steady rhythm. From behind he heard Jeff York join the dance. Marv Fletcher cried out and spun to one side, hit by two slugs at the same time. He fell like wet wash. That left only one.

Vern Draper backed up in the direction obviously taken by the fleeing Miguel Selleres and the hostages. He fired repeatedly as he gained what speed he could in his ungainly walk. Beyond him, near the mouth to the alley farthest from the activity around the hotel, Smoke caught sight of Jimmy Tucker's towhead flashing white in a ray of sunlight. Geoffrey Benton-Howell yanked the boy by his collar. Another man, whose identity Smoke Jensen did not know, dragged the other children along. Miguel Selleres roughly shoved Martha Tucker in the desired direction.

Unwilling to risk their lives, Smoke Jensen holstered his right-hand .44 and drew his coffin-handle Bowie. He hefted it and closed fingers around the grips. A swift up and down motion of his arm, and he released the blade. It turned one full time in the air, and buried half its length in the chest of a surprisedVern Draper.

The six-gun fell from numbed fingers, and Vern's eyes bugged at the enormous, hot pain in his chest. Draper went rubber-legged and staggered to one side. Smoke Jensen pushed past him, and only faintly heard the thump of Jeff York's six-gun when it ended the life of the snaggle-toothed outlaw. Smoke started running, with Jeff pounding along behind.

Beyond the fleeing conspirators and their captives, a coach had rumbled into place. The armored carriage of Miguel Selleres.

At the direction of the corrupt *haciendado,* three burly Mexican bandits, who had accompanied the coach, stepped between their leader and the two lawmen. Each wore the wide, floppy sombrero of a *charro,* with bandoliers of ammunition crossed over their chests. Beneath the cartridge belts they wore short, open bolero jackets, white shirts with string ties and lots of lace ruffles. They were large men, but not with puffy fat, yet their bellies protruded over the belts that supported their holsters.

Each had a brace of Mendoza .45s, canted forward so to provide easy reach to a man in the saddle. Their tight trousers, the outer seams trimmed with silver conchos, pegged down to slender tubes where they met the tall boots. They all sported flowing, long, thick moustaches that drooped to their jawlines. Without comment, they swiftly drew their weapons.

Jeff York killed the one opposite him before the *bandido* could squeeze his trigger. Beside him, he heard the steady bang of Smoke's .44. Jeff's target flopped on the ground and raised a cloud of dust. The two Smoke had shot staggered forward a step, fired wildly in the general direction of the lawmen they faced, and then took another bullet each.

Impact turned them inward, facing each other, their

foreheads rebounded off one another, and they spun away, arms hooked together in a macabre do-si-do. Meanwhile, Benton-Howell energetically shoved Jimmy Tucker into the coach. He gestured impatiently to his third partner, Dalton Wade, to pass him the other two children.

By then, Selleres' three bandits had been dispatched. Slowly, the cloud of expended powder began to clear. Miguel Selleres found himself facing Smoke Jensen and Jeff York, smoking Colts in their hands.

"It's over, Selleres. Let your hostages go," Smoke Jensen demanded.

Swiftly, Selleres grabbed Martha Tucker under one arm and laid his wrist tightly across her throat, the muzzle of his Mendoza pressed to the soft flesh behind her chin. "Put up your *pistolas, Señores,* or I will kill her before your eyes."

Twenty-six

The sneer on Miguel Selleres's face portrayed more fear than contempt. "We are leaving here. All is lost, *¿como no?* We'll take the woman and these brats for safe passage. Do not come after us."

"Why not? You'll kill them eventually," Smoke challenged.

Selleres shrugged. *"Que obvio. Pero no es importante para té."*

"It's sure as hell important to the woman and her kids," Jeff York growled.

"Holster your guns or she dies," said Selleres coldly.

Jeff York cut his eyes to Smoke Jensen. Smoke considered only for a brief second, then gave a small nod. Both lawmen slid iron into leather. Miguel Selleres began to back toward the armored coach.

Madness glittered in his eyes. "We're leaving now. But we'll be back. Everyone will be made to pay for what they've done to us. The whole damned world will tremble before us!"

At that moment, Martha Tucker managed to dip her chin low enough to get a mouthful of the arm holding her. She sank her teeth in and ground them.

With a howl of anguish, Miguel Selleres jerked his

head upward in reflexive response to the pain. His grip loosened, Martha opened her mouth and fell to one side. Smoke Jensen drew his left-hand .44

"No, we won't," Smoke Jensen barked, as his bullet popped a hole in the forehead of Miguel Selleres.

The Mendoza Colt dropped from a lifeless hand. Selleres had overlooked one vital requirement. He had not cocked his weapon. Driven by desperation, Dalton Wade made the terrible mistake of unlimbering the age-worn, 5-shot Herington and Richards .38 from its long, soft pouch holster. To do so, he had to release the hand of Tommy Tucker. It did him no good, though. A bullet each from Smoke Jensen and Jeff York struck his chest at the same moment. Screaming, Rose Tucker ran after her little brother. A major transformation had come over Benton-Howell. He sank to his knees, hands upraised in supplication, tears streaming down his full cheeks, face ruddy.

"Please, don't kill me. I don't want to die. None of this was my idea. You—you can't kill me," a sudden hope rising in his quaking body. "I'm a peer of the realm! And, after all, no one important got hurt."

Smoke Jensen turned an icy gaze of utter contempt upon the groveling Englishman. "We'll save you, all right, *Sir* Geoffrey . . . for the hangman. Jeff, go after the Tucker kids."

Once they had been restored to their mother, who wept copiously in relief over the safe resolution of their dangerous situation, Smoke Jensen turned his attention back to Benton-Howell.

"Sir Geoffrey?" His lips curled with contempt. "Well, you're sure not a gentleman, let alone a knightly one. You're a coward, a murderer, and a thief. You're so low

and corrupt, you'd have to reach up to scratch a snake's belly. I said we'd save you for a date with the hangman, but I didn't promise what condition you'd be in for the trial." Smoke undid his cartridge bell. "Put up your hands and defend yourself."

Benton-Howell began to splutter. "Bu—but, I'm—I'm your prisoner, sir. You cannot strike me."

In an eye blink, Smoke Jensen hit him with a right and left to either side of the jaw. Benton-Howell sagged and raised a futile left arm in an attempt to block the next solid punch, which whistled in as a sizzling right jab. He gulped and backpedaled. His shoulders slammed against the heavy side of the coach. Jimmy Tucker's head popped out the door.

"Yaaah-hooo! Kick him between the legs, Smoke."

"James Lee Tucker," Martha admonished, scandalized by her son. "Such language. For shame."

Jimmy didn't look the least repentant. "I mean it, too, Mom."

Left arm still up, Benton-Howell darted his right in under its concealing position. Suddenly Smoke Jensen was there. One hand clinched a lapel as Smoke spun Benton-Howell around. Smoke pulled down the frock coat to reveal a concealed shoulder holster that held a short-barreled .44 Colt Lightning. Jeff stepped in and plucked the weapon from its holster. Smoke swung the frothing-mouthed Benton-Howell around and slammed his head into the armored side of the carriage. It made a solid *thunk.*

Smoke brought his dazed opponent face to face, and went to work on the midsection. Feebly Benton-Howell tried to fend off the blows. Clearly this was not a fight,

it was a beating, plain and simple. Every bit of the outrage and frustration of the last mountain man poured out
on the source of it all. Benton-Howell doubled over, his
air exhausted, and Smoke Jensen straightened him up
with a hard left.

The Englishman's knees buckled and his head
drooped. Still Smoke bore in. Blood ran from a cut on
the cheek of Benton-Howell, from the corner of his
mouth, and the corner of an eye swollen shut by severe
battering. At last, Smoke Jensen took control of his anger
and eased off. When the red haze left his eyes, he found
Benton-Howell on his knees, thoroughly battered and defeated.

Disgust plain on her face at having witnessed the sav-
aging of Benton-Howell, Martha Tucker hugged her children to her and spoke with unaccustomed chill to Smoke
Jensen. "It's over then?"

"Yes. All but the roundup of the trash and, of course,
the trial. I've no doubt Benton-Howell will be convicted
of ordering your husband's murder. And he *will* hang."

"Yes . . . of course," she responded stiffly. "At least
that way it will be done according to law."

Her sudden, inexplicable disapproval stung Smoke
Jensen. He started to make some sort of reply, thought
better of it, and shrugged. He retrieved his hat from the
ground, dusted it off, and indicated the way back toward
the hotel with it. Without further comment, Martha
Tucker followed, her children clustered at either side.

They had progressed only a third of the way down the
alley, when a shot crashed overloud in the confined
space, and little Tommy Tucker slammed forward out of
the protective circle of his mother's arm. Martha took

one stunned look at the spreading red stain on the boy's back, and began to wail hysterically. Young Rose Tucker screamed and dissolved into tears. Jimmy hit the ground.

Smoke Jensen reacted quickly also. He jumped to one side and looked beyond the frozen tableau of the Tuckers to where a wooden-faced Forrest Gore worked the lever of his Winchester in a frantic effort to chamber another round. Smoke's hand dropped to the butt of his .44, and he freed it before the bolt closed on Gore's rifle.

Smoke's arm rose with equal swiftness and steadied only a fraction of a second to allow the hammer to drop. Quickly he slip-thumbed three more rounds. All four struck Forrest Gore in the chest and belly. The Winchester flew to the sky, and Gore jerked and writhed with each impact. A cloud of cloth bits, flesh, and blood made a crimson haze that circled his body. Jeff York turned in time to plunk two more slugs into the child-killer. Then he spun, pistol still smoking, toward Benton-Howell.

"That does it! No waiting for the hangman, damn you. It's your scheming that brought it to this. Now you pay."

"No, Jeff!" Smoke Jensen barked harshly. "Let him sit and sweat and wait for that rope to be put around his neck. That way he'll die a thousand times over."

Jeff York's shoulders sagged. "You're right, Smoke. Sorry, I lost it for a moment."

Martha Tucker drew out of her grief long enough to look up with a face drawn with anguish, and addressed Smoke Jensen with some of her former warmth. "Thank you, Smoke Jensen. Thank you for saving a fine lawman's career and self-esteem. And thank you for avenging my husband and my—my son."

All at once, Smoke Jensen felt as though he had been

the one to take a beating. "I did what I had to do, Martha. Now, we have a lot yet to accomplish."

Martha Tucker had been restored to her ranch. A week had gone by since the Arizona Rangers had cleared the streets of Socorro of saddle tramps and low-class gunfighters. They had ridden away after little Tommy Tucker's funeral. Each one had expressed their deep sympathy for the courageous woman who had lost a husband and son within a month's time. Even Cuchillo Negro and his Apache warriors left small, feather-decorated gifts on the raw earth of the grave. Then they, too, rode off to the west.

That left Smoke Jensen alone at the ranch. He recalled the tension and black grief at the burial of the small boy, and a sensation of relief flooded him as he watched Martha Tucker step from the kitchen, smiling and brushing at the swatch of flour on her forehead in a familiar gesture. She smiled up at him as she approached where he stood with his saddled roan.

"I've put a pie on. I—I sort of hoped that you would stay on, if not with your hands, at least yourself, for a while."

"I really can't, Martha. I'm long over due in returning to my ranch."

"With it in the capable hands of men like Walt and Ty, I see no reason why a few days more would matter."

Smoke sighed. "Truth is, I miss 'em. The High Lonesome, the Sugarloaf, and . . . my wife. It's time I got back to them. Goodbye, and bless you, Martha Tucker. You're a strong woman. Strong even if you were a man."

"Why, I—I take that as the supreme compliment," she said, clearly flustered. Then Martha rose on tiptoe and kissed Smoke lightly on one cheek. "Goodbye, Smoke Jensen. You'll be missed . . . awfully."

Jimmy Tucker rushed forward and hugged Smoke Jensen around the waist. He was too deeply moved for words, but his silent tears spoke it all. That made it even more difficult for Smoke Jensen to take his leave, but he did.

Prying the lad's arms from around him and giving a final tip of his hat to Martha, Smoke swung into the saddle and rode off. He didn't look back until he reached the top of the ridge to the northeast. The backward glance did not last long, for his thoughts had already spanned the miles ahead to his secure nook in the Shining Mountains, the cozy log and stone home on the Sugarloaf, and his beloved Sally.

THE BLOOD BOND SERIES

by William W. Johnstone

The continuing adventures of blood brothers, Matt Bodine and Sam Two Wolves—two of the fastest guns in the west.